DRUMS OF THE LOST GODS

DRUMS OF THE LOST GODS

BY

DAN LEISSNER

MIDNIGHT MARQUEE PRESS, INC.
BALTIMORE, MARYLAND, USA

Copyright © 2010 Dan Leissner
Cover Design by Jeff Duke
Cover Layout and Interior Design by Susan Svehla

ISBN 978-1-936168-09-5
Library of Congress Catalog Card Number 2010933214
Manufactured in the United States of America

First Printing by Midnight Marquee Press, Inc., July 2010

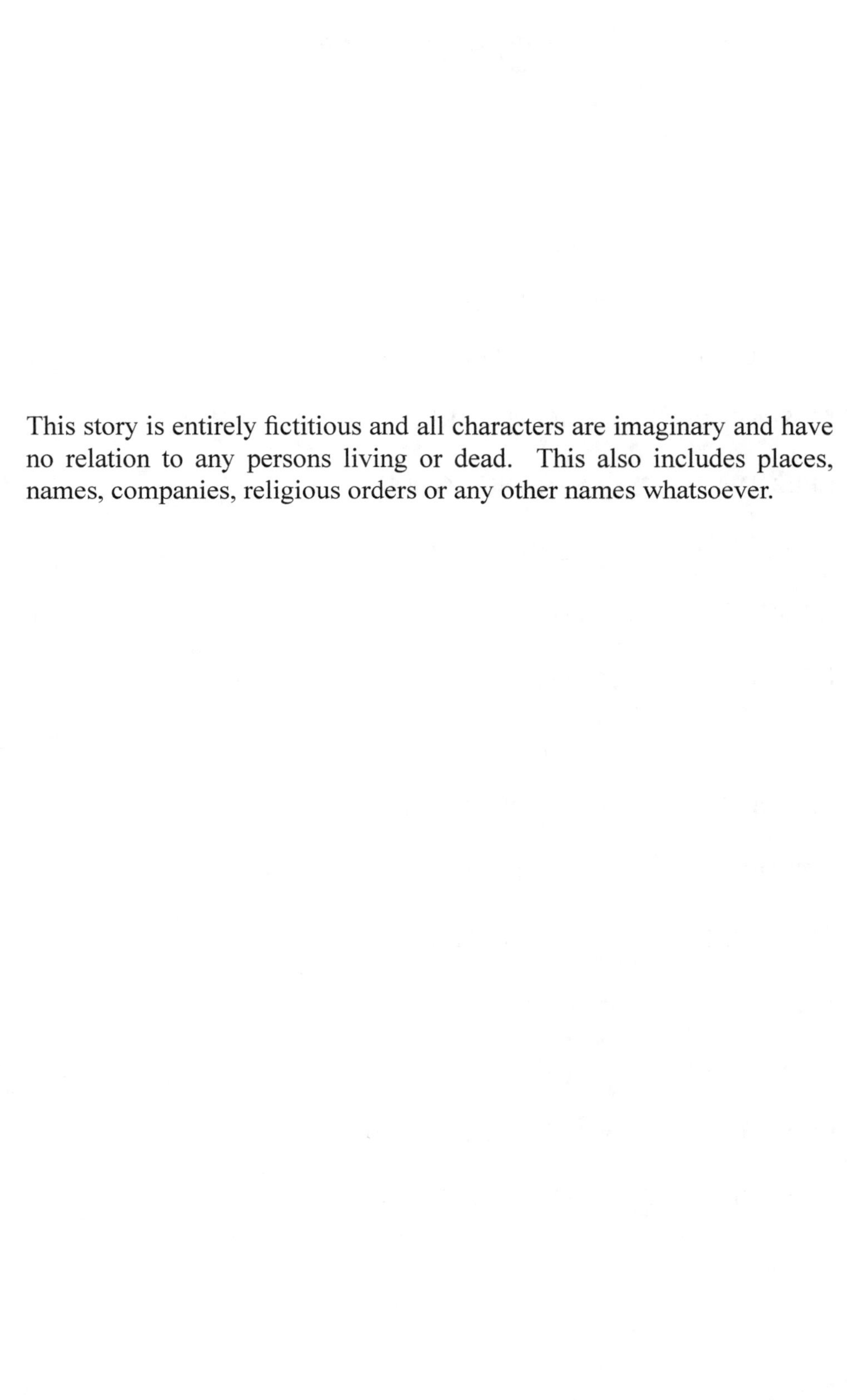

CONTENTS

EPISODE 1:	THE CALL OF ADVENTURE	10
EPISODE 2:	NIGHTMARES	23
EPISODE 3:	STRANGE GOLD	33
EPISODE 4:	KIDNAPPED	43
EPISODE 5:	THE WHIP	51
EPISODE 6:	PIRATES	59
EPISODE 7:	GREED	68
EPISODE 8	THE BLACK LAGOON	75
EPISODE 9:	CAPTURED	83
EPISODE 10:	CANNIBALS	92
EPISODE 11:	GREEN DEATH	101
EPISODE 12:	MONSTERS	109
EPISODE 13:	THE LOST WORLD	119
EPISODE 14:	MAN-EATER	128

EPISODE 15:   THE LAND THAT TIME FORGOT   136

EPISODE 16:   BLONDE VERSUS BRUNETTE   155

EPISODE 17:   LUST IN THE DUST   165

EPISODE 18:   WARRIORS OF AN ANCIENT WORLD   173

EPISODE 19   THAT'S NOT CRICKET!   180

EPISODE 20:   THE DUNGEON   199

EPISODE 21:   A SACRIFICE   209

EPISODE 22:   ATTACK OF THE ROBOT MEN   216

EPISODE 23:   A RECKONING   221

THE PLAYERS

NATE "THE NAIL" O'DWYER: The Big Guy. King of the mobsters. A hood.

TRIXIE MARLOWE: Exotic dancer. The Platinum Blonde. A good-time girl with a heart of gold, hard and yellow. A dame with a strange power over men. And women.

CELIA CAVENDISH: The celebrated tennis champion and socialite. The independent woman.

COLONEL GUSTAV VON SEYFRITZ: A stiff-necked Prussian. A thoroughly bad egg.

ARMAND DUBOIS: A mysterious Frenchman. Soldier of fortune.

PROFESSOR ANGUS MACKENZIE: The world-famous archaeologist.

JEREMY CHARLES ARTHUR WHITTERING-SMYTHE: The ex-public school boy who has everything. The profile of a Greek God and an Oxford rowing blue.

MACK AND LEFTY: Torpedoes.

BRAUN AND GRUBER: Goons.

The England cricket team's tour of Australia has shaken the Empire to its very foundations with allegations of poor sportsmanship leveled against the England team.

Women follow the trend set by film star Marlene Dietrich and are wearing men's clothes.

Condemned for its actions in China, Japan leaves the League of Nations.

Franklin D. Roosevelt is sworn in as President of the United States. He repeals Prohibition and signs the National Industry Recovery Act. It is the dawn of the New Deal.

Adolf Hitler becomes Chancellor of Germany. Books are burned. All opposition parties are banned. "Undesirables"—political prisoners and opponents of the regime—are being held in concentration camps.

Meanwhile, in Gangstertown USA, Trixie Marlowe is shakin' it for 'em down at the Fat Cat Club...

EPISODE 1:
THE CALL OF ADVENTURE

Cymbals splashed, trumpets flared, ripping across the deep booming throb of a big bull fiddle. The spotlights sizzled upon the ivory form of the dancer. Clad only in a few little spangly things, she stood with her arms held high above her head, eyes half closed, lips parted, the wet tip of her tongue darting. Her whole body, poised, vibrated from her shoulders to her knees, every curve glistening.

Her feet stamped. Her head was thrown back, her shoulders barely moved, yet her body was leaping madly. Her body moved in a steady shaking. Now she crouched, now she sprang high in the air. She was writhing like a snake. Eyes closed, she moved her hips sinuously. Waveringly, lambently, her ample bosom shook. She ran her hands over her body, fingertips fluttering, up her thighs to hips and belly and breasts, slippery with sweat. The drums rippled and the brass moaned. Then the crack of a rimshot and she finished in a clamorous throbbing and heaving that left her on her knees, her shining body arched and her head nearly touching the ground, with no movement save her panting breath.

The spot was extinguished to a core of inky blackness. When the house lights glowed again the dancer was gone, to an ocean of applause pierced by shrill whistles and a stomping of feet.

"Sounds like Trix is really giving it to 'em," commented Sam Gianelli.

Sleek as a whippet, he was a thin sharp little man, so thin his bony shoulders could move inside his tuxedo without disturbing the exaggerated padding of its cut. His blue-black hair was slicked back from a high, smooth forehead, his pencil moustache drawn with a ruler. Dwarfed by a massive mahogany desk, he clipped a pair of gold pince-nez to the bridge of his long nose and shuffled through a fat leather-bound ledger.

"She's doubled the takings in less than a month, Boss."

The owner of the Fat Cat Club held his double brandy up to the light.

"So what's new?" he growled. "Ya knows ya can't go wrong with a bit of tit 'n ass."

Nate "The Nail" O'Dwyer was a big man, and he cast a giant shadow. A looming six footer, he was as broad as he was tall, and would have stood taller but for the heavy simian slope of his massive shoulders, weighed down by the bulging muscularity of his long arms and huge, shovel-like hands. He strained every seam of a blue silk suit, his bull neck tormenting his collar and tie. His heavy features were those of a pugilist and hard drinker, his plastered down hairline receding, a sole concession to approaching middle age in a man who kept himself in prime fighting condition.

He stood as always, legs astride, his arms loose at his sides, ever on the brink of exploding into action. Like the big pistol at his armpit, he was well-oiled, always primed. His narrow piggy eyes were watchful and restless, had that unblinking opaqueness of a killer.

"I knows the business, Sam," he rasped in tones resonant with the harsh clamor of the tenements and stockyards, tinted with just a ghost of the brogue. "Give the customers what they want, that's all there is to it, give 'em booze and broads."

Nate slammed back the brandy in a gulp. Sam Gianelli, who fancied himself a more cultured soul, winced to see a refined old Napoleon so abused.

Right on cue, the office door swung open.

I'm ready, Big Guy!"

Trixie Marlowe. Hardboiled good-time girl. The Platinum Blonde.

"How do I look?" she spoke at a rat-a-tat-tat, with a pronounced and nasal twang.

"How do ya like it?"

Trixie paused to strike a pose. Her dress was a second, silver skin. It shimmered sleekly on the swell and alert pinnacles of her unfettered breasts, picked out the dimple of her navel, crowning the pert protuberance of her belly, flowed smoothly on the flaring sheen of her hips, the opulent rolling spread of her rump, her long and shining thighs.

"Well?"

She did a quick twirl. The dress was cut to bare her back right down to the base of her spine, daringly, precariously bare. Her skin was almost translucent, glowing, gloriously sculpted alabaster. There was something foxy in the sharp tilt of her features, her eyes dark and alive and sparkling, the mouth a ripe, ruby rosebud, her hair carved platinum.

"Do ya like me, Daddy?"

She advanced on Nate O'Dwyer. She led with her pelvis, a lithe, slinky, strutting swagger. The oiled, slow shimmy of her shoulders, the quivering peaks, were a blatant provocation. Sam Gianelli swallowed hard. Nate lumbered forward to meet her.

"Ya look just great, babe," he said huskily.

Like a great bear, he bent over her, his huge hands reaching round to seize and knead her buttocks. With a shrill giggle of alarm, Trixie slithered out of his grasp, turning her face aside.

"Not now, Daddy," she laughed. "You'll mess up the war paint."

Nate shrugged and returned to the brandy bottle.

"Dames!" he muttered darkly.

When he pulled out a vast cigar and settled into a plush plum leather armchair, Trixie stamped her foot impatiently.

"Aw, Daddy, get your coat. I'm hungry!"

Nate glowered.

"Just hold yer horses, babe. I got business to attend to."

Trixie pouted and rapped her long fingernails on the desk top. She stopped when Nate stared hard at her. Behind the desk, Sam cleared his throat.

"Uh, sounded like you went over big, Trix."

Trixie tossed her head.

"Huh! I got them mugs eating outta my hand."

Gianelli grinned.

"Yeah, you sure are one hell of a stripper, Trix."

Trixie regarded him haughtily.

"I am an exotic dancer."

She turned to Nate, put a high, wheedling inflection in her voice.

"When are you going to get me that movie contract, Daddy? I've been taking them lessons for six months and...."

Nate rose with astonishing quickness, his bulk seeming to soar out of the padded depths of the armchair. Trixie shrank back instinctively. There was a nervous glitter in his eyes, and when he was nervous he was violent. You steered clear when he had that look in his eye.

"Shut yer yap!" he snapped. "Like a goddamn cracked record!"

He seized her wrist in a grip that made her grimace with pain.

"I pays for them actin' lessons like I pays for the clothes on yer back and the lousy air ya breathe. I'll let ya know when yer ready to be a movie star!"

Released abruptly, Trixie retreated to a far window, rubbing her arm ruefully. When Nate let fly a string of obscenities, she jerked round with alarm, but the big man was now pacing impatiently, glaring at his watch.

"Where the hell are they, Sam?"

Gianelli felt sweat prickle on his brow. He flapped his thin hands placatingly.

"Don't worry, Boss, they'll be here any minute."

Time ticked by. Nate paced, sucking audibly on his cigar. Gianelli pretended to rustle through some papers, while he made a sneaky survey of Trixie's amazing contours. Trixie stayed glued sullenly to the window, watching the late night traffic ebb and flow.

There was a muffled scuffling in the corridor, the sound of angry voices. Nate turned eagerly, Sam rose from his seat.

"Here they come!"

The door burst open. Mole Murphy stumbled into view, his arms flailing, propelled from behind. He was short and podgy, with a round red face topped by a dented grey derby. His fancy check suit had been rumpled by rough handling, the necktie askew and two buttons missing on the vest.

He was followed into the office by Mack and Lefty, a matched pair of torpedoes, collar up and hat brim pulled low, jaws of granite and shoulders like the decks of an aircraft carrier, each with a hand wrapped around the .38 nestling in an overcoat pocket.

"Hey! What's going on?"

Collecting himself, Mole glared all around, spluttering with righteous indignation.

"Whaddaya think you're doin'?"

He stared at Trixie, who responded with a practised flicker of contempt, then at Gianelli, who removed the pince-nez and slipped them into his breast pocket. When he lit upon Nate O'Dwyer the bluster evaporated and his blood turned to ice water.

Nate stepped forward to loom over him. He jumped backwards and ran up against Mack and Lefty, could only struggle feebly when they took an arm each and held him fast between them.

"Glad ya could make it, Mole," Nate growled. "I wants a word with ya."

Mole's face shone out of O'Dwyer's shadow, as white as a sheet. Nate fixed him with a frozen, reptilian gaze, and he stared back like a paralysed jack-rabbit. His mouth dropped open, a thin strand of spittle dangling from his chin. Stark terror radiated from him, you could taste it on the air.

"I hear whispers, Mole," O'Dwyer grated. "Them whispers tell me the Polack's gonna try his luck."

His guest just stared at him and gulped. Sam sat back down behind the desk. Trixie was watching closely, her eyes flicking eagerly between them.

"How about it, Mole? Ya keeps yer ear to the ground, ya hears them whispers too."

Mole struggled fitfully, a spasm of panic. Trixie's eyes widened.

"Is the Polack feeling lucky? Has he put the finger on me?"

Mole shook his head desperately. Drops of sweat flew from his forehead.

"I–I dunno what you're t–talking about," he stammered. "I….."

O'Dwyer's fist looped up from his side. It traveled in a lazy arc, hardly seeming to move at any speed. Mole jerked as if struck by lightning, and Mack and Lefty had to hold on tight. The grey derby was catapulted all the way to the door. Startled, Gianelli jumped in his seat. Trixie wrinkled her nose and said "ugh," but her tongue tip teased her lip.

The torpedoes took the strain as Mole sagged between them. Nate's huge fist had enveloped the whole of his face, mashing his nose to pulp and ruining his mouth. There was blood on his chin, splattered down his shirt front.

Nate took out a handkerchief and wiped his knuckles.

"Let's have it, Mole."

He strolled over to pick up the derby, then jammed it back securely on Mole's head, wedging it down to his eyebrows. Trixie took a deep breath. The room was suddenly hot. She giggled nervously.

Mole coughed and spat teeth.

"If I tell ya he'll k–kill me!"

O'Dwyer grabbed a fistful of his soiled lapel.

"And if ya don't I will," he snarled. "After I've let the boys loose on ya with a pair of pliers and piano wire!"

On cue, Mack and Lefty tightened their grip till Mole heard his arm bones creak.

"Okay, okay!" he yelped. "The Polack's got a squad stashed at the Metropole, independents from outta town, been there for a week, still makin' plans!"

O'Dwyer grinned viciously.

"That dumb lug!"

Chuckling, he patted Mole roughly on the cheek.

"Thinks he can outsmart me!"

At a barely perceptible nod from his boss, Lefty brought the Smith & Wesson from his pocket and applied the butt smartly just behind Mole's ear. He collapsed like a sack of potatoes. Trixie winced and nibbled on a fingernail.

"Take the garbage out and lose it somewhere."

While the torpedoes removed the unconscious Mole, O'Dwyer was pacing the room again, not nervous now, but suffused with the light of battle. Gianelli was back on his feet, Trixie looking from one to the other with mounting excitement.

Then Nate stopped short, banging a fist into his palm.

"Okay, Sam. We'se gonna arrange a little welcomin' party for those boys at the Metropole. And then we'll bury the Polack!"

Gianelli nodded, smiling thinly.

"It'll be a cinch, Boss, but you'd better get out of the country for a while, till the heat dies down. We can handle it."

Nate frowned, then threw back his head and laughed.

"Yeah, why not, I could do with a vacation."

He thought it over, rubbing his chin.

"How about the Old Country?" Gianelli suggested.

"Oh no, Daddy!" Trixie pleaded. "It didn't stop raining for a month!"

"How would ya know?" Nate retorted. "Ya never got that big ass of yours outta bed!"

He moved in on her and Trixie tensed. But he was in a good mood now and didn't see her flinch as he flung a mighty arm around her shoulders.

"Okay, okay!" he boomed. "Ferget it. We'll find somewhere with lots of sunshine, somewhere real exciting!"

"Forty-thirty!"

High noon shone down upon Surrey's most exclusive tennis lawns, pampered greens confined to a close-knit elite, to those with the proper social credentials, or the national title.

"Match point!"

Celia Cavendish had both the credentials and the title. Her first serve deep and true, she followed it in to the net and punished the weak return with a killing volley.

"Game, set and match!"

Celia was already on her way before the ball struck home, an inch from the inner tramline. Turning her back as it bounced into the shadows, she strode briskly towards an empty terrace of benches. Her opponent picked himself up from the manicured grass and bounded forward to leap the net and pursue her eagerly.

"I say, old thing, spiffing shot!"

Jeremy Charles Arthur Whittering-Smythe. A rowing blue, with the shoulders and profile of a young god. Barely into his twenties, he was secure in the knowledge that this was all that he would ever need. He bounded through life with the blithe carelessness of one who past, present and future, had not a worry in the world. Eternally optimistic, as are all those who can afford to be, he left the human race to its own devices and desired only that it should do the same for him.

"Well, I might be approaching the autumn of my career," Celia plucked her towel from its perch on the spars of the empty umpire's chair and dabbed deftly at her brow. "But I hope I can still manage a simple volley."

Turning to meet her young opponent, she extended her hand, permitting herself to mellow, bestowing a rare smile.

"Well played, Jeremy."

She patted his cheek fondly and electricity surged through him. When she smiled like that, his heart flipped over. Oh, he had bagged his crop of giggling debs, but here was a real woman. Her grey eyes were steady, her chin determined, the set of her features cool and aristocratic. Her bearing was regal, her superb body poised, sheathed in crisp tennis whites, a flawless, breathing harmony of curves. Top to toe, she was a thoroughbred.

Celia let him stare. Sweet boy, so young, so beautiful, such a wealth of uncomplicated pleasure. A memory of the dawn tinting his bare shoulders flickered past her mind's eye. She felt so deliciously self-indulgent.

Absently, she wiped the handle of her racket. Then she paused.
Its tackiness, something so familiar to her, seemed oddly distasteful. It
was clumsy and ridiculous, and she glared at it and threw it down on the
benches with an alarming clatter.

"I say, steady on!"

Jeremy stooped to rescue the offending object and fingered the
frame where its curve had splintered. Celia sighed heavily, tilted her head
back, her face up to the bright blue sky.

"Oh, I'm bored with tennis!"

Her companion stared at her, amazed. The woman dubbed the
Queen of the Court, disenchanted with the game!

"Chasing after a silly little ball!"

Jeremy was aghast.

"Come off it, darling. Not with the Championships a week away!"

Celia tossed the towel over her shoulder, then sniffed with disdain.

"Hang the Championships!"

Jeremy looked about in alarm. Not the sort of thing to proclaim in
public, not with half the nabobs of the Association lurking somewhere on
the premises. He glanced at Celia warily. Her eyes were blazing and her
chin was more determined than ever. By Jove, she was in one of those
moods, no telling what she might do.

He jumped back as she snatched the broken racket from him, drew
back her arm and hurled it in a looping spiral down the length of the court,
till with a hearty thwack it met the wall of dark green canvas.

"They can jolly well do without me this year!"

She stamped her foot decisively, glaring at her surroundings.
Suddenly, she flung out her arms, reaching up to the sky. Her movements
put a noticeable strain on the front of her blouse, and Jeremy gulped
audibly.

"Let's steal an aeroplane," Celia cried. "And fly around the world!"

Jeremy shuffled his feet and forced a sheepish grin.

"Ah… er… smashing idea, C. But neither of us can fly….."

Celia rolled her eyes and groaned.

"Oh, where's your sense of adventure?"

She cocked her fist and thumped him in the chest, making him gasp
and rock back on his heels.

"That's what I want, adventure!"

While Jeremy caught his breath, Celia was drawn to the distant
rooftops of the rambling, mock-Tudor clubhouse. In an instant, she had

snatched up a large brown leather holdall and was striding towards the narrow gateway that led from the court.

"Come on, we can discuss it over a drink."

The silver-skinned Trimotor wallowed in the turbulence that rose up from jagged mountains. All around, dirty yellow clouds boiled and bubbled. In the distance, lightning flickered. Blue sparks crackled from the wingtips.

This spectral electricity lent a ghoulish tinge to Nate's grey-green pallor.

"Jesus H. Christ!"

He wrenched himself away from the window. Tugging out a vast handkerchief, he smeared his shining forehead greasily. Behind him, Mack and Lefty sat as still and stolid as stone. Only a brittle glitter in their eyes betrayed them when the aircraft lurched and dipped into a trough.

At Nate's side, Trixie lifted the lid on a large box of chocolates.

"What's the matter, Daddy?"

The narrow passenger cabin seemed to spring upwards abruptly, hang still for a moment before plummeting again. O'Dwyer's stomach jumped into his throat.

"What's the matter!" he spluttered. "This lousy crate's buckin' like—!"

Trixie made her selection and popped the candy into her mouth. Smiling, she chewed slowly and extravagantly. The plane climbed an invisible mountain and went down the other side. Nate stared in stark horror. Ashen-faced, he groaned and lurched to his feet. With his hand clamped over his mouth, he staggered off down the aisle, making for the tail. Trixie shrugged and picked out another chocolate.

Several rows behind her, Jeremy noted Nate's passing.

"By Jove, we are having a rough time of it!"

The airframe shuddered violently. Everything rattled. The bulkheads rattled. The spars rattled. The sparse furnishings rattled. Celia's teeth rattled.

"Bloody hell!" she gasped, clutching the arms of her seat till her knuckles bled white.

Jeremy swallowed hard and bent across to pat her hand.

"Steady, old thing."

The light from the window tinted their drawn features with a sickly shade of sulfur. Something up front slid and fell with a crash. Celia winced.

"When I said I wanted adventure this isn't quite what I had in mind."

Jeremy managed a weak smile.

"Chin up. One day we'll look back on this and laugh."

The Trimotor bounced like a stone skipping on water. Jeremy clutched at his belt buckle. Celia closed her eyes.

All blue and brass buttons, a steward materialized at her side. He hovered there attentively.

"Good afternoon, Sir, Madam. Will you be requiring wine with your lunch?"

He didn't bat an eyelid when Celia was sick all over his shoes.

The river stank. The color of lead, it wound sluggishly between crumbling banks of black mud, overhung by the ragged, mattering walls of the jungle. The sky above was a glaring blank, the air thick and stifling.

The boat's propeller stirred up eddies in a skin of swirling slime. A flaking, off-white barge, its senile motors coughed and stuttered uncertainly, as it tacked around a rotting tangle of driftwood.

"God damn it to hell!"

Nate's fist bruised the worm-eaten rail that girded the blunt prow. For the umpteenth time, he rooted in his pocket and read the words printed on a crumpled slip of paper. SO FAR SO GOOD. STOP. METROPOLE SQUAD TAKEN FOR A RIDE. STOP. POLACK GONE TO GROUND. STOP. EXPECT RESULTS SOON. STOP. GIANELLI.

O'Dwyer scowled viciously. Expect results soon. What the hell does that mean? He glanced at Mack and Lefty, standing close at hand, staring out ahead like Washington crossing the Delaware. This was a mistake. They should never have left the city. He shoulda just gone and taken out that mug with his own bare hands.

He glared at the black, enigmatic walls of the forest. Sweat left dark patches on his tan bush jacket. The salty beads on his forehead attracted a darting swarm and he cursed and swiped vigorously.

The Captain watched him with mild amusement. A lean, swarthy man in faded dungarees and a frayed straw boater, his lip curled contemptuously. Fat, greasy pig of an Americano, he think he come here on a country ramble!

"I say, a trifle sticky, what?"

Jeremy joined the skipper in his rickety wheelhouse. He removed his brand new pith helmet and wiped the sweatband carefully. The gilt of its "by Royal appointment" emblem was already dulling. The Captain looked him up and down, in his tailored safari suit. A milk-sop, he concluded. He knew the type, always the first to go down with the jungle fever, carried home grey-faced and mumbling, wrapped in mosquito netting.

"Like a bally Turkish bath."

The captain mellowed a little when his new companion produced a silver case and offered him a cigarette.

"It will be cooler in the mountains, Senor."

Towards the stern, a half open hatch was heaved up all the way.

"Jeez, this is some flea-bitten old tub!"

Trixie emerged, squinting, into the daylight. She wore a pink silk blouse, tied up to expose a pale flash of midriff, light blue slacks that billowed as she strolled along the deck.

Halfway, there was a tattered awning. There Celia sat wearily on one of a jumble of packing cases, stirring the air tepidly with a paper fan. She tilted her head back and fumbled with a shirt button, perspiration glistening at her throat.

"That's it, dearie," Trixie grinned down at her. "Relax and let some air in."

Celia let go the button and appraised her fellow passenger coolly. She felt Trixie's bright eyes flick all over her and, furious with herself, was suddenly blushing. Trixie laughed abruptly, patted her bare middle, and moved on.

The Captain was riveted to the lazy, expansive swing of her hips. Eyes narrowing, he wiped his hand across his mouth, fingers rasping on stubble.

"Aaii!" he gasped. "What a piece of ass!"

Jeremy was entranced by the lithe, liquid swagger of her stride. Accustomed to the cool and crisp damsels of the Shires, this was a creature from another planet.

"I say, rather, a real American platinum blonde!"

Trixie joined Nate in the bow. Shading her eyes, she looked out over the broad, dull river, its towering black fringes converging to a point lost in the shimmering grease of the heat haze, the pale and distant mountain tops seeming to hang upon the glaring sky.

She turned her back on the landscape, leaning on the rail. Arching her body, she tilted her face up to the sun. Her breasts thrust sharply against the thin material of her blouse. The silken knot rode up, exposing more of her creamy middle. From beneath long lashes lowered to half mast, she saw the Captain lick his lips, that pretty Englishman exhale a gasp of tobacco smoke. She caught Celia's eye, back in the shadows, chuckled when she stiffened and quickly looked away.

O'Dwyer swore, disrupting his collar so as to wipe around the back of his neck.

"Don't ya ever sweat?" he demanded.

Trixie giggled saucily, wiggling her pelvis.

"Oh, you know I do, Daddy!"

Nate glowered and muttered angrily.

"I shoulda never let the wop talk me into this. I—!"

Something whizzed past his ear. The reed shaft of an arrow was quivering in one of the wooden posts of the awning.

Celia sprang to her feet, staring in amazement at the feathered projectile imbedded barely two feet from her head. Jeremy stood staring wildly all around, scanning the impenetrable walls of the jungle. The Captain flicked his cigarette butt into the water and turned the boat towards the middle of the river.

"Holy ——!"

O'Dwyer wore a broad Sam Browne belt, weighed down by a heavy holster. Scrabbling to release the flap, he hauled out a big .45.

"We're under attack!"

Close by, Mack and Lefty were jolted into action, the sharp crack of their .38s mingling with the boom of the heavy automatic. Trixie screeched and threw herself face down on the deck. With O'Dwyer bellowing obscenities, the mobsters bombarded the shoreline. Startled birds burst out of the treetops, flapping crazily in all directions. Gibbering with terror, long-tailed monkeys swung and scrambled to safety. Small branches fell with a splat into the water.

His features lit with excitement, Jeremy waved to a stunned Celia.

"Keep your head down, old thing!"

He turned towards the stern, poised to leap down from the wheelhouse.

"I'm going to get my rifle!"

The Captain swore and seized his arm.

"Don't be a fool!"

He made the wheel secure with a loop of leather, before dashing into the bows, gesticulating furiously.

"Stop it, you idiots! Stop it!"

Out of ammunition, Nate stood with the slide jammed open, fumbling in his pocket for another magazine. Mack scowled as the hammer fell on a spent cartridge. Lefty squeezed off another, raised a spurt of mud on the far bank.

The Captain clamped his hand over the torpedo's wrist.

"Stop making all that damned noise. It's only some bored Indian!"

Nate stared at him, then eyed the shore suspiciously. He grunted and shoved the Colt away. His bodyguards relaxed. Glaring, Trixie scrambled to her feet. She surveyed herself angrily; the filthy deck had left her smudged from head to toe.

"All that for one lousy Indian!" she snapped accusingly.

The Captain shrugged.

"It happens all the time."

He returned to the wheelhouse, growling under his breath about damn trigger happy Yankees. Nate frowned at the jungle with a brow like thunder. He shook his fist at it. Stomping over to the awning, he ripped the arrow from its resting place. Back at the rail, he held it high above his head and broke it in two.

"Aw, fer Chrissakes!"

The Ranchero Blanco was a sprawling, single-storey affair, huddling for shelter in the shadow of rugged foothills that cowered beneath the weight of forested mountains and the leaden, lowering skies above. Its worn whitewash was yellowed and flaking, red tiles streaked with dark moss and slime. Off to one side were rickety corrals and a sagging barn, to the other, a snake of low cabins creaked in the wind.

"Ain't this the pits!"

O'Dwyer glared in all directions, looking for someone to blame. With a cough and splutter, the rusty bus that had brought them from the landing turned and rattled away down the hillside.

The voyagers stood in a bunch, surrounded by their luggage. The rain, which had pounded down all morning, abated to a swirling mist. Mack and Lefty turned up the collars of their oilskins, turning their backs on the wind. Jeremy assisted a glowering Celia with the hood of her cape. Muttering darkly, Trixie struggled to unfurl a large umbrella.

"Goddamn!"

Though it was raining, it was still warm, and beneath his heavy oilskins O'Dwyer was sweating like a pig. What kind of a crazy country was this, where you got summer and winter all at the same time!

Having survived the Trimotor and the riverboat, Jeremy was prepared to look on the bright side.

"I say, cheer up, you lot. Let's go and announce ourselves."

He proceeded to squelch towards the Ranchero.

"Attaboy!" said Trixie, glancing round with a knowing glint in her eye to catch Celia frowning. She didn't see Nate watching her, his face dark with thunder.

Jeremy was barely halfway to the broad doors of the Ranchero when they burst open to exhale a mob of drably clad Indians. They advanced at the double, bare feet slapping in the mud, to gather up the trunks and cases and bear them off towards the chain of cabins.

"Welcome, my friends!"

A short, brown dumpling of a man waddled down off the porch and bore down upon them, straining the seams of a bottle green suit. Scuttling breathlessly from one to the other, he pressed the flesh all round, beaming, unabashed by the torpedoes' monolithic blankness or Nate O'Dwyer's scowl. He could scarcely contain himself when his eyes lit upon the female members of the party.

"Ah, such lovely ladies!"

With a flourish, he stooped to slobber over their hands. In a frosty humor, Celia managed to be polite. Trixie wrinkled her nose, wiping her fingers.

"My name is Gomez," the fat man gestured towards his weather-beaten establishment. "Welcome to the Ranchero Blanco!"

Reluctantly, they dressed for dinner. The dark humidity which clogged the confines of the Ranchero did not encourage formal evening wear.

"Aw, hell!"

Nate snarled at his reflection in the pitted bedroom mirror, struggling to construct his bow tie. The sound of Trixie humming a jazz tune as she preened herself deftly brought his blood to the boil.

"Get over here and give me a hand with this, will ya!"

The dining room was long and low-slung, ventilated tepidly by an Indian who squatted in a corner and pulled unenthusiastically on a rope connected to a fan. When Trixie sailed in, sheathed in something minimal in silk that seemed to breathe with her, the murmur of conversation stuttered and died. The men present leapt up to introduce themselves.

"Colonel Gustav von Seyfritz, late of the Imperial German Army!"

He clicked his heels and bowed. His iron grey hair was cropped close to the skull, an inverted moustache drawing the eye to a criss-cross of old duelling scars, and the glint of a monocle. In close attendance were Braun and Gruber, bullet headed, Prussian equivalents of Mack and Lefty, who stood flanking O'Dwyer. The big men sized each other up warily.

"Armand Dubois."

Being a Frenchman, he kissed her hand elegantly. Trixie lapped up his flowery compliments while Nate glowered and muttered under his breath. Dubois was neat and compact, wiry like a terrier, his moustaches sharp and waxed.

"Angus Mackenzie."

Grey haired and scholarly, but with a vigorous air, his Highland lilt hearty.

"Good evening, Miss Marlowe."

Jeremy greeted her eagerly. A little muscle twitched at the side of Nate's jaw, as Trixie took the young man's arm and let him lead her to the table. As she undulated into her chair, she grinned and winked at Celia, whose face turned to stone.

While Gomez fussed and the Indian servants bustled to and fro, the party settled to its meal. Trixie dug in heartily, but Nate only prodded with his fork. Gomez assured him that it was beef, but it wasn't like any beef he'd ever seen.

As Von Seyfritz contemplated the wine, Dubois drained his glass in a gulp and called for a refill. He saw the Prussian watching him disdainfully.

"Come on, mein herr." Dubois chuckled. "Loosen up a bit, let some of the starch out of your backbone."

"How typical," Von Seyfritz sniffed. "You French have lost what little discipline you had in the Great War."

Dubois waved him away blithely.

"That's all you sausage eaters ever think about is war, never happier than when you're up to your armpits in someone's guts."

Trixie tittered, but Jeremy intervened on Celia's behalf.

"I say, monsieur, there are ladies present, you know."

Celia smiled at him and Jeremy tingled all over. Trixie rolled her eyes heavenwards. Dubois duly apologized.

"Quite right," Mackenzie stated cheerily. "One should never bring politics to the dinner table."

"Absolutely," echoed Jeremy.

O'Dwyer groaned inwardly. He was a man who liked to keep his finger on the pulse, and now he was stranded a million miles away from it all.

When dinner was done, Gomez supervised the clearing of the table. His guests adjourned to the lounge, which boasted the luxury of a carpet and a broad semi-circle of serviceable armchairs. As they lit their cigarettes and cigars, the travelers explained their presence in such far-flung, foreign parts.

"The Big Cat," said Von Seyfritz. "I am a hunter."

"How can I put it....?" mused Dubois. "I have a talent for certain things which certain people find useful. At present I am as you might say, on holiday. It suits me at the moment to be inconspicuous."

"On the run?" Nate perked up a bit.

"Not in the sense you mean," Dubois smiled. "I am simply an adventurer."

"A mercenary," sneered Von Seyfritz.

Dubois never lost that smile.

"At least I only do it for the money, mon Colonel, and not because I enjoy it."

Red in the face, Von Seyfritz jumped to his feet.

"What I have done was in the service of the Fatherland, something you damned Frenchmen could never—!"

Dubois snorted. The Colonel fumed. Mackenzie rose to pacify them.

"Gentlemen, please!"

The Prussian subsided, muttering, Dubois shrugged. Nate was disappointed, a good barney might have livened things up a bit. It would have been a good one too, between that big Kraut and the wiry little Frog.

Celia stepped into a tense silence.

You haven't told us why you are here, Mr Mackenzie."

The Scotsman beamed.

"I am a Professor of Antiquities, Miss Cavendish. Rumors abound of strange and wondrous discoveries waiting to be made in these mist shrouded mountains."

Dubois chuckled.

"Yes, I've heard the stories, lost tribes and cities of gold. There isn't a native in this continent that isn't willing to tell you anything you want to hear, for a bottle of whiskey or a few beads."

"Ah," Mackenzie laughed. "You must have faith, monsieur."

The others told their stories. Celia was well known to them all, through her exploits on the tennis circuit, and they all envied Jeremy.

"I'm in business," grunted O'Dwyer, ignoring Dubois' smile.

"And you, Miss Marlowe?" inquired Jeremy.

"I'm a dancer."

I might have known, read the expression on Celia's face. Dubois lit up like a beacon.

"I knew it would be something exciting!"

Suddenly, Trixie rose from her chair, in a fluid motion that caught the breath in their throats.

"Gosh!" gasped Jeremy. "And I'll wager you're a topping dancer, Miss Marlowe!"

Nate scowled. Trixie threw back her head and laughed.

"You bet yer ass, handsome!"

She caught Celia appraising her, and laughed again when the English girl blushed and looked away.

Dubois, meanwhile, had discovered something. He rose and crossed the room, to inspect a battered phonograph.

"Perhaps, Miss Marlowe, you would care to dance for us."

"Like hell she will!" grated Nate.

But Dubois persisted, with Jeremy's encouragement, and even Mackenzie and Von Seyfritz joined in until at last O'Dwyer threw up his hands and relented.

"Okay, okay, what the hell!"

Trixie leafed through a sheaf of black discs, sliding them out of their paper sleeves.

"Okey-dokey," she made her choice. "Now give me some room!"

They pulled back the armchairs as far as they would go. Trixie put the record on and set the turntable spinning.

The disc was old and its crackly undertones lent the music an oddly faraway effect, something Latin and seductive, performed by an obscure Cuban dance band. Trixie played on its subtlety, and the intimacy of her surroundings. This was not the raw bump 'n grind of her routine at the Fat Cat. Instead, she slithered with gliding steps, the movements of her limbs fluid, the shifting tones and contours of her splendid body, sheathed in its second skin of silk, at first almost imperceptible.

Her arms raised and wafting like willows in a warm wind, she stood before them, a breathing, silver statue. Von Seyfritz sat ramrod straight, his eyes glittering. Dubois sucked sharply on a cigarette and exhaled the smoke in a long, low whistle.

The beat shifted gear and Trixie advanced upon her audience with a lengthy, sliding stride, a liquid motion that rippled gloriously from her toes to the top of her platinum head. The statue sprang into life, till the whole room seemed lit by the gleam of silver and alabaster. Then she stopped and, perfectly poised, turned slowly on the spot and looked at them, round the semi-circle. Dubois murmured reverently, the cigarette bobbing on his lower lip. Nate frowned and growled deep in his throat. Angus Mackenzie just sat there beaming, almost hugging himself with delight. Ah, how nothing ever changes, how for thousands of years women have so exerted their power over men!

A momentary, bursting pause, and then the exotic percussion was throbbing again. Suddenly, Trixie seemed to go into a world of her own. Her sharp features misted over with a mysterious veil, her eyes half closed, ruby lips parting. While yet hardly appearing to move, she used the expanses of the room. Her whole body shivered and vibrated, a quiver of the shoulders, a twitch of the hips. O'Dwyer looked surprised and cleared his throat nervously. Von Seyfritz's collar was suddenly tighter. Mackenzie's smile glowed with wonder. This magnificent creature was dancing to some other tune, to some music only she could hear.

Trixie rotated slowly to display the glorious opulence of her fundament, the shining silk stretched taut by the flare of her pelvis and the ceaseless movements of her thighs.

"I say!"

Jeremy's jaw dropped open. Celia's eyes flickered to him angrily, her brow clouding. Then she jerked, startled, for Trixie had materialized before her and was sinking to her knees, fixing her with a hooded gaze, from beneath half-lowered lashes. Trapped breath hissed past Dubois' clenched teeth. The monocle fell into Von Seyfritz's lap. O'Dwyer cursed in a hoarse whisper, his fists coiling till the blood drained from them.

Her arms outstretched, Trixie bent back slowly. Her eyes locked on Celia, she began to do things with her stomach, a small, quick flutter that grew into a long, slow undulation, a languid belly roll, as her shoulders rounded and then arched, her hips rocking forward and back.

Nate stared in amazement.

"Ye gods!" breathed Mackenzie. "How wonderfully primitive!"

Celia sat bolt upright, rigid and glaring, blushing hot scarlet. She couldn't tear her eyes away. Her supple body was suddenly brittle, wrapped in suffocating coils of tension. Her breath came in short, sharp gasps, and tiny beads of perspiration were glinting on her forehead.

The night was airless and humid. A dank and cloying stickiness clogged the narrow passages of the Ranchero Blanco and fell like a leaden weight upon its stifled bedrooms.

Naked, Celia padded across the bare boards, to stand before the chipped glass of her long wardrobe mirror. Her skin was clammy, and there were needles prickling all down her spine.

Frowning, Celia faced up to her reflection. The humidity put a sheen on her skin, highlighted by the amber glow of the lamps. She raised her arms, half-turned slowly to the right, then to the left, her eyes exploring, seeing herself as if for the first time. She revolved, looking back over her shoulder. Still frowning, she raised her arms higher. Tentatively, she swung her hips from side to side. She sucked her belly in, then let it out.

"Damn!"

Celia grimaced and turned away abruptly. Angrily, she tugged on a pair of baggy silk pyjamas. Extinguishing the lamps, she plunged the room from warm amber into the cool blue of moonlight. Scorning the blanket, she threw herself down and sprawled across the bed.

Time ticked by. Celia tossed and turned and grumbled, slipped into a dull stupor.

The door clicked open softly. A darker shadow detached itself from the gloom. Trixie stepped into a moonbeam, wrapped in a long, black satin cloak. Baffled, Celia stared. Trixie grinned.

Celia sat bolt upright on the bed, rigid and outraged.

"What on earth do you think you are doing?"

To her horror, Trixie let the cloak fall open. She wore nothing but a pair of tiny silk drawers. Head back, still smiling saucily, she put her hands on her hips, drew the black folds back and thrust the whole gleaming length of her body into the moonlight, her skin shining like white marble.

Celia's eyes widened.

"G–good God!" she gasped. "Cover yourself at once!"

Trixie laughed, a lively exhalation that played little tricks all over her body. Suddenly there was sweat shining on Celia's face.

With a quick shimmy of her shoulders, Trixie let the cloak slide to the floor, naked now save for that little bit of frilly silk. She clasped her hands behind her head. Her hips began to revolve slowly. Her belly drew inward, then sprang out. Her hips were gyrating up and around, grinding voluptuously.

Celia's mouth opened, but no sound came out. Smirking, Trixie bore down upon the bed.

Trixie knelt astride Celia's outstretched thighs. She flexed her naked shoulders and the moonlight sizzled on her skin. Transfixed by her unblinking predatory stare, Celia was paralyzed, barely able to breathe. At her core, all was in a giddy rush, a thrill of horror, an intoxicating assault upon her senses. The dark bedroom was aglow with the radiance of Trixie's flesh, the still air swimming in her natural perfumes.

In a trance, Celia knew that quick fingers had unbuttoned her pyjama jacket. She felt the silk slide away across her skin, a delicious electricity that brought a sharp intake of breath, made her arch her back, her face tilted up to the ceiling. She thought she heard shrill laughter, coming from somewhere far away. Then a firm pressure on her bare shoulders was pushing her down, unresisting, lying full length on the mattress.

Nimble fingers made light work of the knotted cord at her waist. With a whisper of silk, the trousers were gone. Suddenly, the warm air was cool on the sweat that soaked her body, as she lay there sighing, mumbling a protest that sounded somehow like a plea.

Hands were upon her, now quick, now slow, now soft, now firm, roving over her, exploring her. Helpless, Celia shivered and moaned. She shuddered and cried out, writhing insanely. Now the sweat was scalding, and inside she was molten. And when her last and deepest secrets were discovered, she reared up off the soaked sheets, her body a gleaming, straining arch, her classic profile contorted beyond recognition, her mouth gaping to vent forth dark inhuman sounds of ecstacy and despair.

The door burst open.

"What the—!"

The mass of Nate O'Dwyer blotted out the lamplit corridor.

"I thought so!"

The stark moonlight made the twisted mask of rage even more ghastly. He lumbered into the room, his great arms swinging.

"Goddamn!"

His voice rattled the window panes. Celia lay spread-eagled across the rumpled bedsheets, gasping, her body racked by great, convulsive sobs. As Nate advanced, Trixie backed away quickly. Her sharp features ugly with fear, she backpedalled until she bumped up against the wall. She cowered in Nate's shadow, and screeched as he grabbed her by her hair.

"Goddammit, I'm gonna—!"

O'Dwyer cocked his fist. Trixie capered with alarm.

"No, Daddy!" she shrieked. "Not the face!"

Nate grunted. His fist performed a short loop and thudded into her midriff. Trixie's face screwed up, her mouth gaping in a big O. Her legs buckled. When he let go of her hair she jackknifed, clutching at herself, collapsed onto her knees, her forehead resting on the floor. Nate glared down at her, prodding her with his toe.

"Get outta here!"

On her hands and knees, Trixie headed for the door. Nate rounded on Celia, who moaned, writhing on the bed.

"Now it's your turn!"

His vast bulk swelled to choke the confines of the room. His eyes blazed redly in a roaring, whirling blackness that was coming down to crush her. Celia screamed.

She woke screaming. She sat up wild-eyed, panting. The sheets were damp and twisted up beneath her. Sweat glued the thin pyjamas to her skin.

The door was flung open, rusty hinges squealing. A tall silhouette cast a long shadow in the shaft of lamplight that lanced into the dark bedroom.

"Oh—!"

Her heart pounded. The intruder took a step into the room.

"C…! Are you alright?"

Her shoulders sagged with relief as the panic subsided.

"Oh, Jeremy…"

She took long, deep breaths.

"It's n–nothing…a nightmare…that's all…"

He stopped, halfway to the bed, hesitating.

"Ah…righto…"

He began to back away.

"Right then…sleep tight…"

A confusion of images was a whirling blur in her brain. Strangling a cry, Celia leapt from the bed and sprang upon him, seizing a double fistful of his pyjama jacket, ripping away the breast pocket with its embroidered crest.

"I say—!"

Jeremy was reeling backwards. Breath hissing between clenched teeth, she hauled him towards her.

"No!"

Celia tore the jacket wide open, buttons flying. Her nails raked his bare chest, making him shout out loud. She kissed him brutally, crushing his lips with her mouth.

"No!" she gasped hoarsely. "You're staying with me!"

Snoring, Nate rolled over ponderously. A strand of drool dangled from his chin.

"Huh…!"

Hands folded behind her head, Trixie lay staring up at the stained ceiling.

"Well at least someone's havin' fun!"

She jabbed O'Dwyer with her elbow, but only broke the rhythm of his snoring for an instant.

"Bitch!"

She lay in the deep blue, listening to the muffled sounds that filtered through the wall. Her eyes burned with a dark fire.

EPISODE 3:
STRANGE GOLD

Beneath a blank and glaring sky, the jungle muttered fitfully.

Out of the constant chatter of nature grew another, more artificial sound, the rhythmic slash of a machete. The tattered fringe of a clearing parted, its heavy veils shredded by the flashing steel. A file of Indian bearers came trudging into view, a feast of game dangling from poles carried between them.

"Jeez! How much further?"

Nate flapped angrily at the tiny flies that swarmed around his face. His tan shirt was mottled with black patches of sweat. A large kerchief was as oily as a mechanic's rag.

"A good afternoon's march," Von Seyfritz tossed his rifle to Gruber. "I suggest we stop here for refreshment."

Nate growled something, sat down heavily on a fallen log. Supervised by Mackenzie, the natives bustled about setting up camp. The hunting party took possession of the clearing, glad of this respite from the steamy confines of the forest. Dubois fished out a crumpled pack of cigarettes, tossing away a broken casualty. The Indians squabbled briefly over the pieces.

"Gotta match, Frenchie?"

Nate was right, Trixie never seemed to sweat. Looking crisp, she sauntered away, blowing a cloud of blue-grey smoke up towards the treetops.

Dabbing her brow with an inadequate handkerchief, Celia made her way to Jeremy, who was crouched by a small stove, fanning it into life. Coolly, Trixie stepped across her path, intercepting the dark girl as she reached her objective. Showing her teeth, Trixie winked extravagantly. Celia stiffened and sidestepped her, surprised Jeremy by flinging her arm around his shoulders, as he stood back from the stove, satisfied.

O'Dwyer rose from the log and lumbered over to survey the trophies. A small deer stared back at him with a dead, unseeing eye, its mouth ringed by black, coagulated blood.

"A fine shot," Von Seyfritz congratulated him. "Two hundred yards on the run."

Nate shrugged. It was easy when they weren't shooting back.

"Aw, I wanted the Big Cat."

The Prussian smiled, a bleak, fleeting glimmer of ice.

"Not so easy, my friend. One first has to stake out the bait."

Nate watched Trixie take a mug of coffee from an eager Jeremy, her swagger making Celia frown.

"I know what I'd like to stake out for bait!" he grated harshly.

He glared, and Trixie's eyes frosted over. Von Seyfritz paused before a dangling wild pig, flicking the flies away from it with his glove.

"Not a bad shot of mine," he observed. "Right through the eye."

Dubois lit another cigarette.

"That's what you square-heads are best at," he snorted. "Slaughtering the innocent."

The Colonel bridled, his monocle flashing.

"By God, sir," he shouted. "I will endure your insults no longer!"

His right hand slapped the holster at his belt. From where he squatted by the stove, Dubois sprang nimbly to his feet. Trixie squawked and scampered towards the edge of the clearing. Jeremy positioned himself to shield Celia.

"We are both armed, sir," the Prussian boomed. "If you are man enough to give me satisfaction!"

Nate stepped out of the line of fire. His eyes gleamed. Some real entertainment at last.

Dubois was edging sideways in a wide circle, his hand hovering above the exposed butt of his heavy revolver. His course took him towards Trixie, who yelled and retreated further. The forest held its breath, as the Prussian turned to follow the Frenchman stalking around him, a brittle glitter in their eyes. Von Seyfritz unclipped the flap of his holster.

They drew, but when they did it was to wheel as one towards a sudden commotion, beyond the green wall of the clearing. Nate scrambled for his rifle, calling on Mack and Lefty, who, like their Prussian counterparts, were clawing out their pistols.

A slight figure staggered into the clearing. Gesticulating feebly, it lurched forward and fell. Mackenzie was the first to get there. The others clustered round.

"Ye gods!"

It was a young Indian, naked save for a tattered loincloth.

"Ugh!" exclaimed Trixie, wrinkling her nose.

Gasping, Celia turned away, her gorge rising.

Head to toe, the Indian was horribly mutilated. His long black hair was burnt to a stubble, his scalp blistered and bleeding. Down his right side, the flesh and sinew were wiped away, black and bubbling. Parts of his face were melted down to the skull, the bones showing starkly, his lips gone to leave the teeth exposed in a ghastly, chattering grin.

"Good grief!" was all that Jeremy could manage. Even O'Dwyer was pale.

"In all my years," Dubois croaked hoarsely. "I have never seen such wounds!"

The Indian convulsed, babbling something.

"What's he saying?" Nate asked.

Kneeling beside the writhing form, Mackenzie pressed closer.

"I know some of the local dialects."

Froth flecked what was left of the Indian's chin. His eyes rolled frantically.

"Something about men of silver, and gods from the sky."

They glanced at each other, plainly mystified. The Indian's breath rattled harshly in his throat. He stiffened, shuddered, then went limp, his last breath expelled in a long sigh.

"That's it," O'Dwyer stated.

They stood around the body for a little while.

"What could have done such a thing?" Von Seyfritz pondered.

"I've never seen anything like it," said Dubois.

The hunters drifted away, shaking their heads. Dubois offered Celia his hip flask, which she accepted gratefully. About to follow them, Jeremy stopped suddenly.

"I say, Professor, I think he has something in his hand."

Mackenzie knelt back down again.

"By George, I do believe you're right."

The Indian's dead hand was clenched tightly. When Jeremy hesitated, Mackenzie struggled to prise the brown fingers open.

"There!"

Something dropped out on to the grass. It glinted brightly. Mackenzie scooped it up quickly, turning it over on his palm.

"My God!" he exclaimed, his face lit with amazement.

Jeremy bent closer to see.

"What is it, Professor?"

Mackenzie didn't hear him. An odd glaze came across his eyes.

"It can't be," he murmured in faraway tones. "But it is....."

Suddenly, his gaze was bright with fever. Rising, he seized Jeremy's shoulder with a grip of iron.

"Keep this under your hat, my boy. Don't breathe a word of this to anyone!"

He shoved the object into his pocket, buttoning the flap carefully.

"Not until I have consulted my books."

Mackenzie strode away briskly. Rubbing his shoulder, Jeremy saw Celia approaching.

"What was all that about?" she asked.

Jeremy was baffled.

"Beats me, old thing. You know these mad scientists."

The hunters broke camp and plodded on, back along the jungle trails to the Ranchero Blanco. All the way, Mackenzie checked secretly on the small bulge in his pocket. A tide of exhileration was rising within him.

Brandy and cigars. Three days later.

Nate discovered a week-old American newspaper. He seized it eagerly, made its pages rattle.

"Bah!"

No news. No Polack found floating face down in the river or tossed into a ditch. O'Dwyer cursed and crushed the newsprint into a ball, crunching it between his great spadelike hands.

"What's that rat Gianelli doing?" he snapped at Mack and Lefty. "I shoulda never left him in charge!"

Dubois smiled knowingly.

"Business troubles?"

Nate bristled.

"Yeah, that's right!"

The Frenchman chuckled. He swirled his liquor round the glass, then tossed it down in a gulp. Across the room, Von Seyfritz stared at him balefully. Damn Frenchmen, he muttered to the towering Braun and Gruber, the day of reckoning will come.

An hour drifted by. Jeremy, who had vacationed in Germany, tried to make conversation with Von Seyfritz. The Colonel's experiences out of uniform being somewhat limited, his efforts were short-lasting. Dubois proved more entertaining, with a colorful discourse on the seedy delights of Tangiers and Shanghai. Meanwhile, O'Dwyer and Von Seyfritz settled into an earnest debate on the problems of selecting a handgun with sufficient stopping power and the respective merits of revolver and automatic.

The door banged open and Mackenzie bounded into the room. There was a glow of excitement about him that brought the conversation to a halt.

"Gentlemen," his highland lilt rang like a bell. "Your attention please!"

Beneath his arm, the Professor carried an enormous, leather-bound volume. He crossed the room quickly and set it down on a small table. The others rose and followed him. They sensed his excitement and waited expectantly. Mackenzie took a deep breath.

"Gentlemen," he commenced. "Do you recall that poor fellow who came upon us in the jungle?"

"How could we forget," Dubois sucked on his cigar. "It was incredible."

"I have seen flamethrowers have such an effect on men caught in their trenches," said Von Seyfritz. "But it's not the kind of thing that one expects to find out here."

"Yes indeed," Mackenzie nodded. "Militarily, the peoples of this region are still virtually in the Stone Age."

The Professor rooted in his pockets.

"Be that as it may," he exclaimed. "That unfortunate chap has left us with an even greater mystery!"

His hand withdrew from his pocket, clutching the object which he had prised from the dead Indian's fingers. As the others crowded closer, he placed it on the table.

"There!"

It was a three inch figurine, standing to attention. The legs of a stork supported the torso of a man, with distinctly canine features, topped by an odd, square head-dress.

"What do you make of that?"

Dubois prodded it with a fingertip.

"Gold, is it not?"

Mackenzie beamed.

"Aye, pure gold!"

Nate picked it up, weighing the tiny figure on this palm. He passed it to Von Seyfritz.

"Well, what is it?"

A strange light was dancing in Mackenzie's eyes. He flung open the book and leafed through its yellowed pages. He stopped, jabbing with his finger. There, depicted in a rough etching, was the twin of the golden figure.

"Pelath U-Thol!" the Professor declared. "One of the lesser gods of the Fertile Crescent!"

The others stared at him in confusion.

"I say, steady on," Jeremy blurted. "This isn't the Med, you know."

"Ancient Mesopotamia," murmured Dubois. "But what does it mean?"

Mackenzie ushered them to the armchairs, taking center stage.

"My friends, with our ships and aeroplanes, we like to imagine that we are the first of our species to travel further than our own back yards."

He held a dramatic pause. His companions waited impatiently.

"But Man has been an explorer and an adventurer since the very dawn of recorded time."

Mackenzie turned to Jeremy.

"Is it not said by some that the Phoenicians built Stonehenge?"

He inclined to O'Dwyer.

"And by others that the Vikings, and not Columbus, discovered America?"

Nate shrugged. He didn't much care either way.

"I have been preoccupied for some time by such speculations," the Professor continued. "And have devoted my recent studies to the question of whether certain racial and cultural similarities between the ancient civilizations of the Americas and the Mediterranean amount to more than mere coincidence."

With a flourish, he held up the little gold idol. It flashed in the light.

"And this has only served to deepen my suspicions!"

The others looked skeptical, all except Jeremy, who was caught up in Mackenzie's excitement.

"I say, Professor, what was it that the Indian said about men of silver and sky gods?"

Mackenzie hugged himself with glee.

"Mysteries upon mysteries!"

He sobered, banging a fist down on the table.

"The answers, I am sure, lie hidden in the mountains. Who knows what earth-shattering discoveries await us!"

"Hey, whaddaya mean, us?" Nate interrupted.

Mackenzie flung his arms out wide.

"This is an opportunity we cannot afford to miss," he fanfared. "Between us, we have all the resources necessary to mount an immediate expedition!"

There was an uncomfortable pause. Only Jeremy looked enthusiastic. Dubois cleared his throat nervously.

"Come, monsieur," Mackenzie addressed him. "Where is that fabled Gallic dash?"

His hand sawing the air, he turned to Von Seyfritz and O'Dwyer.

"And when has a German officer ever shrunk from a challenge, or an American ignored opportunity?"

He was irresistible. Held on high, the golden idol twinkled.

The Colonel adjusted his monocle.

"Well, the hunting has been unsatisfactory," he stated. "If nothing else, there may be better game in the mountains."

O'Dwyer held his hand out for the little figure. Mackenzie dropped it on his palm.

"I bet there's more where this came from," Nate mused, the glint of precious metal reflected in his eyes.

"Absolutely," murmured Dubois.

The Frenchman grinned and shrugged his shoulders.

"Anyway, I have nothing better to do!"

The old boat was on the move again, chugging up river. The water was like black glass, the wooden prow cleaving it as sharp as a diamond cutter.

"Remarkable!" exclaimed Mackenzie, his eyes bright with excitement.

The Captain let go the wheel just long enough to light a cigarette.

"Si, senor, this old river, she have many faces."

The boat lay low in the water, her foredeck piled high with crated supplies, her aft crowded with Indian porters, all sat cross-legged on the planking, muttering lowly amongst themselves. Their course drew them towards the ragged bank, and an overhanging branch scraped the dirty awning. Celia started, a large canteen frozen halfway to her lips.

Jeremy grinned at her reassuringly. Frowning, she tugged off her bandana, splashed it liberally and began to wipe her face.

"Cheer up, old thing," beamed Jeremy. "Where's your spirit of adventure?"

Von Seyfritz mounted the heap of crates, monarch of all he surveyed. His gaze soared above the dark jungle, up to the forested foothills and the savage peaks beyond. The mountains were brandished like swordblades, each a challenge ringing in the sky.

"Ah," he exulted. "When did a man have such an opportunity to be tested?"

Braun and Gruber nodded, their jaws jutting with determination. O'Dwyer was less enthusiastic.

"Yeah, well, right now," he grumbled. "I'd swap it all for the chance to walk into a bar and order an ice cold beer."

Leaning on the rail, Dubois chuckled.

"There you have my sympathy, monsieur."

Then, suddenly, the Frenchman was alert, his head cocked to one side, listening intently.

"What's that?"

The others were mystified.

"What's what?"

Dubois held up his hand.

"There, can't you hear it?"

The Captain stilled the engine and let the boat drift. The hunters craned towards the mountains, straining their ears.

"You must hear it!"

They heard nothing but the muttering jungle. Then Mackenzie started.

"Yes!"

A pulse that was separate in its constancy, an insistent throbbing, a vibration.

"By Jove!" gasped Jeremy. At his side, Celia shivered.

Mackenzie opened his mouth to speak, then froze, his eyes growing large with astonishment. The others turned, as he pointed amidships.

"What the—!"

Trixie threw down her "Modern Screen" magazine. She rose stiffly, stood rigid, her eyes half-shut and glazed over. The distant throbbing seemed to swell and hang above them. As they stared in amazement, the silver-haired girl began to tremble all over. The drumming pulse grew in its brooding intensity, and she began to dance. She crossed the deck with little shuffling steps, her head lolling, her face now down now up to the sky, her hips swaying.

"Aya!" the Captain gulped. "I have heard of this, but I have not seen it before!"

He crossed himself, but the brief incantation he uttered was in a pagan tongue. In the stern, the natives jumped to their feet and huddled in a bunch, chattering nervously.

"Aw, cut it out!"

Snarling, Nate sprang across the deck. His great arms swinging, he cuffed Trixie round the side of her head. She yelped and staggered, a wild light in her eyes, looking all about, bewildered.

"Ya crazy—!"

A reed arrow hummed out of the jungle. It pinged off Nate's pith helmet and away on a disorientated trajectory, splatting on the black water without so much as a ripple.

Nate measured the distance to the bank. With a great bull bellow of rage, he clawed out the .45 auto. The big pistol roared, and in an instant he had vaulted over the rail. He vanished momentarily, came up spluttering, was wading ashore in water up to his chin. Clambering up the muddy bank, he ripped aside the green curtain and was gone. Mack and Lefty looked at each other, then drew their .38s and followed. Von Seyfritz looked all set to join them, until Dubois caught him by the arm.

"Don't waste your energy, mon Colonel," he grinned. "He's only chasing shadows."

They waited impatiently, able to hear Nate shouting and crashing about. The jungle screeched and chattered, alarmed by the boom of the .45. Jeremy tugged out his binoculars. The Captain sat down and rolled a cigarette. Trixie swayed, still dizzy and confused. Celia curled her lip. Von Seyfritz cursed all lunatic Americans, while Dubois rocked with silent laughter.

"Here they come."

The commotion subsided. Three rather sorry figures clambered back over the rail. Streaked with mud and festooned with twigs and dead leaves, Nate glared, daring them to say something. One Indian was too excited to notice. He approached O'Dwyer, gesticulating wildly. He shouted at the big American, pointing at him, at the jungle, and at Trixie.

"What's he yammerin' about?" Nate demanded.

"Ah, something about the music of the gods," Mackenzie translated nervously. "And, er, you should not have struck the silver dancer."

Nate's eyes glittered viciously.

"Oh yeah, says who?"

His huge fist shot out like a battering ram. His ranting cut short, the Indian ran backwards all the way to the stern. Spitting teeth, he cannoned into the knot of his companions, bowling them over like ninepins. They collapsed in a tangle of limbs, but after a brief struggle were back on their feet, murmuring angrily.

Ready for trouble, Nate released the flap of his holster. Von Seyfritz stepped to his side, but Mackenzie intervened, flapping his hands placatingly.

"No gentlemen, we must maintain their goodwill!"

Cursing, O'Dwyer dug in his pockets. A handful of coins clattered onto the deck.

"Here, that oughta do it."

Nate turned his back and stalked away. The others relaxed. Dubois listened, but could hear only the whisperings of the forest. The Captain lit his cigarette, reaching out to start the engine. Then they all jumped, startled by a squawk from Trixie, a sharp bark of alarm.

"Hey, whaddaya mugs doin'?"

They stared in amazement, as the Indians shuffled forward on their knees, laying the coins at her feet.

EPISODE 4:
KIDNAPPED

A nervous mile along the river, a grey beach swung into view. Jutting from it was a ramshackle wooden pier, and beyond, in the thinned out fringe of trees, a clutch of teetering shanties.

The Captain grunted and altered course. The boat drew alongside the makeshift dock, coming to rest with a wheeze and splutter. It was late afternoon, and the sun slanted in at a narrow angle. The clouds, pierced by the jagged mountaintops, were slowly purpling, as the adventurers stretched themselves and prepared to disembark.

"I suggest we set up camp here on the shore," said Mackenzie. "And tomorrow we can make a start for the mountains."

Nate rubbed a hand across his mouth, stubble rasping.

"Well, I don't know about you," he grated. "But I needs a drink."

He stomped off towards the treeline. With a jerk of his thumb, he left Mack and Lefty to watch over the porters, who were slowly unpacking the tents. Barking orders at his henchmen to assist them, Von Seyfritz wheeled to follow O'Dwyer. Dubois cocked an eye at Trixie, then loped off after the big men. Trixie hesitated, before plodding in his footsteps, making heavy work of the grey sand.

The rickety shacks were spaced out at random, amidst clumps of scrub and stunted trees. Loungers eyed their passage, and the explorers glanced around warily. The locals all looked the same, dark-skinned and ragged, clad in dirty shirts down to their knees and baggy trousers. Most were bare-footed. One or two were distinguished by long cleavers, thrust into a broad belt.

"The police?" suggested Dubois.

"Coppers!" snorted O'Dwyer. "Well, they'd better not make any trouble!"

They were drawn to a shack larger than the others, decorated by a strand of faded bunting, tacked along its awning. From the open door drifted the low murmur of voices, the chink of glasses.

"This looks like the spot."

They clomped up the few steps and filed inside. When their eyes adjusted to the gloom, they saw a dusty barn, a counter made up of a plank across two barrels, bare floorboards dotted with small tables, densely populated. There was only one window and a hanging lamp, so the light was a dirty sepia, hazed with cigarette smoke, the air thick with the smell of mud and sweat and stale tobacco.

"Jeez!" Trixie wrinkled her nose. "Ain't this a class joint!"

Conversation died as they entered the saloon. When Trixie stepped under the lamp there was an abrupt exhalation.

"Hi boys," she grinned nervously. "How ya doin'?"

Nate grabbed her sleeve and steered her to the bar. Their eyes raking the room like guns in a turret, the Prussian and Frenchman followed. The bartender, a singularly greasy and globular individual, flashed a gap-toothed grin and waited expectantly. Everyone was watching them. Trixie could feel their hot gaze crawling on her skin.

"Whiskey!" barked Nate.

His grin unflinching, the barman produced a dusty glass and filled it from an anonymous bottle. Nate slammed it back in a gulp.

"Holy—!"

Gagging, he reeled and clutched at this throat, beads of sweat breaking out on his forehead. Red-faced, he glared at the empty glass with horror and amazement.

"What the hell is that stuff?" he spluttered.

A ripple of laughter rolled around the room. Dubois picked up the bottle and sniffed at it tentatively.

"Whiskey," he confirmed.

"The hell it is!" Nate croaked hoarsely.

"Well," smiled the Frenchman. "It's what passes for whiskey in this part of the world."

Von Seyfritz refilled the glass and held it up to the lamp.

"And how do they concoct this infernal beverage?" he inquired.

"In various ways," Dubois chuckled. "Mix one pint of creosote with one barrel of raw alcohol, add liquid coffee to a barrel of alcohol until the desired shade of gold is achieved, then add red pepper and chewing tobacco to give it extra bite...."

They stared at him. The bartender just carried right on grinning.

"Fill a barrel to the halfway mark with water and then add one pound of burned sugar, one plug of chewing tobacco, and one ounce of sulfuric acid before topping up the barrel with raw alcohol."

Nate was turning green.

"Add grape juice and it becomes brandy."

Sweating, O'Dwyer shook his head. Trixie laughed.

"Aw, c'mon, Daddy, it ain't no worse than the stuff you and the boys used to make in the bathtub."

Nate rolled his eyes.

"I only made the damn stuff," he barked. "I didn't drink it!"

They were approached by one of the local inhabitants. He was taller than his fellows and broader in the shoulder. His straw sombrero sported a snakeskin hatband, and the machete shoved into his belt had brass studs tacked into its hilt. Revealing his tobacco stained teeth in a lop-sided leer, he sidled up to Trixie, twirling his moustaches.

"No thanks, buster," Trixie grimaced. "Not today."

Undaunted, her suitor bent close to murmur sweet nothings in her ear. Wincing, Trixie recoiled from his stale breath. He already had a broken nose and a criss-cross of old scars on his cheek, an effect not improved by the lecherous smirk that twisted his dark features. Clucking his tongue, he reached out to chuck her under the chin.

"Hey, cut that out, ya big palooka!"

Trixie slapped him hard across the face, with a crack that rang like a pistol shot. There was a collective exclamation from the assembled throng. The tall man took a hasty step backwards, clutching his cheek. For a moment, his eyes blazed with fury. Then he laughed and lunged forward, grabbing for her.

The laugh died as his wrist was seized in a vice of iron. The alcohol-fuelled fires turned to ice, as he felt the bones grind in the grip of a glaring monster. Snarling, Nate spun him like a toy, twisted his arm up behind his back and propelled him across the room. He bounced on the floor like a stone skipping on water, crashed into a table and brought everything down in a tangled heap of limbs and broken furniture.

There was a short pause while the tall man extricated himself and rose shakily to his feet. He was aware that everyone was watching him. Stooping, he retrieved the sombrero and wedged it back onto his head. Then, all at once, he let out a shout and hauled the long machete from his belt. He rushed at O'Dwyer, the steel gleaming in the lamplight.

"Okay, bub, ya asked for it!"

Nate stepped forward to meet him. His bulk deceptive, he feinted, dropping his shoulder to let the broad blade whistle by. He swung a short hook to the breadbasket, and his opponent belched and doubled up, the machete clattering on the floor. The big American followed through with a sweeping uppercut. The straw hat sailed across the room. Its owner flew after it, performed a perfect backward somersault, landing with a crash and lying motionless.

A great gasp went up from the crowd. They froze half out of their seats, as Dubois and Von Seyfritz advanced with pistols drawn. Nate glared down at his fallen adversary, before turning his rage on Trixie.

"Wherever ya go, there's always trouble!"

She shrank from him, but he seized her arm so tight she squealed, her face gone pale. He gestured at their ragged audience.

"I oughta let these bums have ya," he rasped. "That would teach ya!"

Dubois cleared his throat.

"I think we should get back to the others," he interjected. "I have a feeling we have tangled with the Chief of Police."

"Indeed," Von Seyfritz agreed. "For once I am of the opinion that discretion is the better part of valor."

Brandishing their pistols, they backed out in a bunch, all the way across the sand. Bringing their bottles, the drinkers followed as far as the porch. By the time they reached the boat, the shadows were falling and there was only a glimmer on the horizon. O'Dwyer grumbled, but there was no way the Captain was going to take to the river by night.

When the moon escaped the clouds, the sand had the dull sheen of pewter. The huddle of tents bunched up by the wharf stood out starkly against the black river. An unseen nightbird clucked nervously.

Feet crunched the coarse grains. With a long rifle cradled on his arm, Jeremy patrolled the perimeter. His eyes roved along the dark treeline. His imagination conjured big cats stalking, painted aborigines lurking in the shadows, their bows at the ready. He filled his lungs with the tepid night air, excitement tingling within him. He could hardly believe it. Here he was, living the adventures that he had read about at school.

Jeremy marched on, every inch the Great White Hunter. Then a slim shape appeared at his side, a hand falling softly on his arm. The Great White Hunter jumped clear off the ground, his heart leaping into his mouth.

"Oh, I'm sorry," whispered Celia. "Did I startle you?"

She was wrapped in a silken robe, the long tassels knotted at her waist emphasizing her supple contours. In the moonlight, her cool features had the luster of pearl.

Jeremy cleared his throat. The palpitations subsided. Relieved, he flashed a rueful grin.

"Just a bit, old thing."

Celia smiled and squeezed his arm. Her perfume enveloped him and the lump sprang back into his throat.

"I couldn't sleep," she gazed up at the moon. "I thought I might go for a walk."

Jeremy frowned.

"I don't think you should, C," he cautioned. "After what happened today, the natives might be restless."

Celia shrugged.

"Oh, just a little way up the beach and back. I won't go far."

She took his free hand in hers. Her fingers were cool, and a delicious thrill quivered through the young Englishman.

"Besides, I'll have you to guard me."

She set off at a brisk pace, drawing him with her. Jeremy marveled at the moonlight sheening like silver over the liquid contours of the silk. Her stride was lithe and determined, that athletic swagger which had graced the grass courts. Jeremy's adventure was complete, and he stepped out eagerly.

Suddenly, Celia stopped and turned to face him. Jeremy braked hurriedly. With a flourish, Celia flung her arms up to the heavens. Her eyes were shining. Jeremy was intoxicated.

"Ah!" sighed Celia. "This night was made for love!"

Jeremy shuffled nervously.

"Ah, er, w–was it.....?"

Celia laughed somewhere deep down inside, a throaty sound that made his senses whirl dizzily. She tossed her head, her eyes flashing.

"Kiss me!" she exclaimed, striking a pose. "Kiss me, my fool!"

Gulping, Jeremy fumbled to sling his rifle. Celia pounced to wrap him in a crushing embrace. Her hot breath raked his face, and then her tongue was lashing about inside his mouth. Abruptly, she released him, let him reel and stagger back. Stunned, he saw her advance upon him, impaling him with a hooded, predatory stare.

"I s–s–say, C!" he stammered. "I—!"

He didn't see the long cudgel that whispered out of the shadows, descending with surgical precision just behind his ear. With no more than a grunt, Jeremy slumped face down in the sand.

Celia stared at him in mute amazement. Then the shadows split and were dancing all around her. She threw back her head to scream, but a sticky hand was clamped brutally across her mouth.

She whirled and tried to run, but now there were rough hands all over her, the sand slipping and sliding beneath her. Gasping, she writhed and twisted, but only succeeded in falling from one rude embrace into another. Kicking out wildly, she met only thin air, though the dark shapes pressed in close upon her.

Panic boiling over, Celia felt herself being lifted clear off the ground, her whole body heaving against the iron grip that was fixed upon her limbs. For an instant, she was free, fell heavily, the breath wrenched out of her.

Rolling on the sand, Celia tried to scramble to her feet. The next thing she knew, there was a fearful impact to the side of her head. She was tumbling through a blaze of black sparks. Oblivion.

Groaning, Jeremy rolled over. Blinking sand out his eyes, he groped for the fallen rifle. His fingers hooked the sling and he dragged it towards him.

His head pounded like a hammer as he strained to sit up. The dark treetops were revolving dizzily. He struggled to focus, looking wildly all around.

"C–C–C….?"

She was drowning, clawing her way out of roaring black waters.

Celia's vision cleared abruptly. Her head was lolling and the lamplight stabbed into her eyes. A wave of nausea rolled over her, left a prickle of cold sweat down her spine. The bitter tang of bile rasped in her throat.

She was slumped awkwardly on a plain wooden chair. Her hands were bound tightly behind her back, the rough twine chafing her skin. The silken robe was crumpled and askew, pulled down over one shoulder and rumpled up above her knees. Celia fought down a momentary spasm of panic, a hot flash of perspiration breaking out all over her. She studied her surroundings. A bare, whitewashed cell, flaking and peeling, sealed by an ironbound door. She listened intently, but heard nothing. Fear gnawed at her, turning her stomach to water. Then, a rising anger.

There were voices outside. Bolts clashed and the door creaked open. Celia stood quickly. She tugged at her bonds. The room swam dizzily for an instant, then came back into focus.

A man entered, the tall, swarthy individual with the snakeskin hatband and brass studded machete. At his heels scuffed a subordinate, long shirt-tails flapping. The tall man stared at Celia, cursed and turned to cuff his underling soundly. Gesticulating, he flicked at his hair. Celia thought she recognized the word for silver.

The Chief of Police shoved his henchmen out of the door and slammed it behind him. Feet astride, thumbs hooked into his belt, he stood there surveying his captive. Chin up, Celia stared back defiantly.

"How dare you!" she crushed the tremor from her voice. "I am a British subject!"

The tall man laughed, a vicious bark. He strolled towards her and Celia willed herself to stand her ground. His scarred features twisted into a hideous leer, he stopped to loom above her. His acrid breath enveloped her and her eyes flickered, frosting with distaste. Muttering to himself, his eyes slits of fire, he reached out to touch her bare shoulder. He laughed when she flinched despite herself.

Still murmuring his crazed incantation, he tugged at the cord about her waist. Celia's eyes widened abruptly, but she remained absolutely rigid, focusing on a point beyond him. The knot dissolved and the robe parted. Breathing heavily, he pulled it from her shoulders. It fell away, sliding with a hiss of silk. Hanging from the ropes that bound her wrists, it draped down to the floor behind her.

She was perfectly naked. Her smooth skin glowed in the lamplight. Aieee......!"

The Chief of Police just stood and gaped, his mouth opening and closing. Beads of perspiration stood out on his forehead. In a trance, he reached out and wiped a sweaty palm along the curve of her hip. With a gasp, Celia expelled her pent-up breath, triggering a violent shiver that made her body quiver.

The Chief's eyes bulged in their sockets. Groaning out loud, he seized Celia's shoulders and hauled her towards him.

"Swine!"

Celia's shout reverberated off the stone walls. Her knee jerked up with all the power of a finely tuned thigh. The tall man screeched and collapsed at her feet, thrashed around bent up double, clutching at himself.

Celia jumped over him and ran for the door, stumbling over the dangling robe. With her hands tied behind her, it was ridiculous. Desperate, she turned her back on the lock, fingers scrabbling blindly.

A hand like a claw fastened on her hair. Celia shrieked, her eyes blurring with tears. Spitting curses, the Chief whipped his arm around and slapped her savagely. He slapped her again and again, spinning her, driving her along the wall until her legs gave way and she sagged in the corner.

Snarling, he stood over her. Celia cowered, trying to curl into a ball. The Chief drew back his foot, an effort which caused him to grunt and double up again, holding his groin.

The door opened and shut. Bolts clanged. Suddenly alone, Celia lay on her side, her breath grating harshly.

Jeremy burst into the darkness of Nate's tent. He was promptly ejected. Sprawled in the moonlight, he was sat on by Mack and Lefty, their .38s jammed in his face.

"I say, you chaps, steady on!"

The moonbeams were blotted out by the lumbering bulk of Nate O'Dwyer.

"What the hell's goin' on?"

Drawn by the commotion, the others came running, rubbing the sleep out of their eyes. Released, Jeremy sat up gingerly.

"Celia's been kidnapped!"

Nate quelled a chorus of dismay.

"Whaddaya mean, kidnapped?"

Shamefaced, Jeremy explained.

"A lady in distress," grinned Dubois.

"To arms, gentlemen!" Von Seyfritz trumpeted. "We must act immediately!"

EPISODE 5:
THE WHIP

Celia moaned.

They had returned and retied her wrists, left her suspended from a beam above her head, her toes just touching the floor. She seemed to have been dangling there forever. The ropes bit sharply when they jerked them tight. Now she felt only a tingling, and her fingers were numb. Her distended shoulders ached horribly.

She struggled fitfully. It felt as if red hot needles were being driven into her flesh. She groaned and gritted her teeth, sweat streaming down her face. It was hopeless. She gave up, panting.

The sentry trudged wearily between the leaning shanties. Hefting his meat cleaver, he glared at the moon. He rubbed his chin thoughtfully, then stowed the blade under his belt. A small flask appeared. He popped the cork, raising the bottle to his lips, his head tilted back.

In a single bound, a slight figure sprang to his side. A steel sliver flashed. The sentry staggered, his scream emerging as a ghastly, gargling rattle. His hands flapped at his throat, a dark stain spreading on his shirtfront. He lurched forward, then crumpled, kicked once and was still.

Dubois stooped to wipe the blade clean.

Celia's back was to the door. When it creaked open, she tried to twist and see, but the fire across her shoulders stopped her.

The Chief of Police stepped into her field of vision. Murmuring, he stroked her cheek with the back of his hand, cold sparks glittering in his eyes. He laughed out loud when she gasped and turned her face away.

He ran his fingers through her hair.

"You monster!" she exclaimed hoarsely.

The tall man reached up to test her bonds, jerking on the rope. Her body lurched, her toes barely brushing the ground. She cried out, and a low moan shuddered from her. Sweat glistened and rolled. Her head hung down.

There was a knock on the jailhouse door.

Grumbling, a fat policeman waddled down the passage, his bare feet slapping on the stones. He opened the narrow viewing hatch.

"Argh!"

A hairy hand shot through and clamped its blunt talons round his throat. The guard was lifted clear off the ground. He kicked and gurgled, eyes bulging.

The Chief of Police tugged something from his belt. With a fistful of hair, he lifted Celia's head so he could show it to her.

Celia's eyes widened. Her parched lips parted, but only a slight, meaningless sound emerged. The Chief was flourishing a short-handled whip. Leering, he uncoiled it deftly, with a flick of the wrist made it slither like a snake across the floor.

Inching forward on tiptoe, they came to a junction in the dim corridor. Then, as Dubois was about to offer an opinion, a dark figure came round the corner and walked slap-bang into them.

Before the policeman could shout a warning, Jeremy had clipped him with a straight left that would have made the Marquis of Queensbury proud. The turnkey staggered, but still tried to claw out his machete. Von Seyfritz rapped him sharply with the butt of his pistol. The guard collapsed in a heap.

"British fair play!" the Prussian snorted.

A piercing scream echoed through the building, a high sound curdled with pain.

"Celia!" cried Jeremy. "What are they doing to her?"

Nate was already pounding down the passageway.

"Come on!"

Celia writhed uncontrollably, her naked body twisting. A shriek ripped from her throat as she threw her head back.

Laughing insanely, the tall man waited for her convulsions to subside. A wrenching groan burst from her, as she hung there shuddering. Laboring for breath, she strained to take the weight on her toes.

The whip was raised again.

"Yaaahh!"

The heavy door exploded inwards, its locks and bolts fragmenting. It sailed across the room as light as a playing card, but landed on the Chief of Police like a ton of lead. He lay pinned to the hard floor, squirming like a pierced insect. Bellowing, Nate jumped on top, stomped down hard with both feet, pounded till his victim stopped screaming.

They cut Celia down. Jeremy helped her back into her robe.

"The fiend!" he exclaimed.

Celia managed a watery smile.

"You took your time."

The Europeans regarded her admiringly.

"Can you walk?" inquired Von Seyfritz.

Wincing, Celia rubbed her arms, flexing her shoulders gingerly.

"Slowly," she stated.

Brandishing the .45, Nate was pacing the shattered doorway.

"Okay," he barked. "Then let's get goin'!"

They took the quickest route, creeping through the village. Seemingly boneless, Celia leant on Jeremy for support. She ached all over, bands of fire constricting her.

Up front, Nate hefted the big automatic, oiled steel glinting dully. A rearguard, Von Seyfritz turned this way then that, gun muzzle jabbing. Dubois crossed quickly from one flank to the other, up on his toes, catlike. The shacks slumbered, or at least pretended to. The blue shadows were humming, electric. Their wide eyes showed whitely.

There was no sleep that night. As the first tint of dawn picked out the jagged edge of the mountains, they held a hasty council of war.

"They might thank us for ridding them of that swine," mused Von Seyfritz. "But then again they might not."

O'Dwyer slapped the holster at his side.

"Oh yeah?" he growled. "Just let 'em try!"

He had the light of battle in his eyes, but more sober heads prevailed.

"We'll be safe on the river," said Dubois. "We can always come ashore again further on."

"Indeed," agreed Mackenzie. "All roads lead to the mountains!"

The sky acquired a dirty yellow pallor. The horizons grumbled, flickering nervously.

Twirling the wheel, the Captain took his craft out to the middle of the river, seeking the deeper channels marked down on his charts. His stubble bristling, he sucked on a cigarette, inhaling sharply. He wasn't happy. The etchings on the paper went just so far, and then the winding vein of the river was a blank.

"Is something wrong, mon ami?"

Dubois offered a tarnished hip flask. The Captain bared his stained teeth appreciatively.

"By sunset, senor," his eyes narrowed as thunder rumbled in the distance. "We will be going where no white man has gone before, or at least returned to tell of it."

Sternwards, Mackenzie fussed amongst the crates and packing cases. The Indians stared dully at the water. Jeremy leant out over the rail, scanning the jungle eagerly.

"Professor," he called out. "What do you think we'll find?"

Mackenzie beamed.

"If I am not mistaken, my boy," he declared. "Wonders beyond our wildest imaginings!"

At the bow, Mack and Lefty struggled with a canvas chair.

"Go easy, ya mugs!" Nate barked. "Don't break it!"

When O'Dwyer took his throne, the wooden frame creaked in protest. He plucked a fat cigar from his breast pocket.

"Smoke?"

With a curt gesture, Von Seyfritz declined. Nate shrugged. Clamping the stogie between his teeth, he bit off the end and spat it out over the rail. Von Seyfritz dimmed a flicker of distaste. Unmannered louts, these damned Americans.

"This accursed humidity," he said to the ever-present Braun and Gruber. "But soon the storm will break."

Unfurling his bandanna, he mopped his forehead, wiped round the inside of his collar. A mutter of thunder rippled across the heavy sky. Lightning shimmered.

In the shade of the tattered awning, a hatchway grated open. The pale oval of Celia's face glimmered dimly in the shadows. She paused, then climbed out carefully. Trixie looked up from her fan magazines.

"How's your ass, babe?" she grinned maliciously. "Still smarts, huh?"

Celia stared at her stonily and moved towards the stern and Jeremy. He advanced to greet her, all smiles.

"Hullo, old thing, how are you?"

Celia smiled wanly.

"Sore."

Jeremy frowned.

"The rotter!"

Tossing away the magazines, Trixie chuckled to herself. Her sharp eyes lit upon the wind-up gramophone, liberated from the Ranchero Blanco. Soon, to the amazement of the natives squatting in the stern, the scratchy syncopations of a hot cornet were added to the plodding throb of the engine, the constant whispers of the forest.

A breeze tickled the river, fragrant with rain.

"Jeez!"

O'Dwyer recoiled as lightning exploded in his face. Thunder boomed overhead, and the old boat wallowed in the shockwaves.

A splatter of heavy raindrops spotted the deck and awning.

"So!" said Von Seyfritz.

The thunder crackled, ripping across a filthy sky. The breeze gusted again, and the heavens disgorged a deluge. Cursing, the voyagers made a dash for the shelter of the awning, flinching and ducking low, as if they were dodging bullets. The rain plummeted in sheets, blurring the outlines of the jungle. Hissing, the river boiled. A dark huddle in the stern, the natives muttered fearfully.

Through it all, through the sizzle and drumming, the tinny crackle of the phonograph.

"What the—!"

Trixie was dancing. Out in the rain, she was high-stepping and twirling, laughing out loud. Her hair was plastered down, accentuating the sharp angles of her features. Her face gleamed, tilted up to the sky.

"Sacre bleu!" exclaimed Dubois.

"I say!" said Jeremy.

Toe-tapping, Trixie splashed across the shining deck. Soaked, her light garments stuck to her. The billowing slacks clung to her thighs, her shirt smoothed over the peaks of her plainly unencumbered breasts.

"Indeed," gulped Mackenzie. "A most elemental young lady."

Nate was sweating. He felt like molten lava was flowing through him. It boiled up in his chest and rose into his throat, choking him. Snarling he scooped up the phonograph and hurled it in a looping arc, far

out into the river. Continuing the motion, he heaved himself into the rain.
Trixie screeched as his iron hand was clamped around her wrist.

"Owww!"

O'Dwyer dragged her back under the awning. He shoved through
the gaping throng, heaved open the hatchway that led below.

"Get in there!"

The cabin was a murky box with barely room for a rickety bunk.
Faded pin-ups were its only decoration, lit dimly by a stained porthole.
Trixie didn't have far to back up before she hit the wall. Panting hoarsely,
Nate lumbered in after her.

"Goddam bitch on heat twenty-four hours a day!"

Up above, the thunder crashed. Trixie jumped. Through the
porthole, lightning lent a momentary, garish glare to Nate's distorted
features. He reached out and Trixie flinched as he seized a fistful of her
blouse. The thin cloth shredded like tissue paper. Her wet skin gleamed
in the dimness of the cabin, her eyes dancing with a crazy light of terror
and excitement.

Nate stared. His lips worked soundlessly. Then he muttered
something and began to fumble with his belt buckle. Spitting obscenities,
he grabbed her bare shoulders and shoved her down so hard her kneecaps
thudded on the planking.

"Come on, ya knows what I want!"

The storm evaporated. The river glittered, beneath a blaring, brassy
sky. Sluggish currents twisted and turned, confined by the high, ragged
walls of the jungle. Her wet decks steaming, the riverboat plodded on,
tacking warily.

Nate hauled himself up from below, tucking in his shirt-tails.
Dubois sat cross-legged on the packing cases, cleaning his nails with the
point of a stiletto. When the big American lumbered out into the glare
of daylight, the Frenchman winked at Von Seyfritz, his sharp features
creased into a knowing grin. The Prussian curled his lip.

"These Americans," he said to his bullet-headed cohorts. "They are
powerful but decadent, rotten to the core!"

He snorted disdainfully.

"It will be their downfall, mark my words."

O'Dwyer tested the canvas of his deckchair. The resurgent sun had
already baked it dry. He sat down heavily and tugged out a fat cigar.

Mack beat Lefty to it, igniting his lighter with a flick of the thumb. Nate sat back, his eyes half-closed, savoring the rich flavors of the fine Havana. The lava flow was off the boil, and he felt mellow. Dames, he mused smugly, ya gotta know how to handle 'em, ya gotta let 'em know who's boss. As the glowing tip of his cigar dimmed slowly, he slipped into a doze.

Trixie sat slumped on the edge of the bunk. Her shoulders sagged forward till her head hung down to her knees. Her hair was in disarray, its platinum sleekness tugged askew. In tatters, the shreds of her blouse dangled from the waistband of her slacks. The smooth alabaster of her skin was mottled with dark bruises, beads of sweat glinting on the bowed ridge of her spine. The bite of raw bile rose in her throat. She hawked and spat, wiped her smudged lipstick clear across her cheek, scrubbing with the back of her hand.

"Son of a bitch!" she groaned. "Lousy no good son of a—!"

A violent scraping vibrated through the hull, progressing from the bow towards the stern. A dull twang bubbled up from somewhere near the rudder. There was an abrupt frothing, and the whole craft began to shudder, her bridge and deckhouses creaking, the awning all a-shiver. The engines whined and moaned in anguish, the tall stack belching great gasps of black smoke.

"What the—!"

Wide awake, Nate sprang to his feet.

"Merde!"

Dubois pricked himself with the stiletto, drawing a bright bead of blood. Von Seyfritz reached instinctively for the flap of his holster.

"I say!"

Beneath the quivering canvas of the awning, Celia jumped and flung an arm round Jeremy. The rifle he was cleaning tumbled onto the planking with a crash. With a convulsive start, Mackenzie ripped a page clean out of the weighty volume resting on his lap.

In the stern, the spasms from below brought the natives to their feet. Pushing and shoving, they crowded to the rail. Cursing, his teeth clenched on the stub of a cigarette, the Captain set about his valves and levers.

The frothing and grinding subsided, the boat floating in an oily haze. The sudden silence was startling.

Mackenzie cleared his throat nervously.

"Ah, er, what seems to be the trouble?"

The Captain clambered down out of the wheelhouse. Shoving through the muttering Indians, he made his way to the stern. The others followed hard upon his heels. Reaching the rail, the Captain peered down into the dirty water.

"Vines," he declared. "The propeller has become tangled in a web of vines."

Nate's brow furrowed, clouding darkly.

"What the hell?" he rasped. "Since when do vines grow underwater?"

The others exchanged nervous glances. Von Seyfritz unclipped the flap of his holster, the click of the catch sounding loud in the stillness.

"Listen!" exclaimed Dubois.

Mystified, they looked around them.

"Listen to what?" asked Celia. "I don't hear anything."

Dubois drew his pistol with a rasp of steel on leather. The heavy revolver gleamed in the sunlight.

"Precisely," eyes narrowing, his gaze flicked along the riverbank. "No birdsong, no chattering monkeys."

Mackenzie nodded.

"It's too quiet."

The Captain rubbed his chin, fingers grating on stubble.

"I don't like it."

A thin piping swelled to a high-pitched whistle. As one they spun to the dark walls of the jungle. Alarmed, they twisted all about, then became aware of the sound rising high above them, high into the bright sky.

"What—?"

"I—!"

"There!"

Dubois jabbed with the barrel of his pistol. Hands for visors, they shielded their eyes against the brassy glare.

An arrow leapt the river in a great, looping arc, its tip pierced to make a whistle. Reaching its zenith, it seemed to hang for an instant, the high note wavering. Then its nose dipped and the arrow plunged earthwards, the whistle growing till it rent the sky.

The natives cowered. Celia flinched, cupping her hands over her ears. Some craned out over the rail, seeking the source of the arrow. Others followed its trajectory, saw it swallowed by the trees.

The whistle died abruptly, left a singing in the ears.

"Mes amis," said Dubois. "I think we have a problem."

EPISODE 6:
PIRATES

Beyond the bow, the river vanished, sucked around a bend overhung with tattered shrubbery. Hidden by this ragged screen, a new sound broke the nervous silence, a dull throb which grew in volume, assuming an irregular beat.

The adventurers crowded forward.

"Ach so!" exclaimed Von Seyfritz.

A strange craft churned sluggishly round the bend and out onto the broad, glittering sweep of the river. It was a wallowing wooden tub, dirty white paintwork blistered and flaking. Strung in fluttering strands, faded pennants decorated a crazy, teetering superstructure. A single tin chimney belched oily vapors. Her engines banged and rattled.

"I don't like the look of this," Nate turned to Mack and Lefty. "Go break out the choppers."

Her flags and bunting flapping, the wallowing riverboat plodded towards them. A crew of eight to ten became apparent, decked out in garish motley, the baroque, mock-military of some local town band. A jagged rent here, a bullet hole there, ringed by brown stains. This circus finery had not been parted with voluntarily.

"Garcia, my friend, this is our lucky day!"

The Pirate Captain and his First Mate perched atop the rusty scaffolding of the bridge. The patent leather of their caps was cracked and dusty, the tall plumes tattered and askew. High collars were curling, gold braid threadbare, brass buttons chipped and dull. The Captain was too big for his tunic, his hairy belly ballooning out over the waistband of his striped trousers.

"Our lucky day!"

Beaming, the Pirate Captain ran his fingers through the greasy tangle of his beard. In startling contrast to his leader's imposing bulk, the First Mate was stooped and impossibly thin, skin and bone, so thin he could move around inside his patched and tobacco stained uniform. His dark features were all nose, a mighty flaring beak with beady black eyes tacked on either side and a wispy moustache drooping beneath.

"I hope so, my Captain," he bared broken yellow teeth. "I have not eaten for three days."

On the foredeck below, the pirate crew crowded to the rail. They were lean and swarthy, long cutlasses shoved into their belts, hefting ancient muskets and big horse pistols, their eyes glinting narrowly. The Pirate Captain extended a small brass telescope, focusing on the riverboat stranded on the shining water. He scanned the promising jumble of packing cases. He saw white faces. Then, with a sharp intake of breath, he made out the unmistakable curves of a woman.

"Ayieee!"

Bellowing orders, he shoved the First Mate aside, reaching for the wheel.

Across the water, Dubois checked the loads of his revolver. Von Seyfritz snapped the toggle of a Luger, feeding a round into the chamber. He nodded curtly to Braun and Gruber. Clicking their heels, they followed his example.

The Captain rubbed his chin till Mackenzie feared his fingers would ignite on the stubble.

"Do you know these people?" the Professor inquired nervously.

The Captain spat a string of obscenities.

"The big one," he sucked on a cigarette stub, exhaling viciously. "He is El Diablo, the King of the River Pirates."

Mackenzie sighed heavily.

"Oh dear," he dabbed at his brow with a damp handkerchief. "Well, I am sure we can come to some amicable—"

The Captain snorted.

"El Diablo, he will cut our throats just for fun!"

Jeremy passed by, ushering Celia to the shelter of the awning. The Captain's gaze followed the smooth undulations of her shapely form.

"And now that he has seen our cargo...."

Mackenzie mopped his face. The Captain rolled his eyes.

"We are fortunate he has not yet seen the silver haired one."

Nearby, Nate tugged the .45 from its holster. He let the magazine drop out of the butt and onto his palm, savored the gleam of the fat brass cartridge held in its lip. With a grunt, he slapped it back in, working the slide with a flick of the wrist. The sheen of blue steel sent a shiver down his spine. The light of battle was dancing in his eyes.

"If them birds is lookin' for trouble," he rasped. "They've come to the right place!"

The pirate craft churned onward, closing on the entangled riverboat. Cursing, O'Dwyer dashed into the bow.

"Hold it!" he boomed, brandishing the automatic. "That's far enough!"

Below decks, Trixie screeched and wrapped her arms around herself. Without so much as a passing glance at her semi-nakedness, Mack and Lefty crashed by the open door of the cabin, pounding down the dark and narrow corridor.

The pirates plodded on till they were broadside to their intended victim. Their engine died with a cough and splutter. The sudden silence was broken by a nervous clucking in the treetops.

Celia settled deep into the shadows of the awning. Jeremy collected his hunting rifle, stuffing a box of ammunition into his pocket.

"Be careful," Celia tugged at this sleeve.

Jeremy grinned, his head swimming with feats of derring-do.

"Chin up, old thing. We'll sort these bounders out."

Across the short span of water dividing them, they eyed each other warily. The pirates cocked their long muzzle-loaders, the click sounding thinly in the coiling stillness.

"State your business!" barked Von Seyfritz.

El Diablo beamed. His gap-toothed grin put the sun to shame.

"You seem to be in some kind of trouble, my friends!" his bellow echoed up and down the river. The jungle muttered fitfully, then fell silent again.

"Yeah," Nate grated. "And I don't suppose ya knows anythin' about that."

Flanking him, the others kept their weapons in plain view. Mackenzie murmured fearfully.

"Better get your head down, mon ami," Dubois chuckled. "Before the fireworks go off."

The Professor retired towards the awning. El Diablo flung his arms out wide, the picture of hurt innocence.

"Why so suspicious, my friends?" he protested. "All we want to do is help!"

Snarling, O'Dwyer took aim, zeroing in with the big .45.

"Ya got ten seconds to scram," he declared. "Before I parts yer hair with lead!"

The pirate's grin vanished. His arms fell to his side. The First Mate's fingers crept towards the worn butt of a pistol, protruding from the folds of his ornate tunic.

"Now that is not very nice, Senor," El Diablo's booming tones were edged with steel. "What have I done that you should threaten me?"

Mackenzie joined Celia in the shade amidships. She was pale and taut with apprehension. The Professor forced a wan smile, patted her hand reassuringly.

The blue steel of the .45 flickered from the Pirate Captain to his First Mate.

"You tell that clown to keep his paw offa that gat or I'll—!"

"Fuego!"

"Fuego!"

"Fuego!"

El Diablo's shout was swamped by the sudden rattle of musketry. Blue-grey powder smoke blossomed along the rail of the pirate ship as her crew cut loose with a ragged volley. The air crackled with hot lead. Wood chips and splinters spurted.

"Let 'em have it!"

Standing full square to the enemy, Nate let fly, the big Colt belching flame, roaring and bucking, the ejected empties winking in the sunlight.

"Give 'em hell!"

Dubois ducked as a musket ball gouged a chunk out of the rail. Bobbing and weaving, he scampered for the cover of the crates piled high in the stern. The natives yelled with alarm, threw themselves flat, pressing their faces to the deck. Ignoring them, Dubois flung himself full length to safety, popped up to bang off a shot, up and down like a jack-in-the-box.

Flanked by Braun and Gruber, Von Seyfritz struck the pose of a duellist, side on to the foe, pistol arm extended, free hand on hip. He emptied the Luger methodically, the spent shells tinkling on the deck. Pausing to reload, he eyed the energetic Dubois scornfully.

"So, is that how Frenchmen fight?"

The long rifle wedged precariously under his arm, Jeremy struggled to unwrap the box of cartridges. Buzzing like an angry hornet, a musket ball singed his cheek. With a started yelp, he jumped up into the air. The box slipped from his fingers, burst open, slim brass cylinders rolling on the planking. As he stooped to try and catch them, splinters burst from the wall of the wheelhouse, precisely where his head had been.

"Thanks!" the young Englishman exclaimed, raising his eyes heavenwards.

Suspended on the glare of the river, the ragged craft banged off broadsides at each other like two ancient men of war. A pall of gunsmoke rose and hung above them, pierced by the slanting rays of the sun. The cacophony of shouts and gunfire rang thinly off the flat surface of the water, its reverberations sending shivers through the treetops.

Cursing, Von Seyfritz fumbled with the toggle of the Luger. Behind the packing cases, Dubois refilled the swung out cylinder of his revolver, then snapped it back into place with a jerk of the wrist.

"Ha!" he jeered. "So much for German efficiency!"

Where the riverbank met the water, tufts of reeds glowed in the sunshine. Suddenly, they quivered, single stems detaching themselves and moving out towards the battle, trailing pearly strands of tiny bubbles.

Seeing Jeremy stumble, Celia jumped up with a sharp cry of alarm. As she stepped into the light, Mackenzie reached out to restrain her.

"Please be careful, my dear," he warned her. "I don't think you—"

Stripped down to baggy pantaloons, two dripping figures clambered lithely over the rail, daggers clenched between their teeth. Startled, Celia shrieked. The pirates stopped and stared. Celia froze, then gasped and began to back away along the deck, totally oblivious to the sounds of battle raging all around. Leering, the pirates shuffled after her, leaving a trail of wet footprints on the deck.

"Stop!"

Mackenzie came rushing out of the shadows. Lip curling, the leading pirate swatted him aside, sent him tumbling back beneath the awning with a crash.

Celia's rump bumped up against the rail, bringing her to an abrupt halt. Taut and pale, she stared at the swarthy forms advancing upon her, lean and stringy, their stubbled features ugly with lust.

They approached, muttering darkly. Celia tried to bend back away from them, grimacing at the fetid odors of their breath. The wooden bar dug into the base of her spine, and she gripped the rail till her knuckles bled white. The pirates advanced relentlessly, fixated by the quick panting undulations that strained the thin stuff of her blouse.

Suddenly, the color returned to Celia's cheeks. Her eyes narrowed, anger boiling up inside her.

"Alright, you swine," she shouted. "Is this what you want?"

With both hands, she reached up to her collar. In a single, wrenching movement, she tore downwards. Buttons popped all the way down.

"Come on then. Take a look!"

She flung her arms wide, the torn halves of her blouse parting, ripped from the waistband of her trousers. The pirates choked. Their jaws dropped, eyes bugging out on stalks. They reeled, staggered by the lustrous, creamy revelation, the heaving snowy mounds straining at a little bit of frilly lace.

Celia sneered, her eyes flashing, sparking with rage.

"Well, what are you waiting for?" she spat. "Here it is. Come and get it!"

The pirates gulped and licked their lips. One of them murmured, almost reverently. The other stepped forward, a shaking hand extended, trembling like a child. The knife slipped from his fingers and thudded on the deck. His eyes glazed, he shambled onwards, hypnotized by those twin palpitating, panting globes.

His head disintegrated.

Celia shrieked as her flesh was splattered with hot globules of blood.

The pirate lay twitching in a spreading lake of crimson.

His companion stood staring down at him in shock, the pool of blood lapping at his toes. Then he grunted and staggered, lurched sideways, his limbs out of control. He crashed through the rail and disappeared, rose slowly to the surface, face down, spread-eagled, a dark stain expanding around him.

Celia screamed and flung up her arms.

Catlike, Dubois sprang to her side. Smoke curled from the muzzle of his revolver.

"Are you alright?"

She stared at him blankly.

In the shadows, Mackenzie stirred, groaning feebly. He struggled to sit up, then was nearly trampled underfoot as Mack and Lefty came thundering up from below. They lunged into the sunlight, cradling a trio of Thompson submachine-guns.

"Jeez! Where ya been?"

Nate stowed away the Colt and caught the ugly weapon one-handed.

"How long does it take ya mugs to load them drums?"

Like a well-oiled machine, they clicked into action. The roar of the three tommy-guns stifled the boom of old muskets and the sharp crack of pistols. Between them, the big drum magazines boasted three hundred rounds. The Americans squeezed them dry. Spraying lead as coolly as water from a hosepipe, they stitched the pirate ship back and forth, up and down.

El Diablo gasped in horror as he saw his men literally fall apart, blown away like ragdolls. Beneath him, his vessel shuddered and began to dissolve, pounded into splinters and sawdust, cracking like matchwood. Rattling like a snaredrum, the tin funnel was perforated till it buckled and collapsed with a crash and shower of sparks. Black smoke was suddenly seeping out of the mutilated planking. Tongues of flame began to nibble greedily at the woodwork.

Babbling hysterically, the First Mate threw himself into space. He hit the water with arms and legs flailing and, before the foamy turmoil had subsided, was swimming for the shore. Reeling as the superstructure began to teeter and tilt beneath him, El Diablo shook his fists, howling with rage.

"Damned no-good lousy Yankee sons-of-bitches! You come to our country and —!"

A white flash, a ripping detonation. The surface of the water was withered by the blast. The treetops rippled. A writhing, oily bubble of flame rose into the bright sky, higher and higher, expanding and growing paler, till there was nothing but a dark smudge which slowly evaporated.

The smoke of battle cleared. Dark blotches of oil mottled the water, flecked with debris. Bodies floated face downward, turning slowly on the sluggish current.

Grinning, Dubois slapped Nate soundly on the shoulder.

"Crude, mon ami, but effective!"

O'Dwyer tossed away the smoking tommy-gun. Mack caught it deftly, the weapon like a twig in his hairy paw.

Dazed, Celia tugged the torn halves of her blouse together. Setting down his rifle, Jeremy strode swiftly to her side.

"I say, spiffing show. Knocked the blighters for six!"

He stopped short, startled by the spatter of blood decorating her frontage. Celia shook her head, grimacing.

"Don't worry, it's not mine."

In the shadows of the awning, the hatchway creaked open. Trixie emerged, somewhat restored, blinking in the sunshine.

"Hey, what gives?" she complained. "It sounded like World War Two'd broken out up here!"

She stared at the dishevelled Englishwoman in amazement. Celia regarded her archly.

"So glad you could join us."

Trixie tossed her head and turned away. A groan drew her attention to Mackenzie, struggling to get to his feet.

"Take it easy, Perfesser," she drawled, bending to rescue his spectacles.

She aimed her spectacular rear at the young Englishman. Jeremy's eyes widened, a lump in his throat. Celia glared, till she lit upon a livid weal traced across her companion's cheek.

"Jeremy!" she gasped. "You're hurt!"

Jeremy reached up to finger the wound.

"Oh, it's nothing, old thing," he shrugged blithely. "Just a scratch, that's all."

As he glowed all over, Celia fussed, dabbing with a handkerchief. Hands on hips, Trixie looked on.

"Jeepers, what a performance!"

Dubois discovered that he had been grazed in the ribs by a passing musket ball. Whistling softly, he examined the ragged tear in his shirt. Von Seyfritz eyed him from the rail.

"You are lucky, Frenchman," he commented icily.

Dubois chuckled.

"You sound disappointed, Colonel."

Beaming, he looked the Prussians over.

"I see that none of you squareheads has managed to add to his collection of duelling scars. Such dishonor!"

Von Seyfritz snorted. Braun and Gruber stepped forward, frowning, but the Colonel restrained them with a word. Suddenly, there was a concerted muttering from the stern. Bolder than the rest, one of the Indians was advancing, his fellows crowding close behind. He approached Trixie, cradling one hand in the other, spots of blood pattering down onto the deck.

"Whaddaya want?" Trixie demanded nervously.

Mumbling, the Indian dropped something onto her palm. Turning white, Trixie jumped a clear foot off the planking.

"Yike!" she yelped. "He's given me his finger!"

With a screech, she flung the mangled digit over her shoulder. It landed with a soft thud on the awning. Growling, Nate loomed with a brow of thunder. The native yelled and scuttled away. Shaking his head, Mackenzie hurried to tend him.

"Jesus H. Christ!" O'Dwyer shook his fist at Trixie, who was casting around frantically for somewhere to wipe her hand. "You're back for two minutes and already—!"

A resounding groan spun them all round.

Gasping, the Captain lurched out of the wheelhouse. He swayed, tumbling out to sprawl heavily on the deck.

They crowded round. There was blood all over his shirt front. Pink foam flecked his lips. Eyes screwed up tight, his breath rattled harshly in his throat.

Dubois knelt to unbutton the Captain's shirt.

Shot through the lungs," he whispered. "It's no good."

The Captain opened his eyes. Groaning, he struggled to sit up, then fell back limply. He coughed, a thin stream of blood emerging from the corner of his mouth.

"Easy, mon ami," Dubois squeezed his shoulder. "It'll be alright."

The Captain was racked by a violent fit of coughing. He groaned again, teeth grating.

"Don't be stupid!" he gasped. "I'm done for!"

Startling the Frenchman, he seized Dubois' lapels. His eyes glared feverishly, rolling around the circle of faces above him.

"Turn back!" he pleaded. "From here the river is uncharted. It is death to go on!"

His grip slackened. His eyes turned up and inward, till only the whites showed. His breath burst out in a long and gargling sigh, the pink spittle bubbling on his chin. A shiver passed through him. He seemed to shrivel. His head lolled to one side.

Dubois rose slowly.

"C'est finis."

EPISODE 7:
GREED

Lefty patted down the dirt with the flat of his shovel. Mack mopped his brow. Cramming the stained kerchief back into his pocket, he glanced across the clearing at O'Dwyer.

"Okay," Nate grunted. "That's it."

He turned on his heel, dark patches under the arms of his safari jacket, the back of his bull neck glistening. The cloying dankness of the jungle weighed down upon him, and he made for the open spaces of the river, out there glinting through the trees.

The humidity fogged Mackenzie's glasses. Blinking, he coughed nervously.

"I....I think we should say something."

The Prussians patrolled the edge of the clearing, pistols drawn, eyes flicking warily around the dripping screen of greenery.

"We don't have time for that!" snapped Von Seyfritz.

Jeremy looked down at the sorry mound that marked the Captain's last resting place.

"Oh, I say, you have to give a chap a decent send-off."

Exasperated, Nate flung out his arms.

"Okay," he rasped. "But make it snappy!"

The Professor tugged off a floppy sunhat. Jeremy bowed his head. While something suitable was recited, the Prussians watched the forest. O'Dwyer stood glaring into space, a little muscle twitching by the side of his jaw.

"A lonely place to lie," Dubois observed as Mackenzie replaced his headgear.

"There's worse," growled O'Dwyer, remembering Mole Murphy, forever walking the bed of Blue Lake, his feet encased in concrete.

They thrust aside the leafy screen and stood on the lip of the riverbank. Untangled from the vines, the boat lay moored below them.

Mackenzie eyed it thoughtfully.

"Well, gentlemen," he sighed. "We must come to a decision."

There was a long silence, laden with doubt. Nate cleared his throat. Dubois stroked his moustaches.

"Just ignore us, why don'tya!" Trixie complained, joining Celia at the rail.

Nate's eyes narrowed.

"Ya'll do what I tell ya!"

Celia frowned.

"I think our situation merits some serious discussion, Mr O'Dwyer."

The big American swore under his breath. Dames! Shouldn't be allowed outta the bedroom.

"Dash it all, C!" Jeremy exclaimed. "We can't give up now!"

Dubois smiled indulgently.

"Your spirit does you credit, mon brave, but we are without our Captain and will soon be without our charts."

Mackenzie squared his shoulders, gazing out to where the winding expanses of the river melted in the heat haze.

"For my part, my friends," he declared. "I am eager to press on. After all, the unknown is my business."

Jeremy beamed.

"Bravo, Professor!"

He embraced the old boat with a sweeping gesture.

"I can handle her. Piece of cake. I'm jolly nautical, you know."

Von Seyfritz cocked an eyebrow, the monocle dropping to dangle on its cord. Scowling, he screwed it back into his eye socket.

"You English!" he snorted. "You treat everything like a damned picnic!"

Dubois laughed and slapped his young companion on the shoulder.

"What the hell," he grinned. "I have nothing better to do."

Nate ran a finger round the inside of his collar.

"You got that little doo-dad on ya, Perfesser?"

Mackenzie rooted eagerly in his pocket. The tiny golden idol lay gleaming on his palm. They bent closer to see, its reflection glittering in their eyes.

Nate prodded the little figure with a blunt forefinger.

"Uh, ya think there's more where that come from?"

Mackenzie nodded vigorously. He saw himself lecturing to the packed houses of worldwide geographic societies. Professor A. Mackenzie, on the earth-shattering discoveries of the Mackenzie Expedition!

"You know what they say, my dear Mr O'Dwyer. No smoke without fire."

Nate glared at the treetops. He still had the taste of gun powder in his mouth.

"Okay!" he boomed. "Count me in!"

Trixie groaned and retreated to the shelter of the awning. Celia rolled her eyes heavenwards.

"Men!"

Jeremy, his head full of dreams, came back down to earth with a bump.

"It is alright, isn't it, C?"

She shrugged, resigned to her fate.

"Oh, of course, absolutely. Far be it from me to spoil your fun."

Von Seyfritz plucked the statuette from Mackenzie's palm. He glanced at Braun and Gruber meaningfully.

"So!" he barked. "Then we had best be on our way!"

He turned to negotiate the slippery slope that led down to the boat. Dubois watched him, his eyes clouding.

They made barely a mile that afternoon, spent a nervous night moored on the riverbank, their tents set up on the shore. The light of the campfire cast strange, crawling shadows. The jungle whispered all around them, muttering fitfully. Through ragged gaps in the black canopy above, the sky was glowing redly.

Mounting guard on board the riverboat, the twin Prussians snapped to attention.

"Achtung!"

Von Seyfritz's monocle glinted dully. Frowning, he mopped his brow, slick with perspiration. In this damned jungle, the nights were as stifling as the days.

"All is quiet," his henchmen reported.

Von Seyfritz nodded. His hands wrapped around the rail, he leant out into the darkness. Black veils shrouded the river.

"Can you hear it, gentlemen?"

His eyes were lit by a dancing fire. Braun and Gruber glanced at each other uncertainly.

"Destiny!" Von Seyfritz declared. "Can you hear it calling?"

He plucked a silver cigarette case from his breast pocket, ran a fingertip across the regimental crest embossed upon it. His subordinates whipped out their lighters. The Colonel tilted his head to the flame, the predatory cast of his features startling in the momentary glow.

"Yes indeed!"

He offered the case to Braun and Gruber, who accepted with a curt bow and click of the heels.

"Germany is awakening," his voice was charged with a strange resonance. "A new Germany. Young and fresh and ready to take its true place in the world!"

He paced the deck, his eyes blazing with a messianic fervor, clenched fists battering the air. His henchmen stood to attention, quivering with excitement.

"We have learned the lessons of 1918, but America is decadent, and Europe is weak and flabby and ruled by frightened old men!"

His forefinger jabbed into the blackness.

"The riches of the New World once fueled the ambitions of Imperial Spain. If there is gold in those mountains, it will be ours. It will belong to the Fatherland!"

The Colonel's voice floated across the black water, penetrating the deep, overhanging shadows of the riverbank. Dubois paused as he buttoned up his flies. He stood there for some time, head tilted to one side, listening.

When the distant conversation had faded to a murmur, he left the shadows and returned to the tents and firelight. Mackenzie was perched on a folding stool, a heavy volume draped across his lap. The Professor looked up, smiling. Dubois waved, then veered towards a small table set up in the wavering glow of the campfire.

"Hiya, Frenchie!" Nate slapped down a deck of cards. "Wanna join me for a hand or two?"

Dubois grinned.

"Don't mind if I do."

Nate slid the cards out of their carton.

"That's the spirit. Pull up a chair."

As Dubois settled down, O'Dwyer shoved a fat bottle across the table. He cursed, swiping at the swarm of insects drawn by the light of the fire.

"This goddamn place is drivin' me crazy!"

Dubois smiled, lighting a cigarette.

"The smoke will drive them away."

He leant over to light Nate's cigar. The big American sucked on the thick stogie till its tip sparked brightly. He bent forward in his seat, juggling the cards deftly.

"Yeah, well, it'll all be worth it if there's gold in them thar hills."

Dubois filled his glass and held it up to the firelight, admiring the amber glow of its contents.

"I think we can rely on the Professor," he said quietly. "He strikes me as a man who knows what he's talking about."

Nate laid down the deck. Dubois cut. Nate cut, then grinned.

"So far so good. I deal."

About to give Dubois his third card, O'Dwyer paused, his brow lit by a sudden thought.

"Say, Frenchie," he rasped. "You'se a pretty cool customer. I likes the way ya handle yourself. Ya ever decides to pay a visit to the good ol' U.S. of A, I sure could use ya."

Dubois pursed his lips thoughtfully. Then Trixie sauntered by, humming a tune. The Frenchman whistled lowly, drawn to the liquid undulations of her spectacular anatomy.

"Ya like that, huh?" Nate asked casually.

Dubois raised his eyebrows.

"She is an extraordinary woman."

Nate snorted, dealing out the rest of the cards.

"Dumb broad! There's plenty more where she came from."

"Indeed?" Dubois chuckled. "Then the United States may well be worth investigating."

Nate studied his cards.

"Yeah," he growled. "She was nothin' when I found her. A lousy, two-bit taxi dancer."

"Taxi dancer?"

"Yeah, a buck to cop a feel out on the floor, two bucks for a blow-job in the alley. Fun for the truckers and drillers, till the crash came along and the whole caboodle folded."

Dubois ditched two of his cards. Nate exchanged them for fresh ones.

"That's when she wasn't trying to win the Marathon."

Dubois was astonished.

"The Marathon? I can't quite picture Mlle Marlowe as an athlete."

Nate guffawed, poured himself another shot of whiskey and tossed it down the hatch.

"Athlete? Haw! She's some kinda athlete alright!" His heavy shoulders shook with laughter. "I mean the Dance Marathons. The mugs dance all day and all night, round and round, dance till they drop. Last couple left standing wins the big prize."

Dubois nodded soberly.

"Ah yes, of course. These are hard times."

Grinning, O'Dwyer spread out a winning hand.

"Only for deadbeats and losers," he grated. "Bums who ain't got the balls to reach out and take somethin' if they wants it."

He held a great spadelike hand up to the light. Heavy gold and gemstones glittered.

"Me, I done okay!"

Dubois scooped up the cards, weighed them on his palm.

"Yes," he said quietly. "I'm sure you have."

Mack and Lefty patrolled the perimeter, hefting the Thompson submachine-guns. They proceeded with a heavy, measured tread. Their eyes glinted narrowly in the shadow of broad hat brims, blue steel jaws set firmly, a butt drooping from the lower lip.

"I say, you chaps," Jeremy hailed them. "How goes the watch!"

They grunted.

"Mind if I join you?"

They grunted.

Moving on, they waded through deep pools of shadow. The young Englishman could scarcely contain his excitement.

"I must say I never thought I'd ever meet an authentic mobster!"

Mack and Lefty exchanged glances.

"I say," Jeremy searched for the right words. "Have you ever taken anyone for a ride?"

They stopped and turned to look at him. The span of their shoulders blotted out the starlight.

"Oh!" said Jeremy. "Ah!"

Celia stood in the narrow space between two camp beds, each draped in its canopy of mosquito netting. The sloping, buff-colored roof of the tent glowed with the smokey radiance of a hanging lamp.

She stood motionless, lost in thought. The minutes dragged by unnoticed. Then, with a sharp intake of breath, she pulled herself together. She undressed quickly, shedding the stale garments and casting them aside. Twisting this way and that, she surveyed herself. The welts had faded, but she still blushed at the memory. Frowning, she tugged on her pyjamas, sitting down on the bed.

"Hiya, babe!"

The tent flap was wrenched aside and Trixie swaggered in to join her.

"Whoo! It's a hot night!"

Celia stared stonily. Smirking, Trixie unbuttoned her blouse. Humming softly, she let the creamy V expand until it slid off her shoulders. She wasn't wearing a bra. Yawning, she clasped her hands behind her head, arching her body backwards.

Celia's eyes widened.

"Stop that!" she exclaimed hoarsely.

Laughing, Trixie kicked off her shoes, balled up her socks and tossed them over her shoulder. She peeled off her slacks, disposing of the last little wisp of silk with a mere flick of the wrist.

Her eyes dancing, she struck a saucy pose.

"How do ya like it, honey?"

The whiteness of her was startling. Celia paled, her dark eyes burning, growing wider and wider. Trixie's palms traced the smooth flare of her hips.

"Peaches and cream."

Tiny beads of perspiration glistened above Celia's upper lip. She couldn't breathe. Trixie's sculpted shoulders shimmied, sending delicious ripples through her.

"Jelly on a plate."

Fire raced in Celia's veins. Her heart pounded, seeming to leap up and choke her. Suddenly, her skin was crawling with sweat. Trixie's eyes shone with a brittle, mocking light, her smile hard and impossibly bright. Then, with a high-pitched, rattling giggle, she spun to extinguish the lantern, drowning the tent in darkness.

"Night, night, dearie. A gal's gotta get her beauty sleep!"

Within minutes, Trixie was snoring. Celia lay in the hot, inky blackness, boiling inside and out, furious.

EPISODE 8:
THE BLACK LAGOON

The sun blared out of a brassy sky. Steaming, the jungle constricted the long, slow bends of the river, its sluggish currents marbled by whorls and eddies of slime. High above, a bird of prey croaked hoarsely, flapped its black wings and resumed its leisurely, corkscrewing glide upon a thermal.

Shielding her eyes against the glare, Celia squinted at it balefully.

"Jeremy, are you sure you know what you're doing?"

Beneath the broad brim of a jaunty Panama, the young Englishman's eyes twinkled merrily. He beamed at his frowning companion, radiating confidence.

"Absolutely, old girl," he assured her. "Boating is in my blood, you know."

Celia was not convinced.

"Yes, darling, but this isn't the Norfolk Broads."

It was stifling in the wheelhouse, and he had unbuttoned his shirt down to the belt buckle. Tiny pearls of perspiration glistened on his chest. Celia stared, nibbling unconsciously on a fingernail, recalling long hot summer days, delicious interludes spent in the fragrant shade of a weeping willow.

"Or punting on the Cam."

Jeremy was blushing. He felt a sudden flutter deep inside, a ghost of that first thrill of terror, of stuttering clumsiness and fumbling apologies.

"Ah.....er.....um.....don't worry, C, it'll be alright."

Celia watched a glinting bead form in the pulsing hollow of his throat, then roll slowly down his skin. A quick tightness gripped her, an ache welling up inside. But with it came other images, in stark, glaring clarity, a palpitating, quivering creaminess, and bright and saucy eyes. Swallowing hard, she turned her face away, so Jeremy could not see the blood rush hotly to her cheeks.

"Well," she snapped tautly. "If you say so."

She left the wheelhouse abruptly, her quick steps thudding on the deck. At the rail, she sucked in a deep lungful of the tepid air, fighting to ease the grip of a fist clenched inside her.

Amidships, two broad-shouldered torpedoes and their bullet-headed Prussian counterparts paused to admire her, their gaze exploring her thoroughbred lines. Braun said something which made Gruber laugh unpleasantly. Mack and Lefty exchanged a knowing glance. Then all four fell to with their oily rags, protecting the weaponry from the penetrating dampness of the jungle.

That same humidity wrinkled the cheap pulp of Trixie's magazines, curling the pages. Reclining in a canvas deckchair, she tossed "Screen Scene" away and picked up "Picturegoer". Leafing idly through its contents, she lit upon Clark Gable resplendent in a razor sharp tuxedo. Her eyes narrowed.

"Oh yeah!" she sneered.

Only in the movies. Men were only like that in the movies, handsome and efficient and clean. Not in real life, not in her life, not the grunting gorillas who had poked and prodded and pawed her since she was thirteen, who slobbered and farted and fell asleep on top of her when they were all done.

Trixie flicked through the pages. She came to Dietrich, Marlene in a stark studio portrait, the lights like ice on that beautiful death's head, with its hypnotic, heavy-lidded stare. A slow chill trickled down her spine. Unforgettable, the lightning bolt that jolted through her, hidden in the darkness of the movie house, as Marlene swaggered across the silver screen, across that smoke-filled cabaret, to plant a big wet kiss on that stuck-up dame, right on the lips.

"Morocco........"

That electric shock was a mystery to her then, but not for long. Nate got it with his money and muscle. She wove her spell with a glance, with a twitch of her hips.

Nate crushed the charts into a ball.

"Okay," he declared. "From here on in we're flyin' blind."

With a twist of the wrist, he propelled the useless paper out beyond the bow. Close by, Von Seyfritz frowned.

"I don't like it," he muttered. "I don't like this sailing without charts."

Dubois chuckled.

"Indeed, mon Colonel. It is an offence against German efficiency."

Von Seyfritz curled his lip.

"One day, my friend, that mouth of yours will get you into trouble."

A slow tension squared his shoulders, thumbnail brushing the flap of his holster. The Frenchman's eyes gleamed viciously.

"At your service, monsieur, at your service."

O'Dwyer stepped back a pace.

"Aw, fer Chrissakes!" he complained. "C'mon already, quit the jawin' and get down to swappin' some lead!"

The Europeans stared at him in amazement. Then Mackenzie bustled into view, gesticulating energetically.

"Gentlemen! Look!"

They turned as one to gaze out across the shining span of water.

"Goddamn!" groaned Nate. "Just what we need!"

The river forked, split in two by an arrowhead of dark foliage. Two identical ribbons of glittering water veered away at an acute angle, melting into the heat haze. Chartless, the explorers stared at each other, dumbfounded. Behind them, Jeremy poked his head out of the wheelhouse.

"I say, you chaps, may we have a decision?"

Von Seyfritz turned away, scowling. Dubois shrugged. Nate grunted decisively, rooting in his pockets.

"Okay, Perfesser," he called to Mackenzie. "Heads or tails?"

The copper coin glinted dully as it turned over in the air. The sun was climbing to noon.

Alarmed, the jungle cackled, as the engine wheezed and rattled spasmodically.

"The Captain had the old thing fine-tuned," Jeremy apologized to Celia. "I'm afraid I haven't the knack."

Celia patted his arm reassuringly and wandered off to lean upon the rail. She watched a troupe of chattering monkeys swing nimbly through the treetops. Von Seyfritz appeared at her side.

"I wish I had my rifle," he commented. "It would make a challenging shot."

Celia turned to gaze upon him coolly.

"Do you always see the world through the sights of a gun, Colonel?"

The Prussian drew himself up. Damned handsome, these Englishwomen, though they tend to be too independent.

"I am a man," he stated. "And man is a hunter."

A faint smile curled Celia's lip.

"Yes, Colonel. You are a man."

Von Seyfritz wasn't sure what to make of that. Celia moved on. She strolled to the stern, where Mackenzie sat absorbed in his leatherbound volumes. The Indians had gathered round him, peering curiously at the odd hieroglyphics etched across the yellowing pages. As the dark-haired woman approached, they fell back respectfully.

"Well, Professor, tell me all about the Fertile Crescent."

Mackenzie glowed all over.

"The cult of Pelath U-Thol!"

"Really?" murmured Celia, thinking about green lawns and strawberries and cream, about ice tinkling in a long cool gin and tonic.

"Indeed," Mackenzie's eyes sparkled. "During the first phase of the Third Dynasty. A cult rumored to have indulged in dark practices, including human sacrifice."

"Charming."

"They were implicated in a plot to overthrow the Royal House, but were discovered and brutally suppressed."

He held a dramatic pause.

"But then the survivors seem to have simply disappeared."

The Professor dug in his pockets. The golden idol gleamed.

"And unless I am very much mistaken...."

"Hey!" Nate exclaimed.

The American stood in the bows, waving to attract their attention. Jeremy popped his head out of the wheelhouse.

"I say, what's up?"

O'Dwyer gestured vaguely.

"Ain't we goin' faster than usual?"

There was a long silence. Trixie stepped out from the shade of the awning. She peered, blinking, at the river.

Dubois frowned.

"I think you are right, monsieur."

And suddenly, the old boat was sliding on the water faster than the slow plod of the engine could possibly propel it. Despite Jeremy's hand on the wheel, she began to veer off line. Surprised, the young Englishman made the necessary adjustments. Within seconds, the boat began to drift again.

Trixie startled them with a sudden squawk of alarm.

"Jeez!" she pointed. "Willya look at that!"

In the distance, the glassy surface had become agitated, slashed with white foam where fangs of black rock projected greedily.

"Hang on, everybody!" shouted Jeremy.

The sawtooth rapids spat and sizzled. Her ancient timbers groaning, the boat was sucked into the churning white water. She dipped into a trough so abruptly that, for an instant, they were levitated from the deck.

"Holy—!"

The old tub wallowed broadside into the broiling foam. The wheel was wrenched from Jeremy's grasp, spinning crazily. With a yell, Nate overbalanced, teetering over the rail, his arms flailing. Mack and Lefty sprang to haul him back to safety. Yelping, Trixie slipped, bouncing on her rump across the tilting deck.

Bobbing like a cork, the boat was battered on and on in circles, clattering and grinding, her keel grating on the rocks. Celia flinched from a lacerating burst of spray. Mackenzie reached out to assist her, only to be flung flat on his face, sliding sternwards on his belly, spluttering, the decks awash, till he fell amongst the Indians, all tumbling in a bundle wide-eyed and babbling with terror.

The rush of seething water drowned a bellow from Von Seyfritz. As he clung to the creaking superstructure, a great wave exploded over the rail and drenched him from head to toe. His henchmen dripped stolidly. Screeching, Trixie rolled in an untidy backward somersault. Nate reached down to grab her by the scruff of the neck. Sheltering beneath the awning, his arm locked around a wooden support, Dubois caught Celia by the waist and drew her in beside him.

"Thank you," she gasped, her hair plastered to her face.

"My pleasure," Dubois grinned, as the spray swirled around them.

A thin scream needled through the booming of the rapids.

"Man overboard!" shouted Mackenzie.

A sudden lurch of the stern had hurled one of the Indians into the rail. The worm-eaten woodwork snapped under the impact, and he hurtled into the flood. As the boat plunged and churned perilously, he was swept along parallel to them. Now and then a flailing limb jutted above the foam.

His fellows gesticulated frantically, tugging at Mackenzie.

"Can't we do something?" the Professor cried.

No one moved. Then Jeremy sprang from the wheelhouse, binding a heavy rope around his waist.

"Stand back there!"

He dashed across the rocking deck, tossing the free end of the rope to a dumbfounded Dubois.

"Secure that, will you."

The Frenchman hitched the rope to a stanchion. Celia paled.

"Jeremy, what on earth are you doing?"

As the would-be rescuer strode manfully to the rail, Nate intercepted him, seizing a fistful of his sodden sleeve.

"Are ya outta yer cotton-pickin' mind?" he bellowed. "It's just some lousy nig—!"

But Jeremy slipped the American's grasp and was gone, his body cleaving the boiling waters like an arrow.

Celia screamed. The river roared. Spray blurred the dark, dizzy fringes of the jungle. Water and sky seemed to blend and tumble, rolling over and over.

"That's it, old chap. Cough it up."

The Indian lay face down on the deck, gagging and spluttering, while Jeremy pumped discolored river water from his lungs. He was soon fit enough to be borne away by his comrades, laid out and fussed over in the stern.

"Well done, sir!" applauded Mackenzie.

Celia squeezed the young man's shoulder.

"My hero."

Jeremy beamed.

"I always knew the old boy scout training would come in handy some day."

They took stock of their surroundings. After the bellow of the river, there was a startling silence. They were becalmed in a black lagoon, its water as still and as heavy as tar. Beneath a glaring, colorless sky, grey, grassy marshland stretched as far as the eye could see. Along the skyline, there was a dark shimmer of jungled foothills, blue mountains floating in the haze.

The metal sky weighed down upon them, the stench of the swamp stifling and fetid.

Trixie flapped at the top button of her blouse, trying to let some air in.

"Aw, Daddy!" she complained shrilly. "I wanna go home!"

Red in the face, O'Dwyer loomed over her.

"Quit that whining!"

His arm swung in a looping backhand. The smack echoed thinly over the flat black water. With a yelp, Trixie backed up and sat down hard. Celia stood over her, gloating.

"I say!"

Jeremy stepped forward to remonstrate. Growling, Nate batted him out of the way with a mere flick of his great paw. Celia glared, her eyes sparking with anger.

"Mr O'Dwyer, you are an insufferable bully!"

With a brow like thunder, the big American bore down upon her.

"Another one who needs a damn good spankin'!"

He cocked the flat of his hand. Celia stood her ground, glaring. Trixie licked her lips. Jeremy scrambled to his feet, only to be bowled over again, by the Europeans stepping up to defend the Englishwoman's honor.

"I think not, monsieur," Dubois stated.

"You will not lay a finger upon the lady, sir!" Von Seyfritz declared.

Nate's simian features contorted, purpling with rage. His fingers quivered above the butt of the .45. Mack and Lefty stomped forward to flank him. Braun and Gruber matched them.

Celia groaned, throwing up her hands in exasperation.

"Oh, stop it, you bloody fools, I—!"

"Hey!"

Trixie squawked irately, as two of the natives, fumbling clumsily, bent to help her to her feet.

"Hey, hands off, ya mugs!" she protested. "Daddy, get these monkeys offa me!"

Breath hissing between clenched teeth, Von Seyfritz spun on his heel. The Luger rasped from its holster, flashed in a short arc which ended abruptly with the muffled thud of steel on bone.

Senseless, the Indian fell flat on his face. Veins bulging, O'Dwyer seized his companion and hoisted him high above his head. With a grunt, Nate hurled the kicking native into space. He hit the black water, which absorbed him without a splash. For a second, he vanished, and then his head bobbed into view.

Snarling, O'Dwyer rounded on Jeremy, who was struggling shakily to his feet.

"There ya go, hero, there's another one for ya to fish out!"

Celia gasped. Mackenzie shouted something.

Around the floating Indian, the black water was suddenly bubbling. He shrieked, an exhalation of pure terror.

"What the—!"

The water was churning, a black froth tinted purple. His eyes starting from their sockets, the Indian howled in agony, thrashing desperately with his arms. As the purple stain spread, his struggles grew weaker, till his face, horribly distorted, subsided beneath the black bubbles.

Ripples faded. The flat black surface reflected their pale faces.

Nate stood dumbfounded.

"Fascinating," murmured Von Seyfritz.

Dubois stared in amazement, his pistol frozen halfway from the holster. Mackenzie shook his head, horrified. Trixie gulped. Eyes darting nervously, the torpedoes scanned the surrounding marshland. Their Prussian counterparts held the cowering natives beneath the muzzles of their guns.

Gagging, Celia turned away. Jeremy moved quickly to support her.

"Tell me it isn't true," she muttered. "Tell me this isn't happening."

Dubois leant out over the water, to inspect the purple stain. A sudden strand of bubbles startled him. Then a pale glimmer revealed itself to be a severed brown hand, bobbing abruptly to the surface.

"Ugh!" exclaimed Trixie, beating a hasty retreat.

Dubois cursed violently.

"What's the matter?" Nate demanded, breathing heavily.

Dubois strode swiftly to the hatch that led below.

"We are lying low in the water."

He disappeared from view. The others dashed to the rail, peering at the waterline. They clustered anxiously, awaiting his return. He was back within minutes, his trousers soaked to the knee.

"The timbers are smashed," he informed them. "And there is water coming in."

Shading his eyes, he surveyed the sweltering swampland.

"We have about an hour in which to unload our provisions. From now on, my friends, we are on foot."

EPISODE 9:
CAPTURED

The boat lay grounded in the grey reeds, black water creeping over her decks.

"Okay, let's go!"

They squared up to the drab and baking marshland, the dark girdle of forested foothills, supporting the blue shimmer of the mountains. Behind them, the baggage train of Indians shuffled into line.

After some discussion, they settled on a formation. Braun and Gruber fanned out in front, the tip of a shallow arrowhead completed by Mack and Lefty. The rest followed at a safe distance, with O'Dwyer and Von Seyfritz on the left, Dubois and Jeremy to the right, all shouldering long hunting rifles. Safe between them, Mackenzie escorted the women. Bringing up the rear, the native bearers were strung out in single file.

Time dragged its heels. The sky was a steaming ochre, while the swamp stank, turning brown. Dark patches of sweat stained them. Cursing, they slapped and flapped at a stinging swarm.

"Achtung!"

A thin cry echoed flatly across the mire. Alarmed, the main party dashed to catch up with the vanguard.

"Quicksand!"

Where Braun had been, there was only a spasm of bubbles, rising to the surface of the grey-brown slime and bursting with a puff of oily vapor. They arrived just in time to see the foresight of his rifle vanish.

"Hilfe! Hilfe!"

Gruber thrashed desperately, wallowing in a grey glue that sucked greedily at his thighs. His struggles only served to submerge him to his belt buckle.

"Stay still, man!" barked Von Seyfritz.

The Colonel sprinted to the baggage train. Shouting, shoving the Indians this way and that, he rooted among the packs, the bearers chattering in confusion.

By the time Von Seyfritz returned, uncoiling a length of rope, Gruber had sunk to his breastbone. His eyes rolled in panic, palms splatting on the rubbery surface of the quicksand. Mackenzie and Jeremy bent as close as they dared, trying to placate him. Celia paced nervously, her hand over her mouth. Trixie grimaced and backed away, as the Prussian's struggles stirred up eddies of foul-smelling gas.

"Here, give me that!"

As Von Seyfritz fumbled with the rope, Dubois snatched it from him. Deftly, he fashioned a noose, expanding it with a flick of the wrist.

"Stand back!"

The Frenchman stepped out to the edge, whirling the lasso above his head. The loop of rope floated for an instant and descended in a broad hoop around the struggling Prussian.

"Put it under your arms!" Dubois shouted. "Under your arms!"

The khaki slime was up to Gruber's armpits. Dubois tugged to draw the noose tight. Then he flung the trailing end of the rope to Von Seyfritz. At a gesture from O'Dwyer, Mack and Lefty lumbered forward to assist him.

Grunting, they hauled Gruber free from the sucking sands. The swamp gave him up reluctantly, slurping greedily.

They stood around for a while staring at the spot where Braun had been. The Indians had set their burdens down and were squatting in the long grass. Bellowing, Nate got them back on their feet.

The sun was already caking the mud on Gruber. He spat and muttered lowly. Von Seyfritz squared his shoulders, his jaw jutting fiercely.

"He died doing his duty to the Fatherland!"

The Prussians snapped to attention and flung out their arms in salute. Behind them, Dubois was watching, his brow furrowed darkly.

They plodded on grimly. Gradually, the dark wall of the jungle drew near. The baking marshland was weighed down by a crushing silence, broken only by the squelching suction of their footsteps.

Suddenly, the leading bearer seemed to stumble. Looking faintly surprised, he staggered and fell heavily.

"Get up, ya.....!"

The Indian didn't move. The others clustered around, looking about them nervously.

"Come on, get up!"

Nate prodded the prostrate native with the toe of his boot.

"Look," said Dubois.

The Frenchman crouched down by the body. There was a bright bead of blood on the Indian's neck. From it projected a tiny, feathered dart.

As the others craned to see, Dubois plucked out the little arrow and held it up for inspection.

"Poisoned, no doubt," Mackenzie speculated. "Direct into an artery, poor fellow."

Then Nate started, cocked the bolt of his rifle, the click ringing out loudly.

"Jesus H. Christ!"

All around them, tussocks of brown and grey grass rose and revealed themselves to be garishly painted aborigines, wielding long blowpipes.

The air sizzled with the zip and whistle of the darts. Trixie yelped and hopped on one leg, clutching at her calf.

"Quickly!" shouted Mackenzie. "You must remove it!"

Trixie yelled again as Dubois stooped to oblige. Then he and the Professor hustled the ladies towards the ragged curtain of the jungle, while the others unslung their rifles and laid down a barrage, the boom of the long guns rolling across the flat expanses.

The Prussians knelt and squeezed off their shots methodically. Mack and Lefty didn't feel at home with this thoroughbred weaponry and banged away spasmodically, raising distant spurts of discolored swampwater. Jeremy bobbed about, dashing hither and thither, hopping with excitement. Once or twice, his eager eye glimpsed a fleeting target, but by the time he raised his rifle, it would be gone. He rattled off a round or two anyway, just to make himself feel better.

The reeds to Nate's left parted and a painted gargoyle burst upon him, lunging with a short spear. With a single thrust, he transfixed the nearest bearer. His victim shrieked, squirming like a pierced insect. As the grotesque figure struggled to wrench his lance free, O'Dwyer fired from the hip, blowing him backwards off his feet.

Roaring, Nate ripped out the spear. The hapless Indian howled, kicked once, then curled up into a ball and lay still. His eyes blazing, Nate hurled the shaft high into the sun.

"Yaaaaa!"

The smoke of battle cleared. They were left confronted by the empty, mocking marshlands.

"I think we've seen the blighters off," ventured Jeremy.

Von Seyfritz surveyed the huddled clump of natives, the bodies sprawled close by.

"To date, we have taken four casualties and have lost our transport," he observed. "Not an auspicious start."

Nate snorted, wiping the sweat from his face.

"Yeah, but two of them was Indians, and they don't count."

They had to herd the bearers at gunpoint, moving on swiftly to join the others in the shelter of the jungle.

They paused to catch their breath, deep into the dappled gloom, far below the whispering canopy of the treetops.

"Jeez! I..... uh..... I don't feel so good...."

Trixie staggered dizzily, sitting down with a thump.

"The dart!" Mackenzie exclaimed. "There must be some poison left in the wound!"

Trixie sighed and sprawled out full length on the mossy floor of the forest. Celia surveyed her stonily. Dubois sprang to kneel down beside her. He rolled her over onto her stomach and folded up her trouser leg. Seizing her ankle, he sucked noisily on her fleshy calf.

"Hey.....!"

Trixie squealed, then giggled drowsily. Dubois sucked and spat for some minutes. All done, he grinned and patted her on the rump. Nate advanced, glowering.

"Cut it out, pal," he growled. "Ya can look, but don't touch."

He reached out to tug the Frenchman away. Eyes narrowing, Dubois casually slipped the stiletto from his belt. Nate stopped short and took a step back.

"Lefty, gimme yer shiv!"

Mackenzie was about to remonstrate, but Von Seyfritz caught his arm.

"Go ahead, Frenchie," Trixie mumbled into the moss. "Stick the big palooka."

A high-pitched whistle welled into a shriek. A roaring metal thunder burst upon them, something unseen above the impenetrable screen of the treetops. The dark canopy reverberated, a rattle of leaves and twigs raining down upon them. The earth trembled.

The Indians cowered. Then, as one, they threw away their bundles and ran in all directions, scattering into the shadowed depths of the jungle. Their shouts sucked away by the roaring overhead, Nate and Von Seyfritz struggled to unsling their rifles, their loud report dimmed by the concussion battering down from above.

In an instant, the howling faded to a diminishing whine, then silence, abrupt and startling. They all stood staring at each other, pale and mystified. No one dared to ask.

"Well," Mackenzie blurted eventually, as he wandered amongst the discarded baggage. "All we can do now is shoulder the bare essentials ourselves and carry on."

Celia gasped.

"Carry on!"

Mackenzie shrugged apologetically.

"I am afraid that we have gone beyond the point of no return, my dear."

Trixie groaned, sitting up gingerly. Celia sneered and turned on her heel. Glaring at Dubois, Nate told Mack and Lefty to look after Trixie. They lumbered forward to help her to her feet, but she waved them away irritably.

"Lay off, you bums, I can manage."

She laid a hand on Dubois' shoulder and heaved herself to her feet. The world span about.

"Aw, Jeez!" she gulped. "I think I'm gonna upchuck!"

Celia rolled her eyes. Nate's great shadow fell across the dizzy blonde.

"Don't," he said flatly.

Trixie swallowed hard. The torpedoes treated Dubois to a flinty stare. Grinning, he sheathed the stiletto and, whistling a jaunty tune, turned to slap Jeremy on the shoulder.

"Come, mon brave, let's help the Professor."

With a great deal of fuss and bother, they went through the bundles which the Indians had left strewn upon the ground. They separated the wheat from the chaff, preserving the bare bones of the camping equipment, and the bulk of their ammunition. As Von Seyfritz observed, the forest would provide them with fruit and fresh meat.

As they fell into line and set off slowly, Jeremy at long last voiced their anxieties.

"I say, Professor," he gestured towards the treetops. "What was all that noise about?"

Mackenzie's eyes twinkled. He seemed to glow with excitement.

"Wonders upon wonders, my boy!" he declared. "Great discoveries lie before us!"

Night fell like a black curtain and wrapped its heavy folds around them. They huddled in the wavering glimmer of their campfire, all too aware of the jungle watching them. Drawn by the fire's glow, furry moths zig-zagged, wings whirring.

"Aw, heck!" Trixie complained, her shoulders hunched, arms wrapped around knees drawn up tight.

Celia sat nearby, within the amber pool cast by the flames. She surprised Jeremy by stopping Dubois as he strolled by and asking him for a cigarette. The Frenchman lit it for her, murmured a few pleasantries before moving on. Celia sucked audibly at the slim paper cylinder, then exhaled in a long sigh. Staring out into the darkness, she let Jeremy gaze upon her. The young man felt a slow warmth seeping through him. Her pale face was lovely in the glow of the firelight.

"I didn't know you smoked, C."

She smiled wanly.

"I don't."

In the deep blue between the fire and the surrounding blackness, Dubois and Von Seyfritz stood at sentry duty. Somewhere in the hidden distance, there was a shrill cackle, an abrupt whoop and hooting, followed by the rumbling cough of the jaguar. The sound struck sparks in the Prussian's eyes. He licked his lips, tasting death. Dubois fingered the bolt of his rifle.

The growling ignited into a full-throated roar. A gibbering shriek of terror was choked off in its prime. Celia jerked and then flapped at herself angrily, as ash dribbled down her shirtfront. Trixie looked up, alarmed.

"Don't worry," said Mackenzie. "It won't come near the fire."

Broad shadows in the gloom, Nate shrugged and Mack and Lefty relaxed. The low mutter of their voices droned in counterpoint to the whisperings of the forest, their conversation taut and monosyllabic.

Celia tossed the cigarette butt into the flames. Grimacing, she rolled her head from side to side, trying to ease the kinks out of her neck.

"Oh, Lord," she groaned. "I'm exhausted!"

Mackenzie drained his cocoa to the dregs, setting down the chipped enamel cup.

"Yes indeed," he yawned. "We must try to get some sleep."

The tents had been too bulky to carry. Grumbling, they crawled into their sleeping bags. Swathes of mosquito netting had also been abandoned, and they were obliged to resort to a particularly obnoxious ointment. They lay nervously in the pale wash cast by the flickering campfire, their eyes straining to pierce the dome of blackness that hung above them, listening to the rustle and click of tiny things crawling.

Nate's machete rang like a gong. The impact jarred all the way to his shoulder. Cursing, he rubbed his wrist, then drew back his arm and swung the blade savagely.

Seeping through the treetops, sunlight dripped down to the dappled floor of the forest like a heavy syrup, thick enough to squeeze between the fingers, all a musty glow of green and gold. The air was warm and wet to the touch, muffling the incessant murmur that seemed to clog the narrow spaces between each mossy tree trunk.

Sweating, they hacked their way laboriously through a tangled web of undergrowth. It resisted them at every step, at times absorbing their scything strokes with a soggy crackle, then repelling them as if rebounding off steel. Their phalanx soon blunted, they chopped and wallowed, their futile battering echoed by a derisive clucking from the branches above.

"I say," Jeremy's voice floated thinly in the distance. "This looks promising."

O'Dwyer tossed down his machete. It stuck in the dirt, the hilt quivering. Tugging a canteen from his belt, he sloshed lukewarm water onto his face, then unfurled his kerchief and scrubbed vigorously. Puffing out her cheeks, Trixie sat down, but stood up again, grumbling, as she felt the dampness of the forest floor seep through the seat of her trousers.

"I say.....?"

Jeremy's voice seemed fainter now. No one replied. Panting, Mackenzie leant on a tree trunk. He nodded gratefully as Dubois offered him his canteen. Up to his armpits in greenery, Von Seyfritz scowled, wiping the condensation from his monocle.

"Hullo.....?"

They could hardly hear him. Trixie cursed and threw away the remains of a cigarette, the soggy paper dissolving in her hand.

There was a seam in the shrubbery. Barely perceptible at first, it expanded to a ragged path.

"You see," Jeremy beamed at Celia. "I was right."

Celia nodded dumbly. Beads of perspiration trickled down from her hairline. There was a black stripe of sweat where her shirt clung to her spine, dark patches under her arms.

"Where there's a will there's a way!"

The trail meandered through the dripping undergrowth, criss-crossed by dusty shafts of sunlight. Jeremy advanced boldly, Celia struggling in his wake.

"I think we've come far enough," she gasped. "Let's go back and collect the others."

Twenty minutes later, Jeremy had to admit that they were lost. Celia hung her head and sighed. Taking a deep breath, she shrugged and plodded on. Jeremy hesitated, then hurried to catch up. The path expanded into something of a clearing, a pool of gold amongst the green.

"Chin up, old thing. We'll find them, don't you—"

Something snagged Jeremy's ankle, then tugged violently at this leg. The world turned upside-down, ground and scraps of bright sky winking through the treetops, all topsy-turvy.

"Jeremy!"

Gaping, Celia stared in amazement at her companion, now swinging up above the undergrowth, his arms flailing helplessly, suspended by the ankle.

"Hold on, I'm coming!"

She ran forward to help him. Suddenly, the earth dissolved beneath her feet and she was falling, down into a deep, dank pit. Her short scream ended abruptly. The impact jolted the breath from her body. A flash behind her eyes dimmed to a pinpoint, and all was darkness.

"To hell with 'em!" Nate barked.

Mackenzie shook his head vigorously.

"No, we must find them!"

Von Seyfritz hefted his rifle.

"That milksop boy is not worth the effort," he stated. "But we cannot just leave the lady to her fate."

Dubois flexed his shoulders, easing the weight of his pack.

"For once I agree with you, squarehead. We cannot desert a damsel in distress."

Trixie sneered. Huh, if it was me, you'd leave me out there to rot!

Nate swore, bending to snatch up his rifle.

"Okay, okay!" he rasped. "Let's go find 'em!"

Celia awoke to a swaying and jolting and juddering, to an ache in her limbs, and the panorama of the treetops flowing above her, a dark lacework pierced by sharp needles of sunlight.

"I say, C, are you alright?"

She had to strain to raise her head and try to find him. Everything seemed to be bobbing around. Her arms and legs ached dully.

"Speak to me, C!"

He was somewhere out in front. She released the strain on her neck muscles and let her head loll back. A pair of bony brown knees confronted her, then a roughly woven loincloth, a wiry torso and a grinning, painted skull.

Panic rose to choke her. Crying out, she lifted her head again, saw fibers lashing her wrists and ankles to a sagging pole, a sinewy brown back, feathers bobbing.

"Jeremy!" she screamed. "What's happening to us?"

Elastic, the long pole sagged and bowed. Celia could hear her joints creaking. Her protests grew louder as her backside bounced on the hard ground.

"I can think of better ways to travel," agreed Jeremy, somewhere in front.

The path wound narrowly through vicious thorn bushes, thin and whippy branches barbed with spikes a full inch long. Celia shouted as they made short work of the thin stuff of her blouse, raking scalding trails across her skin. She twisted and struggled, the vines that bound her chafing.

Nate examined the dangling noose. The others clustered round the rim of the empty pit.

"Oh dear!" sighed Mackenzie. "This is dreadful!"

Frowning, Dubois wiped the moisture from the barrel of his rifle.

"Yes, those two seem to attract trouble like a magnet."

O'Dwyer stomped over to Lefty and rooted in the torpedo's pack. Producing a bulky canvas satchel, he tested its weight for a moment before slinging it across his broad shoulders.

"Let's go!"

EPISODE 10:
CANNIBALS

A shallow plateau, crudely deforested. A jumble of conical huts, fashioned out of mud and straw. Yellow fumes rising, a sickly-sweet stench of decay.

Center stage, Jeremy and Celia stood bound to tall stakes. Jeremy's right sleeve was missing, his shirt hanging in tatters. Her dark hair in disarray, Celia's blouse had gone altogether. Her modesty was preserved only by a little bit of silk, her creamy skin smudged and cross-crossed with fine lacerations.

"I don't like the look of this," gulped Jeremy.

Turning pale, Celia could only swallow hard, biting back the bile that rose in her throat. A few feet away, a human torso was turning slowly on a spit. It crackled, dripping, and Celia groaned, her gorge rising at the ripe aroma. She turned her face away, only to be confronted by a dangling assortment of brown-skinned limbs. All around, grinning skulls glared from atop long pikes.

"By Jove!" exclaimed Jeremy, "I'm afraid our bearers have come to a sticky end."

The jumbled encampment was a hive of activity. Clad in brief aprons of grass, young women with black eyes and flat faces crouched in chattering bunches, whetting stone daggers. Capering naked children helped stoke fires, fanning the stinking yellow smoke. Wrinkled old women with dried out teats sucked their gums gleefully, tending a vast and bubbling cauldron.

Jeremy struggled fitfully. The binding fibers quivered but refused to yield. Celia shuddered. She ached all over and the scratches on her bare skin were burning like fire.

Somewhere, drums were throbbing. Chattering excitedly, the garishly painted warriors gathered around their captives. Grinning wolfishly, they displayed stained and yellow teeth, filed crudely into points. One prodded Jeremy's ribs. Another tested his bicep. They ripped away the remains of his shirt, shook their heads, disappointed.

"I think I'm too tough for them," Jeremy laughed weakly.

The cannibals turned their attention to Celia. She recoiled from their carrion breath. Eyes glowing, they kneaded her arms. Palms slid stickily across her supple midriff. They squeezed her thighs, cackling, fumbling with the waistband of her trousers. She writhed, protesting loudly. Jeremy strained at his bonds, sweat starting on his forehead.

"Swine!"

There was the dull thud of an explosion. A plume of earth fountained up into the bright sky. Two cannibals lay face down, twitching. A third sat staring dumbly at stumps where his feet had been.

A flash. The huge pot rose, seemed to hover for an instant, then fell with a crash. It shattered, its boiling contents hurled outwards in a great, steaming splash. Scalded, the old women thrashed about, screaming.

The band of warriors split in all directions. One remained, poised to thrust his spear into Jeremy. A small red hole materialized between his eyes. The back of his skull erupted. Shrieking, a painted harpy rushed at Celia, her bare breasts bouncing, brandishing her stone dagger. Celia shouted, twisting frantically against her bonds.

The earth detonated between the native woman's feet. Horrified, the captives saw her disintegrate, dismembered in slow motion. They flinched, ducking their heads as they were peppered with clods of dirt and smoking fragments.

A grey pall drifted across the encampment. There was shouting, a slap of bare feet running, the boom and crack of explosions. Shapes took form in the mist. O'Dwyer stepped into view, juggling an odd metal egg from palm to palm.

"Ya never knows when these little pineapples might come in handy."

The smoke cleared to reveal Von Seyfritz stalking out amongst the deserted campfires. A child crawled, leaving a dark and spotted trail. The Prussian prodded it with the muzzle of his rifle, while Mackenzie turned away, throwing up his hands in horror.

Nate went to join in the body count. Whistling, Trixie strolled over to the stakes, stood there grinning at the captives. Licking her lips, she let her eyes roll all over Jeremy, then closed in on Celia until their bodies were almost touching.

"Now ain't this nice," she cooed, letting a fingertip creep across Celia's skin and onto the rough fibers that bound her.

Celia reddened furiously. Trixie laughed, then turned abruptly and sashayed away, hips swinging.

"Oh, this is too much!" groaned Celia.

Dubois crossed into their field of vision. He surveyed them, shaking his head.

"Well don't just stand there," Celia shouted. Untie us!"

Chuckling, Dubois drew out the stiletto.

"Babes in the wood," he laughed as the fibers parted. "Babes in the wood."

They hardly slept that night, their dread imaginings stirred by every click and rustle, the baleful stare of yellow eyes glowing in the darkness. Some tossed and turned, their nightmares filled with demons. Others sat up in the wan flicker of the campfire, chain-smoking.

Dawn was bland and dripping. By noon, they wallowed in the molten gold and cloying dankness of the greenery, slapping at the swarms of tiny flies, cursing and complaining loudly.

Nate stopped suddenly, his brow furrowing.

"We're goin' up."

Imperceptably at first, the ground took on an upward slant. As it did so, the forest thinned. The undergrowth began to shed its clinging density and the distance between the trees expanded, the great, mossy columns replaced by stunted saplings. The patches of bright sky grew broader, and now and then there was the tantalizing suggestion of a breeze.

Panting, the travelers pressed on with renewed vigor.

"This is more like it!" Jeremy exclaimed cheerfully.

"Yes indeed," Mackenzie agreed. "We are approaching the foothills."

O'Dwyer forged ahead. Now he could sheath the machete. Mack and Lefty flanked him, hefting the long hunting rifles. Birds chattered in alarm at the crash and bang of their rapid progress. Small rodents scurried, but had vanished down their burrows before Von Seyfritz could take aim. Gruber tried a shot, but missed by a mile. Nearby, Trixie winced, her hands cupped to her ears. Dubois shook his head scornfully.

"Oh dear," said Mackenzie.

Jeremy's shoulders drooped noticeably.

"Dash!"

A steep escarpment teetered precariously above them, looming dark against the glare of the sky. Raw and jagged, it was overgrown by a wiry tangle of brush and shrubbery. Where the slope had crumbled, there were stark gashes of startling red ochre.

They all stood rooted for a moment, stunned.

"Yipes!" commented Trixie.

Celia sighed heavily. The straps of her backpack were chafing, its bulk rubbing on the scratches still raw across her skin.

"Are you alright, my dear?" Mackenzie inquired. "Perhaps we could distribute the load amongst us."

Jeremy stepped forward eagerly. The others looked decidedly reluctant.

"Do me a favor!" said Trixie.

Rolling her eyes, Celia waved Jeremy away.

"I can manage," she said stonily.

Nate sucked in a deep breath, let it hiss out between clenched teeth.

"Never mind all that," he grated. "What the hell do we do now?"

Von Seyfritz's finger jabbed upwards to the sky.

"We go up of course!"

Dubois was grinning. The Prussian rounded on him.

"Well, do you have a better suggestion?"

The Frenchman shrugged.

"Not at all, mon ami," he chuckled. "Not at all."

Nate tugged out his canteen. Surveying herself in a small hand mirror, Trixie made a face, groaning. O'Dwyer glared at her. The mirror vanished. Jeremy took a deep breath and approached the frowning Celia.

"I say, old thing, are you sure that you can manage?"

Screwing the cap back onto her flask, she raised a faint smile.

"Don't worry, I'm alright," she spoke with some determination. "We all have to pull our weight."

Mackenzie beamed.

"Bravo, Miss Cavendish!"

Trixie snorted.

"Oh, ra ra!"

Shading his eyes, Dubois wandered along the foot of the escarpment, picking his way through an accumulation of broken stones and other debris.

"There!" he pointed. "That's the spot."

"Well," admitted Dubois. "It could be that I was mistaken."

Von Seyfritz scowled. The monocle dropped from his eye socket, dangling on its string.

"Damned Frenchman!"

Strung out in no particular formation, they straggled across the ragged scar of a bare scree strewn with rubble. Crawling on all fours, they clung to a slope that had proved far steeper than it looked, unable to proceed or go back.

Trixie yelped, surveyed a broken fingernail, her pencil-thin eyebrows arching in dismay. Sweating, Nate stared at her.

"What am I doin' here?" he rasped hoarsely. "Stuck up here on the side of a mountain with this dumb bimbo and.....!"

Spluttering with rage, he shook his fist at the sky.

"Gianelli, ya lousy wop. I oughta have my head examined!"

Puffing, Mackenzie wiped his brow.

"Please keep your voice down, Mr O'Dwyer, you might cause an avalanche."

Nate's face purpled. Spittle flecked his chin.

"Avalanche, ya crazy old loon," he half rose from a crouch, his great arms swinging. "I'll give ya an aval—!"

The big American lost his balance. Bellowing, scrabbling furiously on his hands and knees, he slid downwards on a rattling, rolling carpet of small stones and other rubbish. Reaching out, Mack and Lefty caught him, grunting as they took the strain, all three sliding, locked together. Trixie screeched, alarmed by the onrushing bulk of the three giants. Her legs slid out from beneath her, but she grabbed an exposed root and hung on.

Gritting their teeth, the torpedoes brought O'Dwyer to a grinding halt. Lefty's shoulder flicked Mackenzie. Though barely a glancing blow, it was enough to flip the Professor over, sending him bouncing down the scree in a spray of pebbles, skidding on his backpack like an overturned beetle, his arms and legs waving in the air.

"Help!"

His passing raised vibrations that dissolved the ground beneath Celia. Shouting, she rolled like a log, till Dubois flung himself full length across her, pinning her down. Jeremy set himself like a fielder in the slips. The impact of the Professor's arrival knocked him flat on his backside, but he held on tight.

"Don't worry, sir, I have you!"

A pall of red dust floated out into the treetops, glowing in the sunlight. The rattle of rolling stones faded to a trickle of sand. Gasping, they lay sprawled across the slash of baked ochre.

Celia coughed to attract Dubois' attention.

"I think I'm alright now, monsieur."

Grinning, the Frenchman raised himself from her. She rolled away and sat up, picking bits of dirt from her hair.

Up above, the Prussians were climbing steadily. Nate swore, dark streaks mingled with the sweat on his face.

"Hey, if them Krauts can make it, so can we. C'mon ya mugs, move it!"

Mack and Lefty hauled themselves up, grunting and wheezing, their feet slipping. On all fours, Trixie froze. Heaving his great bulk over to her, Nate planted his palm squarely on her rump. Shoving with all his might, he propelled the protesting blonde forward.

"Get up there!"

Dubois gave himself a brief once-over. Whistling tunelessly between clenched teeth, he began to climb. Jeremy turned Mackenzie the right way up, helping him to reorganize the straps of his pack. Celia scrambled over to join them. Puffing out her cheeks, she looked around anxiously.

"Surely it can't get any worse!"

It could, and it did.

A path angling up the steep slope became a narrow ledge going nowhere. They were pinned against the jagged red scar, the wiry brush hanging above, while below them the scree plummeted to the treetops. Panting, wiping the sweat from their faces, they glanced at each other despondently, their shoulders sagging.

"Aw, dammit!"

Trixie stooped to rub a cramp in her calf. The brittle lip of the ledge crumbled and she lost her balance, lurching forward into infinity. Nate hooked his fingers into her waistband, jerking her back abruptly.

"Stand still, will ya!"

Shrinking from the edge, Celia paled. She swallowed hard, her stomach churning queasily. Startled, she jumped when Jeremy touched her shoulder.

"I'm not very keen on heights," she explained.

Mackenzie cleared his throat apologetically.

"I'm afraid we are barely into the foothills, Miss Cavendish," he sighed. "And the mountains lie beyond."

Celia gulped, turning grey.

"M–mountains? Must we.....?"

The Professor shrugged helplessly.

"Our only hope of returning to civilization as we know it lies beyond the mountains."

Celia threw back her head, her voice raised in anguish.

"Oh, bloody hell! Bloody, bloody, bloody hell!"

Further along the ledge, Von Seyfritz rolled his shoulders, easing the weight of his pack.

"This is all very well," he barked. "But at present we are going nowhere!"

"Correct," confirmed Dubois. "It would be pointless to try and go back down again, and there would seem to be no way up."

There was a long and gloomy silence. Then, all at once, Mackenzie brightened.

"Well, we can't go up and we can't go down," he stated. "But we can go in!"

The silence was deafening.

"Go in?" said Jeremy at last.

Smiling, Mackenzie pointed up ahead. Their eyes lit upon a bulging outcrop of rust red rock.

"There, look!"

A dark cleft split the stony protrusion, as tall and as broad as a man, in shape ominously reminiscent of the lid of a coffin.

They all looked at each other. Nate shook his head.

"Ya gotta be kiddin'!"

Mackenzie quivered with enthusiasm.

"I'll wager these hills are honeycombed with caves and tunnels used by the natives since ancient times. Where there's a way in, there's bound to be a way out."

He beamed at them expectantly.

"Come, come, my friends. What do you say?"

Trixie's eyes widened with alarm.

"I say forget it, Perfesser. I ain't—"

Then Jeremy was pointing.

"Jupiter! What's that?"

Mackenzie brought his hand up for a visor.

"What is it, my dear chap?" Your eyes are younger and keener than mine."

Jeremy shuffled to the head of the line and began to inch his way along the ledge. The others hesitated, then followed nervously, freezing each time the edge threatened to melt away beneath their feet. At last, they clustered on a bit of wider ground, pressed close to the bulge of red rock, grabbing onto fistfuls of scrub for reassurance.

"Well I never!" exclaimed Mackenzie.

Beside the dark cleft, there was a slab of flat stone. There were pink scratches on the red which, as they studied them, slowly formed into a pattern.

"It's a man, ain't it?" said Trixie.

It was indeed a humanoid figure, standing legs astride, arms extended at an angle from its sides.

"A queer-looking cove, if you ask me," observed Jeremy.

The hands and feet were enormous, the limbs oddly bulbous. Convoluted hieroglyphics were etched across its broad torso. The head was a featureless ball, topped by several curly projections.

Mackenzie fingered the deeply incised inscription.

"It can't be," he murmured. "It can't be."

Trixie giggled suddenly, nudging O'Dwyer with her elbow.

"Hey, Daddy, don't it look like Buck Rogers?"

Nate scowled. Mackenzie bent forward into the cleft, his head and shoulders lost in shadow. When he emerged into the sunlight, his eyes were shining with wonder.

"We must go in!" he cried.

The others looked doubtful.

"Give me one good reason why I should go groping around in the dark," frowned Von Seyfritz.

Mackenzie plucked the little golden idol from his pocket.

"This!"

The Prussian's eyes narrowed. Dubois chuckled. Nate licked his lips.

"I say, Professor!" Jeremy exclaimed. "Do you think so?"

"Trust me," smiled Mackenzie.

Celia opened her mouth to protest, but shut it and turned away, shrugging. Trixie went "hey!" as O'Dwyer pushed past her, his bulk blotting out the narrow entrance to the cave. He stared into the darkness, then turned to face them.

"Well, like the Frog said," he grunted. "We ain't got nowhere else to go."

EPISODE 11:
GREEN DEATH

Their lamps cast capering shadows, leaping phantoms that danced wildly all around them.

"Stay close together!"

Nate's rasping tones seemed to shiver tinnily, thin echoes shimmering into infinity. The cleft expanded into an ample corridor, a dark artery winding deep into the hillside. Two abreast, the travellers crept forward in a bunch, the pale lanternlight casting an eerie luminescence upon their taut and anxious features.

"Jeepers!"

Trixie hugged herself, rubbing her arms. The air was chill and metallic. Close behind, Dubois stopped suddenly, his brow clouding with puzzlement.

"This is very strange."

He ran his hand along the tunnel wall. It was smooth to the touch, gleaming like glass. The lamps revealed a subtle rippling, as far as the eye could see. Light and shadow flowed with a constant, stark fluidity.

Exasperated, O'Dwyer paced impatiently. The twin torpedoes waited silently, the lanterns held at shoulder height. Trixie kept close, glancing nervously at the black void up ahead. Their lamps extended before them, Jeremy and the Professor hurried to join the Frenchman. They left Celia in a chill twilight, her wide eyes deep and dark in the drawn, pale oval of her face.

"What is it now?"

Von Seyfritz advanced with a long and martial stride, thumbs hooked into the straps of his pack. Shaking his head, Dubois stroked the glassy wall.

"Look at this," he encompassed their surroundings with a sweep of his arm. "This tunnel, it is like a tube."

Mackenzie rubbed his chin thoughtfully. Von Seyfritz merely scowled and shrugged his shoulders.

"So?"

Dubois rolled his eyes.

"Think about it, man!" he exclaimed. "It's too perfect. It's not real!"

Mackenzie frowned.

"I agree it is rather peculiar," he murmured. "But....."

"And the air!" Dubois interrupted. "Smell it, it's not natural!"

Their nostrils quivered. The atmosphere in the tunnel was strangely crisp, and had a decidedly metal flavor.

"Bah!"

Cursing, Von Seyfritz turned away.

"This means nothing to me!"

His long stride carried him past O'Dwyer. With Gruber hard on his heels, he surged forward, the blackness receding before the pale wash of his lantern, the shadows leaping. At a grunt from Nate, Mack and Lefty jumped to follow, the big American urging on his hesitant companions with a great, looping swing of his arm.

"Wait for me, Daddy!"

Stumbling, Trixie floundered in their wake.

"Men of action," Celia commented dryly.

The hollow ring of their footsteps echoed far into the darkness. Pale and ghostly, their reflections danced alongside them, distending and fracturing, a mad funhouse hall of mirrors. The retreating shadows leapt and writhed.

"Ah," said Mackenzie. "Oh dear."

At the wavering fringes of the lamplight, the tunnel split, forking neatly into two. Perfect twins, the broad blank black circles confronted them, enigmatic.

The hair prickled on the back of Nate's neck. He could smell it. Danger.

"Well?" barked Von Seyfritz. "Which way?"

O'Dwyer grunted decisively.

"Lefty," he snapped his fingers. "Take yer pick."

The torpedo squared his broad shoulders. Holding the lamp up high, he plodded forward warily. Hesitating at the fork, he leant left, before abruptly veering right.

They watched him proceed in his bubble of light. Fingers hooked around the chequered grips, he hauled out his .38. He advanced with wary, shuffling steps, the shifting shadows wrapping themselves above and all around him. A spring coiling inside, his companions held their breath.

"Okay!" shouted O'Dwyer. "Hold it there. We'll come and—!"

The ground melted. With a yell, Lefty teetered, his arms pinwheeling. He lost his grip on the pistol. It clattered to the floor, skittering across the smooth surface. The lamp swayed precariously, the glassy walls of the tunnel splashed by a dazzling cacophony of light and shadow.

With a thin wail of despair, Lefty vanished into a well of blackness below.

"Okay," said Nate. "Mack, try the other one."

Celia gasped.

"How can you be so callous? That man may just have died!"

Nate merely shrugged.

"That's what I pay him for, baby."

The lamp shattered. Yelling, Lefty sailed through space, a black wind roaring all around him. He came down so hard his teeth rattled. Tumbling head over heels, he rolled to the brink of a vast and crumbling pit. A cascade of small stones preceded him, their rush and rattle silenced abruptly as they fell. The silence seemed to last forever, then he heard them patter down, somewhere far below.

Lefty sat up slowly, his feet dangling in thin air. Blinking, he rubbed grit out of his eyes.

"Huh?"

High above, the sky poured in through a jagged hole, a flood of ghoulish, glowing green. A sepulchral luminescence was pulsing down below, a slow, steady beat that sent lazy ripples up to the ragged scrap of sky.

The torpedo grew accustomed to the tomblike gloom. The high walls of the pit formed a broad, symmetrical bowl, held in place by great curving ribs of steel. Massive, dull buttresses were spiked with smaller spars, all snapped and bent and twisted.

"Jeez.....!"

Leaning out over the edge, Lefty looked along the broken, fallen backbone of an enormous metal fossil. The glowing green shivered, effervescent, on a silver skin which sagged like a leaking, wrinkled balloon. Through ragged tears in the metal membrane, strange shapes were black against the beating heart of radiant green. Spikes glinted viciously.

Propping up the walls of the deep bowl, the huge ribs were perforated at regular intervals, all the way down. Lefty hesitated for a moment, rubbing his chin. Then he swung his bulk over the edge and began to descend.

The giant buttress made a natural ladder, down and down and down. He thought it would go down forever. His breath rasped harshly, arms and legs aching, beads of sweat glinting like green gemstones.

"Uh-oh!"

About to put his foot down, he lifted it quickly. Cautiously, he prodded with his toe. A skull rolled over and grinned at him. Ribs rattled faintly. Lefty hunkered down for a closer look, then muttered lowly with surprise.

Yellow-stained and burnt brown, the bone was deeply pitted, in places eaten away down to the marrow, its coarse grain impregnated by the bitter blotches. Lefty juggled the skull on his palm. Frowning, he met its eyeless, grinning glare. He lifted a brown thighbone, the knee joint separating with a dry crackle. Ribs crumpled like paper.

Lefty let the skull roll off his fingers. He stood up straight, flexing his broad shoulders. The green heart pulsed brightly. Head up, he trudged towards it, till the glare melted the outlines of his wide silhouette.

"Yikes!" exclaimed Trixie. "Ain't this grand!"

Bright open spaces burst upon them, the impact stunning after the close confines of the tunnel. Of cathedral proportions, a great dome hung high above them, above a wide plain where fractured expanses were split by rocky shelves and jagged projections.

It took their breath away. From a pinhole open to the sky, the light poured down like silver. Everywhere, quartz sparkled, threaded in veins through the dark rock or sprinkled around in winking speckles.

"Magnificent!" gasped Mackenzie. "We are in a hollow mountain!"

O'Dwyer tilted his head back, squinting at the distant spark of daylight.

"Well, there's a way out," he grunted. "If ya can jump a mile high."

Mackenzie stepped out, waving his arms excitedly. His companions followed, fanning into a line abreast, tiny figures in the vast, uneven landscape.

They advanced cautiously, skirting deep folds in the ground. Wary of hidden danger, they gave each rocky outcrop a suitably wide berth.

Then Von Seyfritz raised his hand.

"Listen!"

They all heard it, a distant tinkle of water. Steam drifted from behind a mighty bulge of glistening stone.

"Hey!"

Nate made a clumsy grab, but Trixie sidestepped him. Her long stride making light of a weighty backpack, she headed for the warm veils of steam.

He couldn't believe his eyes.

A mile of piping gleamed, bent and curled in upon itself like the tubing of a trumpet. Tall cabinets stood humming quietly to themselves. Within glassy domes and bulbs, valves of a most intricate filigree pulsated with an eerie purple, stark against the deep green.

Lefty gaped. Suddenly his collar felt an inch tighter. His fingers crept instinctively to the butt of the lost .38.

A low, dull throbbing made all the broken metal vibrate. Breath trapped behind clenched teeth, Lefty flexed his broad shoulders, his blunt fingers curling into fists.

"Well, hey!" exclaimed Trixie. "How about that?"

Hot water cascaded. Steaming, it frothed over the stones, flowing into a broad basin rimmed with glistening quartz.

"Fit for the Queen of Sheba," Mackenzie observed.

Celia slipped the straps of her pack, letting it fall heavily to the ground. Unclipping the flaps, she dug deeply in its various compartments.

"What's up, old thing?" Jeremy inquired.

Celia plucked out a towel, delving for a cake of soap.

"Well, I may be no Queen of Sheba," she stated. "But I intend to make use of these facilities."

Celia reached for her top button. The others stood and stared at her. She gestured impatiently, waving them away with a flick of the towel.

"If you would care to withdraw, gentlemen. I want to take a bath."

Lefty found himself in a shining metal cone, the thudding pulse a dull compression on his temples.

Within the steel, there was a crystal pyramid, taller than a man. The heart of the green was a white light that sizzled starkly, making Lefty squint and blink. Approaching cautiously, he brought his hand to it by inches. Nothing happened.

Lefty peered through the transparent crystal. A polished well descended in short, concentric terraces. At its foot, perhaps fifteen–twenty feet below him, was a cube of white enamel, decorated with jagged symbols.

Cold sweat beaded the big American's brow. He stroked his granite jaw vigorously, stubble rasping. Each dull drumbeat seemed to tighten a steel band around his skull. All around, the metal hum was droning.

He studied the white cube. It looked valuable.

Stepping back, Lefty searched his wrecked surroundings. He snatched up a broken spar of steel, like a twig in his great paw. Shaping up like a batter at the plate, he put all his weight into the swing. The impact made him judder like rubber. There wasn't a scratch on the crystal.

Celia unbuttoned her blouse. Frowning, she tugged it from her waistband, wrenched it off, with a fleeting grimace for the stiffness in her shoulders. A faraway look clouding her dark eyes, she fumbled briefly with her belt buckle. She pulled off her trousers, flinging them down beside her boots.

She stared down at herself distastefully. The pale silk of her underthings was dingy, her skin clammy. Hands on hips, she bent back, arching the kinks out of her spine. Sighing, she ran her fingers through her hair. It felt coarse and matted. Oh, for a bottle of shampoo!

"Jeez, I'll be doggoned if this ain't the first good idea anyone's had since we came on this lousy jaunt!"

Trixie stepped out from behind a boulder, a long flannel draped across her arm. Celia turned abruptly. The blonde stood grinning at her, bouncing a bar of soap on her palm.

"I love the frillies, dearie," she drawled. "A bit fancy for this neck of the woods."

Furious, Celia felt the heat bloom upon her cheeks. With a sharp chuckle, Trixie crouched to test the steaming water.

"Yep," she declared. "I think I'll join ya."

Celia stiffened.

"If you don't mind," her tone was brittle. "I prefer to bathe alone."

Trixie stood quickly, that saucy light dancing in her eyes.

"Aw, c'mon babe, don't be shy."

She was naked. Instantly.

Celia paled. Her eyes grew wider and wider, her heart leaping to choke her.

Whistling, Trixie sauntered towards the pool. She was dancing, swinging her hips, little quick steps and a sideways shuffle. Mesmerized, Celia was absorbed by her startling whiteness, her gaze drawn irresistibly to the lively palpitations of her snowy bosom, to the flow of her pelvis and the sheen of her thighs.

"There's plenty of room for two."

Strutting, Trixie twirled the towel like a stripper's glove, flinging it up and over her shoulder. Celia snatched at it as it floated down upon her, threw it away, her features pale and stiff with fury.

Trixie waded into the basin, her reflection white and shimmering. With the water lapping at her navel, she pirouetted slowly, her arms held high above her head. Then she sniffed, wrinkling her nose.

"Ugh! I stink!"

Resuming her tune, she began to soap herself, elaborately and luxuriously smoothing the lather slowly across her glorious, supple contours. Celia stared, perspiration prickling hotly on her skin.

Trixie paused, the soap poised above a startled nipple.

"Well?" she demanded. "What're ya waitin' for?"

Rigid, Celia opened her mouth, then clamped it shut. She swallowed hard, wrenching off her underwear so violently that the silk tore. Trixie laughed, anointing herself with the creamy lather. Her undulations stirred expanding ripples, which Celia broke as she stepped into the pool, her movements stiff, her face like stone.

Trixie bent her legs, letting her body dip until the water tickled her chin. She rose suddenly, the milky froth cascading down her thighs. She dipped and rose again and again, till she was clean and gleaming.

Rubbing suds along her arms, Celia tried to ignore her. Trixie grinned.

"How'd ya like to scrub my back?"

Startled, Celia glared.

"You must be joking!"

Trixie advanced upon her, swaggering through the water, her wading tread exaggerating the roll of her hips.

"Aw, be a pal....."

Celia tried to speak, but could only stand rooted, sucked into the wild fire of those bright eyes.

"Why don't ya relax and be friendly?"

They were almost touching. Trixie's sheen sparked electric echoes in the sizzling quartz. Celia trembled, her pulse pounding, her skin dewed with tiny beads of sweat.

"I—!" she croaked. "I—!"

Her senses swam dizzily. Shouting, Celia twisted and shoved. Trixie sat down with a splash, her breasts bobbing on the surface.

"Wooo!" she gasped. "Honey do you play hard t'get!"

Swaying, Celia stood over her, spluttering with rage. She cocked a clenched fist, then froze.

Trixie was staring at something that Celia could not see, something behind her, over her shoulder. Trixie's face turned grey. Her eyes started from their sockets and her mouth gaped to let forth a shrill scream of terror.

EPISODE 12:
MONSTERS

Scowling, Lefty circled the crystal pyramid, looking for a way in. Its bright seamlessness mocked him.

Then, beneath his foot, a plate tilted. As Lefty reeled, off-balance, the pyramid rose, floating up into the gleaming green cone. The dull drumming swelled in volume, a reverberation that was physical. Lefty looked down into the polished well, eyeing the bright cube nervously. The white light needled his eyeballs. He could feel cold sweat trickling down his spine.

He took the first step. Then the next. Step by step, he descended into the well. He could feel the thudding concussion press in upon his ribcage. On the white sides of the box, the bright hieroglyphics seemed to clash and jangle. When he passed his hand across it, the lid sprang open.

The pulse quickened to a shimmering vibration. Lefty frowned. Expecting treasure, he was disappointed. Reaching in, he pulled out a long white cylinder, decorated with red and yellow bands. He grunted softy, surprised by the weight of it.

Shaking the tube, he thought he felt something shift inside. Hope glowed again. Turning the cylinder over and over, he examined it closely. Then he saw it, no more than a hairline.

He tested it, the sinews tightening across his thick wrists. The vibrations intensified, climbing in pitch till they became a shrill whistle. Then a screw thread gave, a metal cap slipping from his fingers to rattle on the floor.

A clutch of boulders were not boulders at all. On the sparkling shores of the basin, a clump of stone shook itself and fragmented into three. Ugly carapaces rose on bent stilts, quartz dust glittering. Eyes like dull bulbs telescoped on stalks, sawtooth mandibles clicking.

Trixie sat bolt upright, her eyes as wide as saucers, her shriek long and shrill and piercing. Celia froze, gaping.

Long jaws clashing like swordblades, the monsters drew up short at the edge of the steaming water. Frustrated, they prowled the perimeter, scuttling sideways, scuffling on the stones. Frantic, Trixie tried to rise, but only fell back with a splash, sitting down hard. Celia opened her mouth. Her screams echoed inside her skull. A tiny, strangled sound emerged.

"Hold on, we're coming!"

Jeremy came bounding over the broken plain. Braking to a halt, he fumbled with the bolt of his rifle. As one, the creatures rotated, stubby antennae tasting the air, seeking out this new danger. The rifle went off before Jeremy was ready for it. Slipping from his shoulder, the butt rapped him sharply on the nose. The lip of the pool disintegrated, shrapnel raining down into the water. Yelping, Trixie ducked beneath the surface.

"Lousy amateur!"

O'Dwyer tugged out the big automatic. As the razored jaw bones chomped greedily, he emptied the magazine, the booming detonations rolling like thunder around the high dome of the cavern. With a sizzling whistle, the slugs were repelled by the stony armor, vented their frustration by whining far into the distance.

Trixie surfaced, gasping, her hair plastered down to the sharp angles of her features. Lead buzzing all around her, she sucked in a deep breath and submerged again. Celia stood rigid, her skin crawling coldly. She strained every fiber of her being, but could not twitch a muscle, her limbs paralyzed, rooted to the spot.

Acknowledging the futility of Nate's efforts, Dubois lowered his revolver. He stepped back hastily as a clicking nightmare tacked crablike towards him.

"Stand away there!"

Von Seyfritz strode into battle, a big, brutal double-barrelled Express cradled in his arms. Stepping up onto a high table of stone, he took stock of the situation.

"Yipes!"

Coming up for air, Trixie saw the boldest of the scuttling monstrosities testing the waters, leaning into the steam. Making waves, she backed away hurriedly. In frozen horror, Celia watched the creature's bent legs swivel it in her direction. Its weak eyes detected the pale glimmer of her, the short antennae identifying something warm and edible.

The elephant gun roared. The beetle-thing buckled in a burst of yellow slime.

"So!"

Eyes blazing, Von Steyfritz let fly with the other barrel, a clap of thunder that made them all flinch, ducking instinctively. The thing stalking Dubois was flipped over on its back. Its legs flailed in the air, jaws grinding and clashing as a yellow slime seeped from the cracks in its armor.

The Prussian broke open the big gun. Brass cylinders were ejected automatically, tinkling on the stones. Von Seyfritz reloaded, plucking the shells from a bandolier slung across his shoulder. He watched as Nate jumped away from great mandibles poised to cut him in two. As the bony blades clamped down on thin air, he cut loose with both barrels, the recoil rocking him back on his heels.

"Holy cow!"

The thundering echoes faded into infinity. Nate grimaced, spattered with slime.

Von Seyfritz surveyed the hideous corpses, suffused with the light of victory.

"What a unique trophy these would make!" he exulted.

Mackenzie wandered from one carcase to another, pale and trembling.

"Unbelievable!" he gasped. "What could have caused such astonishing mutation?"

They gathered round, shaking their heads, arms outflung to measure the span of the giant invertebrates. Jeremy pressed a handkerchief to his nose, frowning at the spots of scarlet.

"Ahem!" coughed Dubois.

Immersed to her waist, Celia stood staring at the seeping wreckage, oblivious to the chill on her bare skin. Grinning, the Frenchman waded out to her. Startled, she blushed as he draped the long towel across her shoulders, wrapping her arms around herself. Her eyes burning darkly, she trudged out of the water, moving away as Dubois offered to assist her.

Exasperated, Trixie splashed to attract the Frenchman's attention.

"Hey! What about me?"

Nate's shadow fell across her.

"You just get your ass outta there!"

Shrugging, Trixie rose. The water slid over her skin like silver, making her hourglass curves gleam. As she swaggered to the shore, there was silence, abrupt and choking. The men stared, forgetting to breathe.

"Magnifique....!" Dubois whispered.

Tiny pearls of moisture glistened on her skin. Her luster lit their faces with wonder. The earth goddess, mused Mackenzie. So infinitely tactile, observed Von Seyfritz, feasting on a fantasy of that white flesh set off by studded black leather.

"I s–say…!" gulped Jeremy.

Trixie reveled in the heat of their wide eyes rolling all over her. Every breathing inch of her pulsated, as she sauntered up the gentle slope that led from the pond, hypnotizing them with the slow roll of her hips. Then she stopped and just stood there, staring right back at them, as bold as brass. Lap it up, you crumbs! Her gaze flickered brightly from Von Seyfritz to the Professor. Brain or brawn, it was the same.

O'Dwyer stepped in front of her. For a moment, ice twisted in her bowels, but the leer that passed for a smile was twisting his heavy features.

"Okay, hotpants, ya had yer fun."

He bent to pat her bare behind, just to show the others whose property she was. Trixie's eyes narrowed, but she kept her mouth shut.

"Ya knows we don't give no free shows."

With a talon-like grip dimpling her shoulder, he shoved her towards the pile of discarded clothing. Celia, clutching the towel to herself, was collecting her things. When she shivered, Dubois rooted for his hipflask. Jeremy pushed past him, going quickly to her side. Smiling, she let him lead her away, slipping her arm around his waist.

"Ain't love wonderful?" Trixie muttered, rolling her eyes.

It took her a lot longer to dress than undress. Having donned a fresh change of clothing, she took the stale garments to the hot water, hefting the cake of soap.

"Hey, ferget it!" Nate snapped. "We ain't got time for that!"

"On the contrary," Mackenzie interjected. "I suggest we make camp."

They followed his pointing finger to the pinhole high above. The day was dimming rapidly, shadows creeping across the rocky plain. Dubois nodded, a newly rolled cigarette bobbing on his lip. O'Dwyer glanced at his heavy wristwatch, and then he and Von Seyfritz were making for the little heap of baggage, shouting instructions to their henchmen.

The lamps cast an eerie glow, deep shadows in the hollows of their pale and tired features. Beyond their modest campsite, the darkness was absolute.

Exhaling a gust of tobacco smoke, Dubois nodded at the lanterns perched on a projection of stone.

"The oil will not last much longer," he observed. "We had better find our way into the daylight soon."

He flicked the butt away, its bright tip sucked into the fathomless black expanses. Nearby, Mackenzie filled his pipe, his eyes misted over, far away. While Nate re-loaded the magazine of his .45, Von Seyfritz stroked the Luger with an oily rag. Trixie stretched out on a blanket, her head pillowed by a folded jacket. Yawning, she arched her body, catlike. Celia stared intently into her tin cup.

A dull clang startled them.

"Come and get it!"

Jeremy beamed as they peered skeptically into the pot, at a stew bubbling darkly.

"What is it?" growled O'Dwyer.

"Lizard!" Jeremy proclaimed. "And some of those spices the Professor found on the trail."

Trixie groaned.

"Aw, not again!"

Jeremy ladled generous portions onto their tin plates. They poked and prodded it reluctantly. Though Mackenzie declared it to be not unlike chicken, his enthusiasm was not infectious. They chewed grimly, Celia grimacing as she extracted a small bone.

Von Seyfritz scooped out a second helping.

"The taste may leave much to be desired," he told his companions. "But it is most nourishing."

They looked doubtful, but he was undaunted.

"The two German aviators who crashed in the Kalahari Desert survived on such fare for many weeks until they were found."

Dubois spat out a bit of gristle.

"Germans eating reptile," he muttered. "I would call that cannibalism."

Nate got ready to roll out of the line of fire. The Prussian's face froze, the monocle glittering.

"You are very reckless, mein herr."

Dubois shrugged, though his eyes were fixed and unblinking. Von Seyfritz smiled thinly, his tone cool and even.

"As long as we are lost in this wilderness, we need each other," he stated. "But when the danger is passed, my friend, we have an appointment, you and I."

Dubois grinned and rolled another cigarette. With a flick of his wrist, he tossed up the slim cylinder and caught it between his lips.

"Hey, that's a neat trick," said Trixie. "Bet ya can't do it aga—"

Startled, Nate leapt to his feet, letting out a yell of alarm. A broad shadow fell across them as a figure lurched into the lamplight.

Celia screamed. Trixie screwed up her face in disgust.

"Lefty.....?"

He was barely recognizable. His face was blotched with horrible burns, the skin flaking and peeling away. The hair was all but gone from his blistered scalp, his ears melted stumps. His eyes were red and weeping.

"Lefty!"

The bulky figure shambled forward, his arms outstretched in supplication. Ghastly mewling sounds croaked from lips that were cracked and festering, encrusted with running sores. Nate seized his hand, recoiling with horror as the skin peeled off like a glove.

Groping blindly, the thing that had been Lefty stumbled past them, out to the pale fringes of the lamplight. He fell heavily to his knees, crumpled forward onto his face, his rear projecting grotesquely into the air.

Trixie groaned and turned her face away. Celia stood pale and rigid for a moment, then suddenly jack-knifed, gagging. Jeremy sprang to her side. The others gathered round the fallen torpedo, guns in their hands, looking all around them nervously.

"It's like that Indian all over again," Nate told the Professor. "The one with that piece of gold."

Mackenzie nodded slowly.

"Yes indeed," he murmured fearfully. "I am afraid that we are dealing with forces that are beyond our comprehension."

Von Seyfritz worked the toggle action of the Luger, feeding a round into the chamber.

"If it can kill, it can be killed!" he barked. "I did not survive the Great War in order to become fodder for some nameless demon in this God-forsaken backwater!"

There was an edge to his voice that sent a shiver down their spines. No one slept that night. All huddled close to the lanterns, their hands on their guns.

The last lantern flickered and died.

"Oh no!"

They were smothered in darkness, a black flood engulfing them. Helpless, they stood where they were, frozen in mid-stride.

Dubois raised his hand, but until his fingertips touched his nose, he couldn't tell that it was there. Celia could feel Jeremy's arm brushing hers, but could not see his face.

"Aw, goddammit!"

The glowing ember of Nate's cigar gave them a point of reference.

"Whaddawedo, Daddy?" Trixie quavered.

The pinpoint of fire twitched as Nate flicked the stogie from one corner of his mouth to the other.

"Well, we cannot just stand here till we rot!" snapped Von Seyfritz.

"Bravo!" said Dubois.

"Yes, we must go on!" declared Mackenzie.

A memory popped into Celia's brain, a fleeting image of fire drills at her old boarding school.

"Form a chain," she said.

There was a puzzled silence. Dubois lit a match. The tiny spark sputtered, his face floating like a mask in amber. Then he cursed and the little flame fluttered down into extinction. The mask vanished and they heard him blowing on his fingers.

"Yes!" exclaimed Mackenzie. "Hold hands, hold on to the person in front of you!"

They shuffled onward, the blind leading the blind.

"Stay close together," called Mackenzie. "Don't fall behind."

Celia and Jeremy groped for each other's hands. Nate hooked his fingers on Trixie's waistband. The rest hung on to the strapping of their packs. The scuff of their bootheels was reassuring, something tangible. The echoing blackness was bottomless. It amplified every sound, the rustle of cloth, the creak and jangle of their harness. They could hear each other breathing. They could smell each other.

Celia felt as though she were floating in a void. She could sense the darkness on her skin, numbing her.

Jeremy felt her tremble.

"Steady, old thing."

She squeezed his hand tightly. Then her heart leapt into her mouth, as Trixie yelped shrilly.

"Hey! Who pinched my ass?"

O'Dwyer ground to a halt, the others piling up behind him.

"Was that you, Dubois?" he demanded.

"Oh, pardon!" the Frenchman exclaimed. "My mistake."

Frustrated by the darkness, O'Dwyer muttered angrily. Chuckling, Dubois hooked his fingers into a pocket on Nate's backpack.

"That's better," said Nate.

Celia cleared her throat.

"May we proceed?"

With Dubois' laughter echoing into infinity, they shuffled on into the darkness.

"Hold on with your left hand," advised Von Seyfritz. "And keep the other on the wall."

Jeremy's grin tingled all the way down his arm, warming Celia's hand.

"Just like Hampton Court Maze, what?"

They could hear Von Seyfritz bristle.

"This is no game!" he shouted. "You English are all such damn schoolboys! You fought the War like it was some kind of school sports day!"

"Ah yes, but we won, didn't we?" Jeremy said stoutly.

The Prussian spluttered.

"Only the first round!" he hissed. "Only the first round!"

"Oh really?" said Dubois.

"Yes!" ranted Von Seyfritz. "We have had our strength drained from us by communists and blood-sucking Jews, but, mark my words, Germany is awakening!"

Gruber murmured discreetly. Von Seyfritz sucked in his breath and fell silent, a silence which stretched interminably, broken only by the steady scraping of their heels.

Time lost all meaning. Their legs were rubbery and their backs ached. The straps bit into their shoulders. Sweat itched all over.

"Aw, Jeez!" wailed Trixie. "We ain't never gonna get outta here!"

"Shaddup!" Nate bellowed.

He was accelerating, lumbering forward, making them all stumble to catch up.

"Shut yer yap!"

They heard him sniffing the air.

"What is it?" asked Mackenzie.

Nate was running now, his feet thudding on the stone.

Their labored breath rebounding off the glassy walls of the tunnel, they pursued a fuzzy scrap of daylight.

Expecting it to expand, it seemed to get further away the faster they ran, lungs rasping, legs pumping, sweat streaming down their strained faces.

Nate's knees were aching. His skull pounded, his blood roaring like fire. Von Seyfritz ran methodically, precisely, Dubois loose-limbed, loping along. Jeremy panted, trying to remember what his old Games Master had taught him; stop bobbing up and down, put all your energy into forward motion.

Trixie was staggering. Celia said a silent prayer of thanks for months of winter training. Losing touch, Mackenzie felt a great weight pressing on his chest.

"Oh dear!" he gasped. "I say, c–could we slow d–dow…?"

They crashed into a barricade of broken boulders.

"What the—!"

"Ouch!"

Gasping, they collapsed in a heap. A rent in the rocky screen, the sliver of daylight hung above them, picking out the pale glimmer of their faces.

Celia sank to her knees, her head tilted back.

"Oh, Lord!" she panted. "Fresh air!"

Mackenzie was groaning, clutching his chest. Jeremy knelt to help him off with his pack, easing him down to lie full length, a folded jacket for a pillow.

"Don't worry," the Professor wheezed. "I'll be alright."

Concerned, Jeremy fanned him. Dubois unslung his canteen. Wiping her face with her sleeve, Trixie sat down with a thump. She flinched as Nate and Von Seyfritz stepped over her, their attention fixed on the shining gash above them. They could feel the flicker of a breeze cooling the sweat on their faces, their eyes glittering greedily.

"Come on!" yelled O'Dwyer. "Give us a hand!"

Mack and Gruber lumbered forward readily. Tossing the canteen to Jeremy, Dubois sprang to join them.

"Hey!" Trixie shouted. "Watch it, will ya!"

Clambering up the heap, they clawed at the stones. They tugged them away, cursing, their fingers bleeding, letting them drop and clatter downwards, Trixie beat a hasty retreat, scuttling on her hands and knees to where Celia and Jeremy sat mopping Mackenzie's brow.

Gradually, the crack expanded. A pale light filtered into the gloom, probing mistily. Then, suddenly, a warning shout, a crash and tumble.

Blinding, the day exploded in upon them.

EPISODE 13:
THE LOST WORLD

They stepped onto another planet.

Blinking in a bleary light, they saw an unearthly landscape stretching out before them, melting into greyness.

"Brr!"

The air was clammy, wet to the touch. All was oddly unreal, intangible, seen through a film of water.

Ragged, overgrown ravines twisted and plunged precariously, dizzy heights teetering, wrinkled folds growing paler with distance, a deep blue-green fading to grey, blending into the colorless mist. Jagged edges were furred and feathered with shrubbery, strange spikes jutting up to a blank sky that merged seamlessly into the creeping vapors.

At their feet, the bumpy turf was carpeted by a mottled swathe of tiny pink and yellow flowers, interwoven with strands of a close-knit, blue cabbage. Dotted everywhere, were rubbery shrubs, each a ball of green blades. Larger plants spread broad leaves out in a bowl, gleaming with moisture. Ancient, shattered tree trunks sagged close to the ground, hung with a drapery of lichen, fuzzy with a purple moss.

"By Jove!"

Jeremy peered over the edge. Far below, the narrow valleys were dark and choked with foliage. Dull murmurings drifted up to him. High above, a metal croaking echoed thinly.

"Incredible!" exclaimed Mackenzie. "It is almost like standing at the bottom of the sea."

His gesture embraced the odd shrubbery, the patches of pink and yellow and purple.

"Amongst the coral and anemonae."

Nate turned up the collar of his jacket, as the chill clamminess crept down his spine. The others rooted for their oilskins, the slick surfaces soon beaded with moisture.

Dubois pointed. Looming over them, the pale ghost of mountains, their floating pinnacles translucent.

"It will be warmer there," he stated. "Where the mist evaporates."

Celia paled, shivering.

"Up there?"

"Absolutely," said Mackenzie. "We must cross the mountains. It is our only way home."

He paused, feeling for the shape of the tiny idol in his pocket.

"And up there, we may find what we are seeking!"

Von Seyfritz's eyes narrowed.

"Do you think so, Herr Professor?" he asked sharply.

Mackenzie smiled. Nate squared his shoulders.

"Yeah? Well, maybe that'll make this lousy joyride worthwhile."

Jeremy brightened visibly. Dubois shrugged. Celia rolled her eyes.

"Who cares!" Trixie wailed. "I wanna go home!"

Through the mist, the sun was a white disk. It nibbled at the tallest peak, edged it with pale gold. They all stood and watched it for a while.

"Yes," said Dubois. "It will be hot up there. Hot by day and cold by night."

A low growl rumbled along the valley far below. Shrill alarm bells rang all along the overgrown escarpments. O'Dwyer held out his hand and Mack tossed him the long hunting rifle. Gruber did the same for the Colonel. The clack of the bolts rebounded tinnily.

"We ain't got no time to waste," the big American rasped hoarsely. "Let's go!"

The setting sun dissolved into the mist, like blood slowly seeping. Clammy veils writhed and twisted all around them, as they plodded wearily along the interminable, looping trails that wound around the jungled cliff faces. The air was cold and damp, suffused with fearful murmurings.

"Oh!"

Celia slipped. Scrabbling for a hold, her foot broke through the flaking edge. Arms flailing, she teetered on the brink. Instinctively, Jeremy hooked his arm around her. Wide-eyed, Celia clung on tight.

"My hero!" Trixie drawled sarcastically.

She yelled when Nate's iron grip fastened on her arm.

"Shut yer trap and keep movin'!" he snarled. "And watch where ya goin'!"

He shoved her on along the path.

"Fall and I ain't comin' down to fetch ya!"

The slippery trail wound on and on. It looped ahead till it was sucked into the mist, gleaming like a snail's track against the dark foliage.

They inched along the silver ribbon. Their hair was lank and dripping. Water coursed in rivulets down the oilskins draped across their shoulders. Inside them, they were sweating.

"Hell on earth," muttered Dubois.

The mist was a swirl of tiny droplets. Von Seyfritz rubbed his eyes, cursing.

"Like nothing on earth!"

Blinking, Mackenzie wiped his spectacles for the umpteenth time. He looked out across the tumbling landscape with its spikes and draperies and blur of bright mosses, now curiously luminescent in the dusk slowly filtering down.

"Most peculiar," he mused. "One could almost imagine this to be the planet Mars."

The others only hunched their shoulders, fumbling with their collars. For Jeremy, however, life was one long adventure.

"I say!" he responded brightly. "Do you think so, Professor? I've heard that Mars is—"

A rattle and peppering of small stones, raining down from the dark crests above them. Ducking, they threw up their arms to ward off this sudden hailstorm.

"Look out!"

An avalanche cascaded down upon them, rumbling and clattering, broken stones and other debris. They crouched down low, hugging the wall, as an aerial bombardment burst all around them. A glancing blow knocked Nate's pith helmet flying, sent it sailing into the void. A stone the size of a football caught Dubois square on the backpack, flattening him, winded.

Silhouetted against the darkling sky, apelike figures capered on the leafy heights, hooting and gesticulating violently, heaving boulders up and hurling them downwards, brandishing clubs.

"Devils!"

Von Seyfritz stepped out into the open, raised his rifle and fired. The detonation reverberated down the twisted valleys. There was a shriek, a frantic gibbering from above. The bombardment ceased abruptly.

Silence. They rose warily. The Prussian worked the rifle bolt, ejecting the spent cartridge.

"I think that has solved our prob—"

With a shout, Gruber dragged him back to cover. Spreadeagled against the dimming sky, a dark figure plummeted, bounced and rolled, crashing through the undergrowth.

Its headlong progress slowed until it rolled gently down beside them on the path.

"Good grief!" exclaimed Mackenzie.

The corpse lay face down. When Mack rolled it over, the Professor started, gasping out loud.

"Hey!" giggled Trixie. "He's a big boy!"

Nate frowned.

"That's the biggest damn chimp I ever seen."

A large, apelike form lay sprawled at their feet. Naked, its leathery brown skin was spiked with stiff black bristles. A dark thatch atop its flat cranium ran down in tufted sideboards that framed a jutting jaw. There was a small red hole between its sunken eyes, bisecting a narrow forehead.

"Fine shot," Von Seyfritz commended himself. "It would make an excellent conversation piece, stuffed and mounted in my hunting lodge."

Mackenzie was quivering with excitement.

"What gives, Perfesser?" asked Trixie.

Mackenzie's eyes were wide and bright with wonder.

"C–can't you see?" he stammered. "The proportion of the limbs, the span of the skull.....!"

Trixie span on her heel, looking for someone to light her cigarette. Jeremy obliged, the damp matches needing some persuasion before they ignited. Trixie grinned, winking at him. Celia glowered. Chuckling, the blonde returned to their victim.

"Put it in a tux," she commented. "And it would look like some of them stiffs that gawp at me at the Fat Cat."

Celia sniffed.

"Yes, I'm sure it would."

Mackenzie danced around the body, his hands flapping excitedly.

"Pleisanthropus?" he speculated. "But it can't be, it's impossible!"

Muttering to himself, he hovered over the prostrate form, its head resting in a dark pool that was slowly spreading. Jabbing with a pencil stub, he made quick sketches in a small notebook, flinging out his arms, making rough measurements.

The sky was slowly purpling, darkness filtering down towards the blurred horizons. The others waited impatiently, shuffling and shivering. Veils of grey mist wafted across the valleys, now drowned in shadow.

"Aw, c'mon, Perfesser!" Nate snapped. "It's only a lousy monkey!"

Puzzled, Dubois was scuffing at something with his toe. The sound drew Mackenzie's attention from the corpse.

"And what have you there, my friend?"

Von Seyfritz made an exasperated sound.

"It is only a rock!" he snorted. "Those damn apemen threw it at us."

Dubois stooped to lift the object in both hands. He stood silent for a moment, studying it.

"Yes," he said quietly. "But how many rocks have you seen that are shaped like a perfect cube?"

The night was starless and full of strange whisperings. Grey mists crept across the cold ground.

"How very odd," said Mackenzie.

Firelight cast dancing shadows. Angular ridges seemed out of place in the mottled, undulating landscape. Here and there, straight edges of stone broke through a crust of moss and spiked grasses.

"Why odd, Professor?" asked Dubois.

His brow furrowed in thought, Mackenzie paced out a long projection that could have been laid down by a rule, stopping where it veered away abruptly at right angles. Suddenly, he stooped and began scraping away the moss.

"There, you see?" he said, wiping his palms. "These formations are not natural."

Von Seyfritz tugged and a brick crumbled and came away in his hand.

"Obviously!" he barked, dismissing the stone into the darkness.

They heard it thud into the undergrowth. For a moment, the constant murmurings stopped, then swelled up again. Dubois yanked at a tuft of grass. A brick was detached along with it and dangled for his inspection, before its weight broke it free and dropped it to the ground. The Frenchman tapped it with his toe, stirred eddies in the crawling mist.

"Perhaps we have discovered a lost civilization," he chuckled.

"Bah!" Von Seyfritz snorted. "Just a native hut."

Mackenzie shook his head slowly.

"No, I think Monsieur Dubois may be close to the truth," he said quietly. "Only, only....."

"Only what?" snapped Von Seyfritz.

Mackenzie bent stiffly to retrieve the stone that lay at the Frenchman's feet.

"Well, the natives are more likely to be living in mud huts or in caves," he explained. "And the ancient civilizations in this part of the world built their cities with stone hewed into huge rectangles, not small cubes such as this."

Dubois shrugged.

"So, there is always a first time for everything."

Mackenzie hardly heard him.

"Bricks such as this," he murmured. "Were baked somewhere very different."

A sudden rattle drew his attention to Von Seyfritz, scrambling up a jagged pile.

"For my part," he declared from the summit. "I am more interested in the fact that this structure does not seem to have eroded naturally."

"Ah, non!" exclaimed Dubois. "I would say that it has exploded."

Leaving Mackenzie, he clambered up to join the Prussian.

"Look here," he pointed. "And here, where the moss is brown and withered."

"And here the stone is black," added Von Seyfritz.

Then Mackenzie gasped, an abrupt exhalation that startled them and brought them down quickly to his side.

"And what do you make of this, gentlemen?"

They gazed down upon a splintered slab fallen at an angle, staring at a figure incised in bold strokes into the sooty patina that marred its smooth surface.

"Hmm?"

Silent, they glanced at each other nervously. There it was again, bulbous of limb and with a bowl for a head, topped by those odd, curly projections.

Dubois crouched down for a closer look, tracing the outline with his finger. Von Seyfritz stepped back, straining to penetrate the surrounding blackness, feeling for the flap of his holster.

"My friends," Mackenzie proclaimed. "We are about to embark upon the most extraordinary adventure!"

Von Seyfritz was not convinced.

"Well," he hissed. "If you ask me…."

Dubois leapt to his feet.

"Listen!"

Out of the dark mutterings, emerged an eerie melody, a thin piping that soared and swooped and seemed to be in the air all around them, strangely discordant.

In the grey mists, a pale phantom materialized.

"Sacre bleu!"

"Miss Marlowe!"

Her eyes wide and staring sightlessly, she glided close by them, her arms outstretched, in a trance, sleepwalking. As the ebb and flow of the pipes broke into a staccato exclamation, they could see her lips moving, though no sound emerged.

Her blank stare bore through them as if they were not there. Von Seyfritz reached out to touch her shoulder, but Dubois grabbed him by the sleeve.

"Don't! It can be dangerous."

A dull pulse now underpinned the pipes, a dark, deep sound that seemed to well up from the bowels of the earth. On tiptoe, the others followed, as Trixie floated over the broken ground. The pipes were shivering, the drums a shimmering vibration. Then she turned abruptly and fell to her knees, pulling away the stones and scratching feverishly, gouging the dark soil.

Nate's bulk swamped the glow of the fire, as he bent to get a light for his cigar.

"Where the hell have ya been?" he demanded. "I told ya I wouldn't come runnin' if ya ran off and got lost!"

Trixie just stared at him. As Nate's brow clouded with thunder, Dubois steered her away and sat her down upon a blanket spread out on the ground. She slumped dumbly, bewildered, a long strand of saliva dangling from her chin.

"Astonishing!" said Von Seyfritz. "It was as if she knew exactly where to look!"

Clamping his teeth down on the fat Havana, Nate stomped over to glare down at Trixie. She shivered in his shadow, looking all around her in confusion.

"Look?" he grated. "Look fer what?"

Something glittered in the firelight.

"This!" said Mackenzie.

A large medallion dangled from his finger, rotating slowly on its chain. Gleaming, it took the form of a stylized mask, pierced where the mouth and eyes would be, a beard and mane radiating like tongues of fire.

"I say!" said Jeremy.

Smiling, the Professor let it rest on Celia's palm.

"It's gold, isn't it?" she whispered.

Von Seyfritz and Gruber exchanged sharp glances. Dubois' eyes narrowed. Sitting on the blanket, Trixie was mumbling. Mackenzie held the medallion up high, so that it swung and revolved, flashing.

"My friends, we are looking upon the face of a god!"

"We're lookin'," said Nate. "At a million dollars."

Their sleep was filled with dreams.

Von Seyfritz rode in triumph beneath the Brandenburg Gate. His chariot was festooned with garlands, followed by a train of wagons piled high with gold and precious stones. The adoring masses were delirious, the laurel leaves held above him, the whisper in his ear: "remember thou art mortal...." His heels crashed together as a grateful Fuhrer stepped forward to shake his hand.

Mackenzie acknowledged the plaudits of packed lecture theatres. Imperiously, he took charge of the British Museum, a frock-coated entourage trailing in his wake, hanging on his every word. Humbly, he knelt as the King laid the sword lightly on his shoulder.

Nate was plunged into a frozen blackness. There was a roaring in his skull, his lungs bursting. He was wrapped round and round with cables, concrete strapped to his ankles. High above, beyond a pearly strand of bubbles and the wrinkled, glassy skin of the river, he saw the distorted features of Sam Gianelli, laughing at him.

Celia drowned in Trixie's eyes. She writhed in agony, her naked body wreathed in sweat that scalded her flesh like acid.

Trixie danced insanely, in an ecstacy of terror, twisting and leaping to a thunder of drums and the shriek of souls in torment, a raw howl that flayed her. Strange figures capered, veiled by sulfurous fumes. Daggers dripped blood. Blood ran from her fingertips. Blood flowed hotly over her skin, the scarlet stark against the whiteness of her.

Mack dreamt about beer and big women.

Gruber dreamt about beer and little boys.

Jeremy wrapped the sausage-like fingers of his batting gloves tighter round the handle of the bat. He squared up to defend his wicket, but the apparition bearing down upon him was not some demon fast bowler, but a headhunter in a feathered headdress, brandishing a long spear.

"I say, steady on!"

Dubois sat atop a haystack, his arm around a giggling girl. Then the sun's warmth gave way to a sudden chill, as he watched a black shadow creep across the golden fields.

EPISODE 14:
MAN-EATER

"Let's go!"

Dawn was a ghoulish green glimmer. Lowering down upon the dark mountains, bruised blue-black clouds bled a purple rain. Shadows crawled in the whispering valleys.

"Keep up the pace there!"

They plodded dourly along the precarious, slippery trail. Strung out in single file, they bowed their heads, shoulders hunched, bent into the teeth of a cutting wind.

Separated from the main party, the Prussians scouted ahead, pistols in hand, slowing to nose warily around each crumbling bend. Their companions would wait anxiously, shuffling their feet and shivering in the chill of the early morning. A short way behind, Mack and O'Dwyer made a nervous rearguard, glancing back at the trail sucked up by the mist, peering up at the dark and glowering heights, down into the veiled depths of the valley.

"Gives me the creeps," muttered Nate, hefting the big .45.

Forcing a grin, Jeremy offered his hip flask to Celia. Shaking her head, Celia smiled wanly, the dawn lending her strained features a waxlike pallor.

"Hey, handsome," drawled Trixie. "I wouldn't say no to a drop of the hard stuff."

Jeremy beamed. Celia scowled as the blonde pushed past her. Jeremy deftly poured a measure into a thimble of silver.

"Hey," chuckled Trixie. "Ain't this grand?"

She knocked back the liquor with a quick tilt of the head, smacked her lips, patting her middle as she felt the slow warmth of it sliding down.

"Have some, dearie," she extended the silver cup to Celia. "Put some fire in your guts."

Celia stared with a face of stone.

"No, thank you."

Trixie shrugged. She flipped the cup back to Jeremy, who bobbled it, then caught it on his second attempt.

"Suit yerself," she grinned. "Thanks, dreamboat."

Passing Dubois, she plucked a freshly rolled cigarette from his fingers. With a laugh, the Frenchman dug a brass trench lighter from his pocket and lit it for her. At his side, Mackenzie leant forward to get a light for his pipe. Wreathed in fragrant clouds, he sucked on the stem contentedly.

Dubois stowed away the lighter, stood with his thumbs hooked into his gun belt, staring far away into the distance. He became aware of Von Seyfritz glaring at him.

"And where was that contraption," the Prussian demanded. "When we had to light a fire last night?"

Laughing, Dubois nodded towards Jeremy.

"Our boy scout over there was having so much fun rubbing sticks together. It seemed a shame to interrupt him."

Jeremy opened his mouth, then shut it again. Celia hid a smile.

Von Seyfritz muttered darkly. He let the monocle drop onto his palm, exhaled on it, polished it with a small cloth and then screwed it back into his eye socket. Dubois just grinned.

Up ahead, Gruber said something. Von Seyfritz grunted, yanking the briefly holstered Luger back into view.

"Come!" he barked. "We have no time to lose!"

The dawn expanded into a bleary, colorless morning, low cloud sour and leaden. The trail bent away from the void and curled through wrinkled crags and outcrops feathered with a tumble of crazy vegetation. Swollen with moisture, the air was alive with a constant rustle, a patter of droplets falling. Thin streams tinkled down the dizzy gradients, glinting through the dark foliage.

"It is as if we have passed through some invisible door," mused Mackenzie. "And stepped into another world."

The path grew wider, till they trudged across a broad and mossy sward, the dark walls rising all around them, the hanging mountains ghostly and opaque.

Fanning out, they lost formation, enjoying a new sense of space, glad to be free from the brooding valley that fell away below them. They advanced in silence, nothing but the suck and squelch of their footsteps.

"Hey!" Nate broke the spell. "Get a load of this!"

They crowded to join the big American.

"Good grief!" exclaimed Mackenzie.

"Aw," shrugged Trixie. "It ain't nothin'."

At their feet, the ground dipped into a shallow bowl. They peered into it warily.

"It's some kind of plant, isn't it?" asked Celia.

Huge, fleshy petals curled into a great bell. The color of dead flesh and finely veined with purple, it was fringed all around by mottled brown blades, blotched with dark encrustations.

"It is not like any plant that I have ever seen," said Dubois.

Cocking the .45, Nate nodded to his henchman.

"Take a look."

His feet slipping, the big torpedo began to make his way down into the broad bowl. He drew his gun and held it out in front of him. Tossing her head, Trixie snorted.

"Aw, c'mon, ya scared of a flower!"

Boldly, she skipped down the slope. Then, suddenly, she stopped short, her face screwed up like a walnut.

"Yuk! What a stink!"

The wind changed and blew a powerful musk into their faces. They recoiled, covering their mouths.

"Good God!" gasped Celia. "What is it?"

Mackenzie reeled, wiping his eyes.

"Death!" he croaked hoarsely. "Death and decay!"

Then Trixie yelped, pointing. Bones, stained green and yellow, littered the lower slopes of the bowl. Dissolving into the moss, they saw ribs and vertebrae, a pelvis and thigh, a grinning skull that was almost human.

His eyes darting nervously, Mack cocked the .38. Trixie gulped and began to back away slowly.

"Aw, heck," she muttered. "I don't like the look of—"

Celia screamed. Nate jumped and the .45 went off, the reverberations ringing all around them. Startled, Von Seyfritz cursed him viciously.

"My God," whispered Mackenzie.

From the hollow of the fleshy bell, long tendrils fountained high into the air, flailing like the thongs of a whip. Trixie squawked as a glistening tentacle snaked around her ankles. It bound them together, tugging her down onto her rump with a jolt that jarred the breath from her body. A sticky lasso dropped around Mack's bull neck, yanking him flat on his back.

"Holy cow!" roared Nate.

He emptied the magazine, but the great petals simply absorbed the bullets, self-sealing.

"Help!"

Trixie was being dragged towards the grotesque blossom, her fingernails leaving a trail of deep gouges in the soft ground. The bell opened, to reveal a bony beak that salivated greedily.

"Get me outta here!"

Mack kicked and struggled. The ropelike strand bit into his neck. He choked and gurgled, his face red and bloated, eyes bulging in their sockets. Still clutching the .38, he blazed away wildly.

Alarmed, Dubois hit the dirt. Von Seyfritz glared at him scornfully, till a slug nicked his sleeve, scalding the skin beneath.

Jeremy just stood and gaped. Shouting, Celia shook him.

"Somebody do something!"

Yelling, Trixie flopped and twisted like a fish on the line, her eyes wide and bright with terror. The beak chomped, drooling. Shoving Mackenzie out of the way, Nate rammed a fresh magazine into the butt of the automatic. He lumbered down to his henchman, but Mack wasn't struggling anymore. He was just being dragged along, his contorted features purple, his tongue sticking out.

Trixie flailed and beat at the ground. She could hear the great jaws clicking together, see a thousand razor-sharp serrations grinding.

"Hey! What about me?"

Plucking out his knife, Dubois was on his feet and bounding down to her side. Crouching, he sawed away at the rubbery tentacle wrapped around Trixie's ankles. The sharp edge made no impression. While Trixie wailed, he frowned and tried harder, then had to jump back quickly as sticky strands snaked across the ground, seeking him.

With a grunt, Nate shoved away the pistol. Stooping, he seized Trixie's wrists and tugged. Meeting with a surprising amount of resistance, he bent and put his back into it. Yelling, Trixie rose off the ground, her body extended between the clutching tendril and the sweating American.

The tentacle twanged tautly, but it wouldn't break. Von Seyfritz ran down to help. Gritting their teeth, the big men heaved with all their might. The sharp jaws slavered. Trixie screamed. Between the hungry plant and her would-be rescuers, she could feel her body stretching.

"Teufel!"

A fan of tentacles descended, coiling around Nate and Von Seyfritz. Cursing, they only tugged harder, making Trixie scream louder. Shaking his head, Dubois crept round behind the laboring American. Staying on the blind side, he rooted in a satchel clipped to Nate's backpack.

"What the hell are ya doin'?"

The Frenchman produced the last of Nate's grenades. As Trixie's yells of pain became curdled with alarm, he sprang forward, pulled the pin, took careful aim and lobbed the metal egg underarm.

"Are you craz—?"

With a gulp, the bony beak swallowed the grenade whole.

"Get down!"

Dropping Trixie, her rescuers flung themselves to the ground.

There was a pause, then a muffled thud. The earth trembled. A great shock convulsed the fleshy petals, which then began to wilt, the dark leaves curling. The jaws clashed violently, and then gaped, oozing smoke and slime. A blue haze wafted. The stench of burning meat clogged the damp air.

Dazed, they unwound the limp tentacles.

"What the heck were you apes doin'?" Trixie complained. "I think I'm a foot taller!"

As she rose gingerly, Nate lunged across Mack's body. He backhanded her savagely, sent her sprawling in the dirt.

"That shoulda been you!" he jabbed a finger at the corpse. "The only thing yer good for ain't no use to me out here!"

They stumbled away to dig a grave. Trixie stayed where she was, fingering a thin trickle of scarlet that ran down the corner of her mouth. Her eyes glowed with a strange fire. Suddenly, it seemed that she could hear drums throbbing somewhere in the distance, an eerie piping high in the sky.

Little crawly things were eating Mack's eyes long before they buried him. They camped for the night well away from the grave.

"Here we are!"

Jeremy brought a piping tin mug to Celia.

"Careful, it's hot."

Smiling gratefully, she hooked her fingers into the enameled handle. As Jeremy sat down beside her, she sipped delicately, closed her eyes and sighed.

"Ah, just what the doctor ordered!"

She sipped again. Jeremy watched her, entranced, drawn to the pale luminosity of her features, tinted by the firelight. Celia drained the cup steadily, then set it down on the ground. A sudden spasm made her shoulders quiver.

"Oh, it's no use," she groaned. "I can't stop shivering."

Jeremy frowned. Toying with a twig, he etched tiny whorls in the creeping skin of grey mist that lay upon the soil.

"The Professor says that it'll be warmer in the mountains," he stated brightly. "When the sun burns away this bally fog."

Celia tossed her head, exasperated.

"The mountains, the mountains!" she exclaimed. "Are we ever going to reach those bloody mountains?"

Her tone startled the young man sitting beside her. She took a deep breath, mellowing.

"Sorry," she smiled. "Stiff upper lip and all that."

A lump rose in Jeremy's throat, something growing, burning deep inside him. Impulsively, he slid his arm around her. Celia twisted abruptly and curled into his embrace, her hands rushing eagerly across his broad shoulders. Her fingers whispered on the coarse grain of his jacket, tracing the concealed muscle, as smooth and hard as marble.

His lips brushed the pale velvet of her throat and a warm honey welled up within her. Then their hungry mouths were joined, melting.

"No!"

Brittle laughter needled into Celia's brain. In the buzzing blackness behind her lowered lashes, saucy eyes were dancing. Her soul froze.

"No, don't!"

Her features drained, she wrenched herself from Jeremy's grasp, shuddering. Jeremy's jaw dropped. He sat there staring in amazement. When he began to stammer apologies, Celia shook her head, raising a hand to quiet him.

"No, it's alright," she gasped, her shoulders heaving. "It's not your fault."

She caught her breath, gulping, ice twisting inside her. Concerned, Jeremy watched closely, but he didn't dare touch her.

"I'm sorry, Jeremy," she said at last. "I can't, I just can't."

He tried to look into her eyes, but she turned her face away.

"I understand," he said, not understanding at all.

A day's forced march later.

They collapsed, exhausted on the lip of a valley that arrowed up and away from them, towards the mountains and the slowly setting sun.

"This is hopeless!" blared Von Seyfritz.

"Damn right!" grated O'Dwyer.

Trixie hauled off her pack and sat on it, slumped dejectedly. Muttering, she flexed her shoulders, which still ached from the tug of war between the two big men and the deadly plant.

Pausing to admire the emphatic effect which this rolling motion had upon her frontage, Dubois offered Trixie a cigarette.

"Thanks."

There was a long silence, broken by the snap of the lighter and the sounds of Trixie smoking. Mist clogged the deep V of the valley, filled it to the brim, a river of smoke that was cut off by a sheer wall of black jungle, dark against the pale mountains and the red glare of the sun.

"We have been going around in circles," said Dubois. "Up and down and around and around."

The mist was tinted pinkly, the mountains edged with blood.

"Dash it!" Jeremy exclaimed. "We're not getting anywh—!"

Celia gasped.

The sun dipped suddenly, the red ball impaled upon a jagged summit. It burst, a ruby refracting, spears of fire fanning from its molten core.

Trixie jumped to her feet. Celia took a step back, shielding her eyes. As they stood gaping, a deep, dark murmur welled up from the valley below. Like a scalding blade, a single crimson ray lanced earthwards. It sliced into the dark wall that dammed the valley, cut a narrow cleft of fire down into the vein of mist which, all at once, was aglow with pulsing scarlet.

"There!" cried Mackenzie, pointing to the bloody rent carved into the black palisades. "There is the way to the mountains!"

His fingers hooked into a gnarled root, Jeremy heaved himself up to the top.

"By Jove!" he gasped. "We've done it!"

Every fiber quivering with release from the strain of the climb, he stood triumphant, grinning down at the grey fog that clogged the valley, suffused with the incandescence of a new dawn.

"Well done, everybody!"

The others ignored him. Dubois unwound a rope that linked him to Mackenzie. When he offered his canteen, the panting Professor seized it gratefully.

Groaning, Trixie struggled out of the straps of her backpack. Shrugging off her long oilskins, she flopped backwards to sprawl full length, gasping, her breasts heaving. Her hair was in confusion, her face streaked with sweat and grime. She fumbled with her top button, and down the creamy V of her neckline, tiny beads glistened.

"Aw, quit yer gripin'!" Nate barked sharply.

Great globules of perspiration coursing down his heavy features, the big American ripped a cigar case from his pocket. Finding it empty, he snarled and hurled it into the void. It winked in the sunlight, was sucked up by the mist crawling far below.

Surveying a broken fingernail, Trixie moaned, cursing vividly. Snatching a canteen from Gruber, Von Seyfritz looked down at her with evident distaste. How unlike our magnificent Fraulein Reifenstahl, he told his henchman, conquering the heights so nimbly in her alpine films, the ripe embodiment of the spirit and vigor of a new, young Germany!

Gritting her teeth, Celia let her pack slip to the ground. Beneath her rain cape she was bathed in sweat, her shirt soaked through, glued to her spine. Wincing as daggers jabbed into every sinew, she slid off the long cloak and let it fall beside the discarded backpack.

"It's so warm!" she exclaimed.

Mackenzie lurched to his feet, leaning on Dubois for support.

"Yes indeed," he croaked hoarsely. "The air is thinner up here and consequently the sun's rays are much stronger.

He paused, gulping, still struggling to catch his breath.

"It will be as hot as the Sahara by midday."

Propped up on her elbows, Trixie rolled her eyes and slumped down flat again.

"Aw, Jeez.....!"

Scowling, Nate flung out his arms.

"Yeah, this is a real garden spot!"

EPISODE 15:
THE LAND THAT TIME FORGOT

Despite Nate's continuing complaints, the plateau came as a relief after the long climb. Flat and level, it was furred by clumps of dark green scrub that rasped at their ankles, scratching at their knees. Its distant horizon was smothered in a curtain of grey mist upon which the forested foothills hovered, cowering beneath the brandished sword blades of the pale mountains.

"Keep up the pace there!"

Mackenzie was inspired, infused by the sight of the peaks almost within his grasp. Those ringing blades were his Excalibur, his challenge, his destiny!

"Come on!"

He surged past an astonished Von Seyfritz, shouldering the big man aside.

"The old coot really has gone crazy," O'Dwyer muttered sideways, drawing up to the Colonel's side.

"His lunacy has brought us here," Von Seyfritz scowled. "But he will pay the price."

"Jeez!" Trixie stumbled, her feet snagging in the wiry scrub. Stepping out briskly, Celia frowned at her, cold contempt frosting her eyes.

"That's it old thing!" Jeremy encouraged her. "Best foot forward!"

"Bravo!" cheered Dubois. Gruber glared at him as the Frenchman blocked his path, before side-stepping around him and marching on, chest out, chin up.

Suddenly they were hopeful, enthusiastic, optimistic. A kind of euphoria gripped them. After all they had been through, traversing the mountains seemed a mere formality, a piece of cake.

"Oh dear…"

The Professor stopped, bending over, his hand on his knees.

"Oh dear…oh dear…"

He was wheezing hoarsely, shoulders heaving. They stared at him, confused. Then it hit them, like walking into an invisible wall.

"Aw…!" Trixie groaned.

The thin air had made them giddy. Reality came crashing down.

"I can't go another step…!" Celia panted.

The big men slipped off their heavy backpacks and let them fall to the ground. Dubois lit a cigarette and offered one to Jeremy, who seized it from him gratefully.

Sighing, Mackenzie sank down to sit cross-legged on the springy turf.

"P–perhaps we should p–pause for…a…moment…"

With a grunt, Trixie flung herself down on her back and sprawled full length, gasping. Celia reclined more decorously, propped up on her elbow. She tugged out her kerchief and mopped her face, suddenly exhausted.

On his knees, Jeremy was rooting in his pack. He tugged out a tiny camping stove and began to assemble it.

"Time for a brew-up, what?"

"Do you have any fuel left for that thing?" Dubois enquired.

"Ah," said Jeremy. "Good point."

His boyish features clouded for a moment, but soon lit up again.

"There's plenty here to work with."

He cast around, ripping at the coarse carpet that covered the ground.

"I'll soon have a fire going."

"That's better", Celia sighed.

She wrapped her fingers around the tin mug. Taking another sip, she felt the rejuvenating infusion spread out from her chest, down to the tips of her toes.

"Aye, much!"

Mackenzie gulped his tea greedily. It went down the wrong way and prompted a spasm of coughing, his shoulders convulsing violently.

Dubois patted him between the shoulder blades.

"Gently, mon ami."

The Professor recovered, breathing heavily. Sat side by side, the big men stared at him grimly.

"I–I'm so…sorry…" Mackenzie managed. "D–don't worry…I'll be alright…"

O'Dwyer scowled.

"Ya sure about that, Perfesser? Ya drop here and we ain't gonna carry ya!"

"Correct!" confirmed Von Seyfritz. "We cannot afford any passengers."

Jeremy stooped to refill the Professor's cup.

"Now steady on," he protested. "All for one and one for all, what?"

Trixie snorted and rolled her eyes. Yeah sure. Ya looked out for number one in the world she came from.

"Quite right," Celia stated. "We must stand or fall together."

Anger flashing darkly in his eyes, Nate opened his mouth but shut it again when Von Seyfritz cleared his throat harshly. The big American stood and stomped away and the Prussian rose and followed him, Gruber hard on his heels.

"Patience, my friend," the Colonel muttered. "Our moment will come."

"Yeah!" O'Dwyer grated through gritted teeth. "And it had better be damn soon!"

Taking deep breaths, Mackenzie nodded at his anxious companions.

"I'll be alright," he repeated. "Please don't be concerned, I'll…"

Dubois sprang to his feet, his head tilted back, one hand for a visor, squinting up at the glaring sky.

"Look!" he pointed. "What's that?"

They looked. Startled, they jumped up.

"It's…"

"An aeroplane…?"

"An aeroplane!"

Despite the obvious absurdity of it they all began shouting, gesticulating wildly.

"Here!"

"Down here!"

"We're here!"

"Look down here!"

Then they all stopped shouting.

"No it isn't," said Dubois flatly.

"Well?" asked Celia. "Then what is it?"

Mackenzie rubbed his eyes.

"No," he replied. "What are they?"

There were four of them. They cruised in a lazy circle high in the bright blank sky, in a precise, staggered formation, line astern.

"Oh my…"

Banking smoothly, they peeled off one by one and descended, one following the other, like a squadron of pursuit planes diving to attack.

"…God!"

A harsh metal croaking rattled the taut membrane of the sky. Trixie's scream was piercing in the thin air. Cursing, Nate clawed at the flap of his holster, hauling out the big .45.

They were plummeting in a tight spiral, corkscrewing down and down. Bony jaw bones were clashing. A hand covering her mouth, Celia backed up hurriedly. Her eyes wide with horror, she stumbled into Jeremy and sent him sprawling. Dubois fell over him and was scrabbling about on his hands and knees, searching for the pistol that had slipped from his fingers, swallowed up by the brush.

The monocle flashing, Von Seyfritz barked an order. Gruber unslung the long hunting rifle and tossed it to him. The big Prussian caught it one-handed.

"So!" he exulted.

As the others scattered around him, fleeing in all directions, Mackenzie stood rooted to the spot, his eyes glowing with wonder.

"Pterodactyl…"

Mottled brown, leathery wings were stretched across a skeletal frame, tapering to a point; a lean streamlined body with a pebbled reptilian hide, trailing short bird-like legs with talons like long curved daggers.

"The Pterosaur…"

A bony crest, projecting backwards from the top of the skull; the keen yellow eyes; the long blades of the beak, armed with glinting teeth.

The raw primitive fanfare of their hunting song seemed to fill the sky.

"Gott in himmel…" Von Seyfritz worked the bolt of his rifle. "The wingspan must be sixty feet at least!"

He lifted the gun to his shoulder and fired in a single fluid motion. They heard the "whack!" of the bullet. High above, the leader seemed to stop in mid-air, then turned over slowly on its back and tumbled out of the sky, rolling over and over, its huge wings flapping limply, till it came down with a crash onto the earth.

"Impossible…" the Professor mused to no one in particular. "These creatures lived in the late Mesozoic period, between two hundred and fifty and sixty five million years ago."

He turned to Von Seyfritz, who stood triumphant over the kill, picturing yet another spectacular trophy in pride of place on the walls of his hunting lodge.

"I am afraid that they are carnivorous."

Nate was wrenching back the slide of the .45 when a giant shadow blotted out the sky.

"Hey!"

The leader's wingman was coming for him, swooping out of the sun.

"Sonofa—!"

Nate ducked. He was almost quick enough. One hooking claw flashed past his ear, ripping the cloth epaulette from the shoulder of his safari jacket. The other fastened on his collar. Shouting, O'Dwyer was hoisted into the air, his legs kicking wildly.

For all of its size, the winged monster was struggling with Nate's bulk. Wings heaving, it hovered ten feet from the ground, ascended briefly, then sank down, strained upwards again, croaking harshly, jaw bones clicking and clacking.

His heavy features purpling with fury, Nate brandished the big pistol.

"No goddamn bird's gonna—!"

He pressed the muzzle to the creature's beady eye and pulled the trigger. The pebbled skull exploded in a spray of pink and grey matter.

"Yaaaaa…!"

The talons sprang open and O'Dwyer fell back to earth, landing heavily on his back, winded. Wings outspread, his victim came down hard, covering him like a blanket.

Bellowing curses, Nate struggled out from under, lurching to his feet, only to be bowled over as a yelling Trixie ran past him, pop-eyed and open-mouthed, babbling in terror.

Flat out, Trixie hurdled Dubois, who was still scuttling about on his hands and knees, ripping up the scrub in search of his pistol. Trixie kept on going, with the Frenchman's curses flying after her.

Then his fingers found the chequered grips of his revolver. Alarmed, he rolled over on his back.

"Merde!"

Giant wings spanned the horizons. Spiked jaw bones were slavering, thrusting for him hungrily. Dubois rolled over and over, the brittle scrub crunching beneath him, trying to get away. The creature hovered close above him, talons slashing, it raucous braying cracking the air.

Holding the pistol close to his chest, Dubois fired again and again. Amazed, he saw the mottled hide repel the slugs like stone. The beast only shook its head, clashed its jaws together and pressed home its attack.

Dubois shouted as the curved claws sliced through his sturdy bush jacket and the shirt beneath, raking his skin. He gagged on the creature's fetid breath.

A dull detonation rolled across the mossy plain. The creature rocked sideways, its skull splitting, showering Dubois with a hot and slimy pulp.

"Ach so!"

At a distance, Von Seyfritz stood cradling the long hunting rifle. He eyed the prostrate Frenchman and his empty pistol with cold contempt.

"How like the French," he sneered. "Unprepared as always."

Dubois rose lithely to his feet.

"You will find me ready when the time comes, monsieur."

Curling his lip, the Prussian turned his back and walked away, Gruber trotting at his heels.

"Eeeeeeek!"

Trixie was still running. She had no idea where she was going. She just ran and ran around in circles.

The thin air grated in her lungs. Her legs were turning to rubber.

"Yikes!"

The coarse brush snagged her ankle. She sat down hard.

Descending in slow circles, a monster was drawn to the flash of her silver hair. Cawing coarsely, it came down like an arrow for her.

"Oh my—!"

Celia stood nearby, knee deep in the brush. Breathing heavily, she leant on Jeremy for support, clinging on tight to his arm, hampering his attempts to cock the bolt of his rifle.

With a yell, Trixie dived sideways, rolling. The grasping talons clawed empty air.

"Aw Jeez…!"

The creature rose, hovered, then came down again.

"Aw heck!" bawled Trixie, pointing at Celia. "Why's it me all the time? What's wrong with her?"

Pale-faced, Celia reached out anxiously as Jeremy stepped forward to intervene. The rifle went off before he was ready for it, the recoil rocking him backwards.

"Blast!"

Fumbling with the bolt, he staggered. Behind him, Celia threw herself down as the flying reptile swooped low, the tips of its claws flicking her hair.

"Uh!"

Its bone hard wingtip cracked across the back of Jeremy's neck. He fell flat on his face, unconscious.

Whining, Trixie curled herself into a ball, as the creature floated above her, talons clicking, jaw blades grinding.

Celia made the mistake of standing up. Panting, she stumbled over to Jeremy and tried to tug the rifle out from under his body.

Distracted, the monster wheeled in mid-air and lunged for her.

"Aaaahhh!"

The sickle claws fastened tightly on the shoulder padding of Celia's fashionable safari jacket. Elevated by its vast wingspan, it lifted her effortlessly.

"AAA–aa–iiiii…!"

Sailing upwards, the beast bore Celia away, veering towards the mist-shrouded horizons and the dark forested foothills, the blue peaks hanging above.

A rapidly diminishing figure left far behind, Von Seyfritz raised his rifle.

"Non!"

Dubois knocked the muzzle upwards, diverting the gunshot harmlessly into the sun.

"You will kill the lady!"

Snarling, Von Seyfritz shoved the Frenchman aside. He took aim again, but his quarry was too far away, a mere speck now, out of range.

The scrappy ground was rushing by below. A cold wind sang in her ears. She began to unbutton her jacket, then looked down past her dangling feet and remembered that the fall would kill her.

"Uuu…uu…hhh…"

Celia groaned. The beast turned its ugly head to look at her with an unblinking yellow eye. It croaked at her balefully, exposing rows of glinting needle teeth. Its carrion breath made her stomach churn.

Terror and incredulity consumed her. She tried to scream. She couldn't breathe. She was choking, gasping in the thin air.

Everything went dark.

Mackenzie sighed heavily.

"Oh dear, oh dear, oh dear…!"

He stood looking down forlornly at the dead beast, its magnificent wings now bent and crumpled. Its dull eye stared back at him sightlessly, brain matter oozing from the gaping hole in its skull.

"A perfect shot, no?" said Von Seyfritz.

The Professor sighed again.

"Do you realize, Colonel, that you may have extinguished a species on the very day it was re-discovered?"

Polishing his monocle, Von Seyfritz screwed it back into his eye socket.

"Bah!" he snorted. "You are a dreamer, Herr Professor. You fail to understand that Man's purpose is to survive and conquer!"

"Damn right!" barked Nate O'Dwyer. "It's kill or be killed, Perfesser!"

His shoulders sagging, Mackenzie turned and walked away, shaking his head sadly.

Wide-eyed, Jeremy ran past him, zig-zagging, looking all around.

"C…?"

Dubois jumped back out of his way. Sat on the ground, Trixie held out her hands, expecting to be helped up. Jeremy almost ran right over her and she had to roll sideways to avoid being trampled underfoot.

"Aw heck, just kick me as ya pass, why dontya?"

Jeremy ran this way then that, turning about, running in circles.

"C—!"

"Ah!"

A hard light stabbed her eyeballs like white hot needles.

"Oooooooo…!"

Blinking, Celia struggled to sit upright. The world span around, once, twice, then slowly settled down. The world was rocking gently. She was reclining in a cosy cradle, a cradle that was rocking gently. A low melody was murmuring softly, a soothing lullaby.

"Uuuuhh…?"

The lullaby was the moaning wind, gusting across a craggy red cliff face. The gentle rocking was the subtle rise and fall of a massive tree limb, jutting out into space. The cradle was a nest, a deep dish woven together from moss and scraps of bark and twigs.

Celia was sitting in the well of the dish. She was not alone.

"What on…?"

Something stirred. In the shadow of the tangled lip of the nest, yellow eyes gleamed dully.

"Good grief!"

Twin fledglings, miniature monsters, their leathery wings mere buds, although the daggers of their bony jaws were already sprouting tiny teeth.

Their infant eyes were glazed over by a filmy membrane, but they sensed the warmth of her, the taste of her. Automatically, the jaws opened and craned towards her, drooling, the small talons clicking and scratching at the floor of the nest.

A chill shivered down Celia's spine. They're hungry. And I'm on the menu!

"C…!"

Dubois seized Jeremy's shoulder.

"Enough, mon brave. The lady has gone."

Jeremy twisted out of his grasp but found his path blocked by Mackenzie, his hands clasped as though in prayer.

"I'm so sorry, my young friend, but I am afraid that Miss Cavendish is surely lost to us."

The fire faded from Jeremy's eyes. He seemed to deflate, his shoulders drooping.

"It's all my fault," he whispered. "I couldn't…"

"Nonsense, old chap," the Professor consoled him. "There was nothing you could have done."

Von Seyfritz bridled, glaring at Dubois.

"Had you let me take a shot—!"

"What's done is done," the Frenchman said quietly. "Now is not the time to mourn."

Trixie made a face.

"Huh!" she muttered. "If it was me none of ya lugs woulda even noticed."

Glowering Nate rounded on her.

"Whaddaya say?" he demanded, looming menacingly over her.

Hunching her shoulders, Trixie flinched away from him.

"Nothin'…nothin'…"

Nate snarled at her, heaving his pack onto his broad back.

"Then let's get goin'," he grated. "We ain't got time to stand around gabbin'!"

"Sorry, chaps, but you'll just have to go without your dinner."

Reaching up, Celia pulled herself onto the leafy rim of the nest. Her heart leapt into her mouth as it swayed precariously, almost tipping her into the void. The red cliffs fell away to the dappled green carpet of the forest, thinly veiled by wafting currents of mist, hundreds of feet below her.

Catching her breath, she crawled out onto the tree limb, as broad as a barrel, furry with moss. Tributary branches, feathered by long leaves shaped like spear points, fanned out towards a distinct ledge carved into the cliff.

"How strange…"

The ledge zig-zagged up and down the cliff face, all the way down to where it vanished in the mist, up to the jagged crest, tufted by clumps of long grass, dark against the glare of the sky.

"If I didn't know better, I'd swear it was a staircase."

Behind her, the fledglings were bleating plaintively, their tinny cries echoing in the deep bowl. They reared upwards, their hungry jaws thrusting above the lip of the nest.

Galvanized, Celia edged out onto the fan of branches. It bowed slightly beneath her, but held firm. Encouraged, she moved on.

"Oh—!"

She slipped. Suddenly, she was hanging by her fingertips, with nothing but eternity below her.

"I just can't believe it," Jeremy said despondently. "I just can't."

Dispirited, he was bringing up the rear, lagging a little way behind. Up front, Von Seyfritz was setting a brisk pace, with Gruber at his shoulder and O'Dwyer and Dubois close behind.

"Come on!" the Colonel blared. "March!"

Trixie floundered in their wake, wading knee high in the tough brush, the straps of her backpack chafing.

"Awww…!" she bawled. "I ain't—!"

Nate stopped and turned to stare at her. Paling, she accelerated.

Keep calm, Celia told herself. You can get out of this. Just keep calm. A slimy skin of moss parted from the tree bark and with a sudden jolt she was hanging by one hand.

"AAAaa–eee–iiii!"

She screamed, despite herself, and was mightily embarrassed, to hear the shrill ululation echo away into the distance, rebounding off the red cliff face.

You bloody fool. Concentrate!

Breathing deeply, she regained her double grip. The branch was flexible and she waited for its rise and fall to diminish.

Far below, the jungle was strangely quiet and the gusting wind had ceased its doleful moaning. Time ticked by. In the silence she could hear her wristwatch ticking. She could see it, glinting on her strained wrist. Its stylish art deco modernity belonged to another world which seemed suddenly absurd and utterly irrelevant, hanging there 'twixt life and death, in this forgotten, timeless wilderness.

She cursed herself. Action not thought! She remembered what her tennis coach had told her: do, don't think! If you have to think about it, it's too late!

Her shoulders were aching.

I can't hang on much longer.

She studied the rugged cliff face, measuring the distance to the stepped pathway that angled up and down.

I can do it.

She imagined herself to be back in the school gym, exercising on the high bar.

Come on, you were district champion. You can do it!

Carefully, Celia began to swing her legs, tight together, forward and back. She put her whole body into the motion. The spring in the branch helped her, adding thrust to her momentum.

She saw the cliff come towards her, then sway back…towards her… then back…towards her…

"UGH–HH–HHH!"

She launched herself into space.

Wiping the sweat from his brow, the Professor fell back beside Jeremy. He offered a small silver hip flask.

"Here, laddie, I still have a good swig or two left."

The young man shook his head.

"I just can't believe it," he repeated. "C was…well…she was sort of…indestructible…you know?"

Mackenzie raised a smile.

"We must keep hoping, my dear fellow. This land is full of wonders. Here miracles can happen!"

"AH!"

Amazed, Celia made it. She landed lightly on both feet, full square on one of the mysteriously cut steps of the path. Behind her, the leafy branches whipped up and down, fanning her.

For one glorious moment, she stood perfectly poised, exultant, congratulating herself. Then the edge of the path began to crack and crumble and she was reeling backwards.

"OOHHH...N–NOOO...!"

Flailing fingers hooked a wiry tuft sprouting from a split in the red rock. She hauled on it and pulled herself back from the brink.

"No!"

She stood for a while, panting, her body pressed to the cliff face. Then she sank down on her haunches, shoulders heaving, sweat rolling down her face.

Slowly, she got her breath back. She took stock of her situation.

"Well, this path was put here for a purpose," she pondered. "But do I go up or down?"

On the ragged heights above, from the tufted crest of the cliff top, keen eyes were watching her.

"Up..." Celia told herself. "I'll go up."

She hesitated.

"No, down."

She pursed her lips, debating with herself. Rooting in her jacket pockets, she found a coin, a dull penny, with the calm profile of the King. She turned the coin over and over on her palm. Suddenly, she was desperately homesick.

"Alright, damn you," she said angrily. "Heads or tails!"

The coin twinkled as it rose into the sky, revolving rapidly.

"Oh no!"

It fell, unheeded, at her feet.

"No!"

A hoarse cawing rent the air. Giant wings were thrashing, stirring fierce currents that pinned her back against the cliff wall.

Its barbed beak gaping, the monster dropped down upon her, talons slashing. Celia threw herself down flat, curling into a ball. She screamed as the curved daggers sliced through her sleeve, nicking the flesh beneath.

"Get away from me…!"

She lashed out and batted the clutching claws away. Startled by this spasm of resistance, the creature squawked, backed up, hovered and then swooped down again. In the nest, the fledglings craned their heads above the parapet, adding a shrill chorus.

Putting her back to the wall, Celia kicked out with both feet, shouting. Frantically, she began crawling up the jagged pathway. Bobbing, lunging, the creature pursued her, braying loudly.

There was movement high above, on the cliff edge. Figures, silhouetted against the bright sky, jogged along the ragged crest, keeping pace with the battle below.

A vicious wing tip fanned her cheek. The jaw bones clacked and clattered, their glittering teeth eager to rip and tear her.

The harsh croaking flayed her. Exhausted, Celia cowered against the jagged wall.

I'm going to die, she told herself with weary resignation. I'm going to die out here in the middle of nowhere and no one will ever know about it.

A new sound penetrated the clamor of the monster's assault. The sound of music. A mellow flute that piped a lilting melody.

Its effect was immediate and dramatic. Silenced, the creature went rigid, its streamlined body extended, long neck stretched out to its fullest, legs trailing behind, the talons folded. It hovered level with the narrow ledge, supported by the merest subtle undulation of its vast wingspan.

The strange tune took on a fresh intensity, a flutter, a tint of urgency. Astonished, Celia saw the creature edge forward a little, prompted by a flick of its wingtips. Its beak tight shut, it laid its ugly head at Celia's feet, the yellow eyes rolling up almost in supplication, as it made small plaintive squeaking noises.

"What on…?"

She resisted the impulse to stroke it, although it appeared to crave forgiveness and consolation, like a lapdog that had soiled the carpet.

"I don't believe it."

She heard a scuffing up above, looked up and saw the darting silhouettes. The flute prompted again. Controlled by precise adjustments of its wing surfaces, the monster slowly rotated, reversing its position, till its long neck angled away from her and its feet rested on the path.

Its intention was obvious. The flute urged once more and this time Celia knew that the message was meant for her.

"All aboard…"

Without hesitation, she stepped forward, off the ledge and onto the creature's back. Suffused suddenly by absolute confidence, she sat down, cross-legged, with the authority of a Maharajah on his favourite elephant.

A musical command. The beast flapped its wings and ascended slowly in a wide, lazy circle, out over the jungle and then back towards the top of the cliff.

They were waiting for her.

"Well, I'll be…!" said an oddly familiar voice. "Is that 'Cavvy' Cavendish?"

"Aw…!" whined Trixie. "I need a break!"

Heaving off her pack, she sat down on it and folded her arms, frowning.

"Ya can do what yer likes," she declared. "I ain't goin' another step till I've had a cigarette!"

Dubois obliged her, flicking the wheel of the brass trench lighter. Trixie took a deep drag and exhaled the smoke loudly and defiantly.

For once, Nate didn't object, merely unscrewing the cap of his water bottle and taking a swig. Snatching his canteen from Gruber, Von Seyfritz looked at him quizzically. The big American shrugged.

"Gotta rest the pack animals sometime."

The Colonel nodded, watching Jeremy help the Professor ease the straps of his backpack.

"Yes, for the present they have a certain value, but that value diminishes with every step we take. I do not intend to drag them with us over the mountains."

"Just say when," Nate grated.

"Good grief!"

Celia's senses struggled to unscramble what she was seeing.

"It is! What-ho Cavvy!"

The monster floated down gently. As it folded its wings, Celia stepped off its back and onto the long grass. The flute trilled again and the beast unfurled its great sails and sprang into the air, wheeled and departed with one last lingering raucous call, descending from the cliff top and returning to the nest.

Brisk figures were advancing towards her. Tall women with handsome, exotic features and gleaming coppery skin. They wore sixteenth-century Spanish helmets, dulled and dented, from which shining waves of long blue-black hair tumbled to their bare broad shoulders. Their proud breasts were supported by leopard skin halters, flaring hips girdled by brief loincloths fashioned from tanned hide, their strong thighs sheathed in high leather boots. Their bodies were toned and muscular, their movements supple, as they advanced with a long lithe stride. Their eyes flashed darkly with a fierce fire, reflecting the light that danced on the long blades of brandished rapiers.

Eyeing the sword points nervously, Celia took a step backwards. A command. The blades were sheathed instantly. The women stood to attention, eyes front, chest out, stomach in.

"Just like the Girl Guides at church parade, aren't they?"

Celia stared in stark disbelief at the apparition that appeared before her, all smiles.

"Oh come along, Cavvy," drawled a voice cut out of the finest crystal. "Don't you recognize me...?"

She wore a Spanish helmet shaped like the others, but hers was gleaming gold and crowned with a rainbow crest of bobbing feathers. Her superb breasts were guarded by sculpted plates of polished steel and her skimpy skirt was woven from chain mail. The sword hilt at her hip was encrusted with sparkling gemstones. The flamboyant mane that flowed down to her shoulders was flaming red and her skin had that pale translucence that only redheads have.

Her body was magnificent. Celia stared in open envy. And then it all came flooding back, the school girl crushes that charged the atmosphere in the dorm, the fever of jealousy directed at those who blossomed and developed early and spectacularly.

"Pamela...?" she gasped. "Is that you?"

The redhead grinned at her and struck a pose, one hand on her sword hilt.

"Pamela Leffingham-Hoare, my dear, the very same!"

Suddenly, Celia felt dizzy, her legs gave way and she sat down on the grass, howling with laughter.

Arm in arm, they went for a walk along the grassy cliff top.

The dark-skinned women waited silently. Nearby, they had tethered a row of winged monsters, buckled into leather harness, tall saddles mounted on their backs. They stood placidly, wings folded, rolling their yellow eyes with pleasure when the women stroked their long necks.

"I see you have them tamed," Celia observed.

Her new companion laughed.

"Not quite the Arabians that Daddy had in his stable at Hartsmere, but they do have their advantages. After all, horses can't fly."

Celia burst out laughing again.

"Good God! Pamela! I just can't believe it!"

Pamela had drawn her sword and was flicking the heads off tall thistles as they strolled along. She flourished the long blade, making it flash in the sunlight.

"Yes, who would have guessed it, my very own tribe of Amazon warriors."

"Well," Celia chuckled. "You were captain of hockey after all."

They paused, looking back at the women and their strange mounts.

"Who are they?"

"Descendants of the conquistadores, the product of their illicit liaisons with the native girls. As illegitimate half-breeds and the consequence of mortal sin, they were persecuted by both sides. So they went and hid in the jungle and learned to fight and fend for themselves."

"But how have they…?"

"Kept the bloodline going you mean?" Pamela flashed a wicked grin. "Oh, we plunder the local tribes, when the fancy takes us. Just like our midnight raids on Hill House Boys', when we were in the Upper Sixth. And there's the odd fallen missionary. I have quite a collection of them."

"Hmmm…" Celia arched an eyebrow.

Pamela tossed her flaming tresses and laughed.

"Oh, if only crusty old Miss Dawlish could see me now! And to think she always said that I would never amount to anything!"

"Indeed," said Celia. "We did all wonder what had become of you when you disappeared in the middle of term and ran off with that sinister Bolivian."

Pamela laughed again.

"Ah, poor Hernando. He persuaded me into some rickety old biplane and off we went on a quest for ancient gold. Completely misguided of course and he came to a sticky end. He was eaten by cannibals. I was blundering about lost in the jungle when these girls found me. Naturally, having never seen red hair before, they made me their queen and their goddess."

Celia was frowning, her brow furrowed darkly.

"Hernando…he sounds like someone I know…"

Now Pamela looked serious. She ceased toying with the sword and sheathed it.

"Yes, I know all about your expedition, we've been watching you."

Celia started, gripping her old school friend's arm.

Then can't you help us?"

The fun went out of the redhead's face. Her eyes steeled coldly.

"No. Absolutely not. Our existence must remain a myth and a legend."

Reaching out, she gripped Celia's shoulders.

"Imagine if we were discovered and word got out. There would be an invasion of scientists and adventurers and publicity-seekers. These women would never survive!"

Celia grimaced.

"Yes, I wouldn't wish my travelling companions on anyone."

"Here we are," said Pamela.

The flight on the creature's back had been far smoother than expected. The saddle, constructed of padded leather and wood, wedged her in securely and countless hours spent on horseback, from the gymkhana to the hunt, ensured that the reins had a feel that was familiar to her.

"You did that very well," the redhead confirmed, as they dismounted.

Celia smiled.

"It was certainly a novelty."

She laughed, stroking the creature's leathery neck.

"I'd love to enter this chap in the point to point."

Chortling, Pamela slapped her ample thigh.

"Golly yes, what a hoot! That would raise a few eyebrows, what?"

Handing the reins to the attendant warrior women, they walked away a short distance, taking stock of their surroundings. The scrubby plateau stretched away in all directions to the mist shrouded horizon.

Pamela turned to consult the senior amongst her troop, who came trotting briskly to her side. Their language had some Spanish, merged with an ancient, pagan tongue.

"An hour's march in that direction," Pamela was pointing. "Will take you back to your lot."

Celia frowned.

"Can't say I'll be glad to see them again, except for dear old Jeremy, of course. But I suppose that they're all I've got."

"I'm afraid so."

Pamela leant close, looking deep into Celia's eyes.

"Now remember, you must never tell about us. Not a soul. Not ever!"

"Never!" Celia replied staunchly. "I remember the old school motto."

"The official one or the unofficial?"

"The unofficial one of course."

"Sneaky is best!" they chorused, laughing.

Pamela took Celia's hand and squeezed it.

"Good luck, Cavvy."

"Thanks. I'm going to need it."

Jeremy stood and stared, his mouth opening and closing.

"Well, say something…"

Perched on an outcrop of red rock, Celia sat grinning down at him.

His hands flapping with excitement, the Professor stumbled forward, ecstatic.

"My dear Miss Cavendish, we had given you up for dead!"

Leaping down to the ground, Celia crushed Jeremy in a great bear hug, squeezing the breath out of him.

"What…? How…?" he spluttered, bewildered, gasping, laughing.

"Oh…I was too heavy for it…" Celia improvised. "It gave up in the end and dropped me, so I just started walking…"

Jeremy returned her embrace, lifting her off her feet and spinning her about. Mackenzie danced around them, performing a jig of delight.

Trixie looked on sullenly, with a face of stone. "Ain't that just dandy!" she muttered to herself, then turned her back and stomped away.

Dubois joined in the celebrations, garlanding Celia with effusive congratulations and flowery compliments, seizing her hand and stooping to kiss it. Celia lapped it up, beaming a broad smile in riposte to the filthy looks that Trixie was darting at her from a distance.

Even the stolid Gruber was caught up in the moment, approaching to click his heels as best he could and make a curt bow. Seeing this, Von Seyfritz darkened, his scarred features contorting with anger.

"Goddamn!" growled Nate O'Dwyer. "Just when we thought we'd got lucky and was ridda one of 'em!"

EPISODE 16:
BLONDE VERSUS BRUNETTE

"Aw, Jeez!"

This world had many faces, each more foreboding than the last.

Mere specks in a vast landscape, the adventurers confronted their new surroundings.

A volcanic desert, a black wasteland stark beneath a flawless blue sky. Great plains were fractured, mighty plates buckled, black slabs jutting. Where the dark crust wore thin there was a continuous, busy crackling. In a crazy zig-zag of cracks and narrow channels, a molten flow stirred up little tongues of fire, pulsing with a deep, dark orange, plumes of white vapor hanging in the bright, still air.

Everywhere, black boils and blisters were bursting. Liquid fire welled from open wounds. Fresh springs popped and gurgled, dark flecks carried away on the fiery flow. Tar-black whorls and ripples marked ancient tides, forever frozen in time. Deep pools throbbed and simmered, bubbles blurting a splat and lick of flame.

Steam seeped from every pore, from every rent and jagged fissure. On the broken, black horizons, unseen pressures forced the boiling below up into the bright blue sky, belching ragged scraps and shreds of fire, or hissing as a towering geyser, an orange spray falling as a fine rain.

The air was hot and dry and had a bitter tang of sulfur. All was a hissing and spitting and a crackling and a bubbling, bright and hard, battering the senses, the stark orange and black, the white steam shining in the blue above.

Far away, the mountains, pale, transparent.

"Ya gotta be kiddin'!" Nate rounded on Mackenzie.

"A somewhat daunting prospect," the Professor confessed gloomily.

Dubois bent to scoop up a handful of dry black dust. Frowning, he let it sift through his fingers.

"As barren as my great-grandmother," he observed. "And I estimate we have only four days' rations left."

Shading her eyes, Celia squinted at the snow-caps floating in the distance.

"And what if we can't find a pass through the mountains?"

O'Dwyer hawked and spat, the glob of saliva shriveling as it struck the dry ground.

"We ain't gonna make it to the mountains!" he shouted. "Not in no lousy four days, we ain't!"

Trixie groaned, hiding her face in her hands. Mackenzie swallowed audibly. Jeremy tried to make encouraging noises, but his voice faded away weakly.

Dubois wiped his palms on the front of his tan safari jacket.

"Mes amis," he smiled bleakly. "We have a choice. We can be baked alive, or we can starve to death."

Tugging the Luger from its holster, Von Seyfritz checked the vulnerable toggle action for any stray flecks of grit. The blued barrel gleamed, its steely glint reflected in his eyes.

"This is no time," he snapped. "For such defeatism!"

Satisfied, he sheathed the automatic.

"The weak will fall by the wayside," he declared. "But not those with the will to survive!"

The night was warm and glowing. They sat around in their shirtsleeves, their rocky surroundings bathed by a pulsing red aurora.

Perched cross-legged at the rim of a pond of bubbling lava, Mackenzie thumbed eagerly through the pages of a dog-eared notebook. The last of his tobacco gone, he was reduced to sucking on an empty pipe, his features suffused with a light that shone from within.

"Penny for your thoughts, Professor."

Jeremy's tall shadow fell across the pages. Drawn from his reveries, Mackenzie looked up, smiling.

"Sit ye down, my boy, sit ye down."

As the young man settled down beside him, the Professor slipped the small book back into his pocket. Plucking the pipe from his mouth, he glanced regretfully at its cold and empty bowl. Then he brightened visibly.

"Dear boy," he signed happily. "We are on the verge of earth shattering discoveries. I can feel it in my bones!"

Jeremy stared into the red cauldron, slurping greedily at the black stone.

So you've said, Professor," he nodded. "But what exactly."

Mackenzie winked with a grin, tapping the side of his nose. Dubois strolled by, tipping them a jaunty salute. Slipping his jacket from his arm, he folded it for a pillow and laid it on a suitable outcrop of dark stone. Reclining, he lay lost in thought, staring up at the red sky as he stroked his thin moustaches.

"That frog is a deep one," rasped Nate O'Dwyer. "I bet he's seen a thing or two."

He sat beside the Prussian, a little way off from the rest, big shadows silhouetted against a fan of fiery spray that was hissing on the skyline. With the bulk of Gruber looming in attendance, they bent in close to each other, their tone conspiratorial.

"A dangerous customer," said Von Seyfritz. "I shall have to settle with him, before this journey is over."

There was a pause. Nate stared up at the jagged black horizon, the fiery geyser sparking in his eyes.

"I've been thinking about what ya said," he muttered. "About the weak not makin' it."

Von Seyfritz ran a hand over his close-cropped skull, across an old scar showing whitely.

"We are carrying too much dead weight," he stated.

He twisted to survey their campsite.

"That damned Frenchman is at least good in a fight, but the others....."

O'Dwyer nodded slowly.

"Yeah, I could croak that Perfesser just fer gettin' us up here on a damn fool wild goose chase, and that college boy is a goddam pain in the ass!"

The Prussian's monocle glinted as he moved his head slightly.

"And the women," he said flatly. "As baggage carriers they have been barely adequate, and now they are dispensable."

Nate turned to look at him, his face lost in shadow.

"We are going to have to travel light my friend."

Von Seyfritz could hear Nate rubbing his chin.

"If we dispose of one we must dispose of them all," the Prussian persisted.

Nate raised a huge paw.

"Hey, I knows my business!"

He turned to look at the camp, his broad back a black monolith against the red glow of lava.

"A stuck-up bitch and a cheap whore."

With a grunt, he swiveled back to his co-conspirator.

"Let's give it a day or two," he suggested. "I ain't got nothin' against beatin' up on a broad, just to keep her in line, but I don't like to ice one unless I really gotta."

His laugh was a sudden bark, raw and brutal.

"A guy's gotta have principles!"

To respect the women's modesty, they had erected a groundsheet as a screen.

"Whoo!" exclaimed Trixie. "Some heatwave!"

She reclined in her skimpy underthings, her pale skin glowing. Tilting it to the ruddy luminescence, she perused a creased and dog-eared playbill.

Her sharp eyes darted over the bold print. Grinning, she flaunted the paper.

"Hey, you wanna see my billing?"

Celia sat up against a bulge of stone. Her eyes narrowed, lip curling.

"No, thank you."

Trixie shrugged. Holding the playbill out at arm's length, she admired a stylized representation of herself strutting in a few beads and feathers.

"Platinum Venus!" she quoted. "Can she dance! Can she flip a quip with an agile hip!"

Celia rolled her eyes.

Trixie laughed. She yawned and stretched, arching her body, laughing again as she felt the heat of Celia's eyes crawling on her bare skin.

"Yeah, I got what it takes, and I knows how to use it!"

There was a long and leaden silence, Trixie smirking smugly, Celia frowning.

Celia couldn't breathe. Suddenly, she was wrenching at the buttons. She tugged off her shirt and flung it aside. Sighing she flexed her supple shoulders, threatening the straps of her brassiere.

Trixie licked her lips.

"That's it dearie. Let 'em breathe."

She patted the rounded mound of her belly. Her throaty chuckle incited little tremors to tingle deliciously through the long lush creaminess suffused by the warm glow rising all around them.

"When I was a kid, we used to sleep out naked on the fire escape, all summer long."

Celia swallowed hard.

"You belong in the jungle," she snapped. "Then you would never have to wear any clothes!"

Eyes dancing, Trixie shook her head.

"Hell, no!" she protested. "I'd have nobody to watch me!"

Celia made a scornful sound. Trixie grinned at herself prancing across the smudged paper.

"And how does it feel," Celia asked, despite herself. "To dance naked for men?"

Trixie threw back her head and cackled.

"It feels great!"

A veil fell across her sharp features, her gaze hooded, predatory.

"It's power, honey, power."

Celia raised her eyebrows.

"Oh really?"

Trixie laughed viciously.

"The Big Guy?" she snarled. "Every time he hits me he needs me a little bit more."

She spat, the blob of spittle sizzling on hot stone.

"The big lug can't live without me!"

Trixie sat up abruptly. Her heavy breasts rose and fell, straining their little, frilly cups. With a quick, liquid shimmy of her shoulders, she leant towards the English girl. Celia paled, rigid, a tautness in her bare midriff, her dark eyes burning.

"And it ain't just the men, sugar. You know what I mean?"

Celia trembled; there was a sudden drumming in her temples. Suddenly, she wanted to rake that ivory skin with her fingernails, rip that firm flesh into bloody tatters.

"W–what are you t–talking about?" she stammered.

"They think I can't see 'em," Trixie's smile was twisted and ugly. "Them fancy society dames and college girls, out for a cheap thrill."

Her eyes were hard and bright, a crazy spark dancing.

"I see 'em lookin' at me. They think I can't see 'em sweatin'!"

Celia felt a thousand red hot needles pricking up and down her spine. An iron fist clenched deep inside her.

Trixie's laugh made her flinch, like the crack of a whip.

"And it ain't just in the big city either."

She leant so close that their flesh was almost touching. Her heat enveloped Celia, who held her breath, paralyzed.

"I got the power everywhere!"

The tip of her tongue teased her perfect, sharp white teeth.

"W–what?" Celia gasped, the violence of the sudden exhalation making her shudder.

"Aw, c'mon, baby.....!"

One moment Celia was ghostly pale, the next scarlet, blushing furiously. She felt a bead of sweat trace a path down her spine.

"You and that college boy of yours."

Trixie's breast brushed Celia's bare arm, a remarkable nipple sharp through the thin silk. Celia jerked as though jolted by an electric shock. She sprang to her feet. Laughing, Trixie stood quickly, her body uncoiling in one fluid movement.

They stood facing each other. Trixie was grinning. Celia glared.

"You leave Jeremy alone!" Celia gasped hoarsely. "Or I'll—!"

"Or you'll what?"

Head flung back, hip forward and breasts high, Trixie parried Celia's fury with a cocky, mocking stare.

"You're just an amateur, doll," Trixie drooled. "When we're outta this mess I'm gonna take that pretty boy on a trip to the Moon!"

A red mist roared, a withering white flash ripped across Celia's eyes. Blind, she heard the slap, like a pistol shot. Then the heat was cold, ice crawling in her bowels. She saw Trixie, chalk white, fingering a red mark that faded slowly on her cheek.

"Okay," the blonde said matter-of-factly. "If that's how ya want it."

She flung out her arm like a pole, her clenched fist splatting full flush on Celia's lips.

Celia shouted. Her head jerked back. Her arms outflung, she back-pedaled, crashing through the screen. Bursting into the campsite, she lost her balance and sat down hard.

"What the—!"

"Sacre bleu!"

They leapt to their feet, startled by the sight of a half-dressed woman propelled backwards into view.

Celia sat on the black rock, fingering a lower lip already puffy and discolored.

"Okay, rich girl....."

Their jaws dropped as Trixie stepped out in her underwear. She seemed to shine, her generous contours incandescent, aglow with the fires throbbing all around her.

"Ya want some more?"

Her features dark with fury, Celia struggled upright.

"You... you...!" she spluttered. "I'll show you...!"

Trixie threw back her head and laughed. Mackenzie's bootheels scuffed on the stone. His old bones creaked as Nate's great paw clamped down upon his shoulder.

"Don't spoil the fun, Perfesser."

Her pale skin gleaming, Trixie moved in a slow half circle. Her shoulders were hunched and her long legs straddled, her fingers hooked like talons. Eyes blazing with an unholy passion, she ran a gloating gaze over Celia's supple torso.

Celia's heart was beating wildly. Her bare shoulders glistened with sweat. She swallowed hard, then bunched her fists and raised them, her back straight and knees bent slightly.

"Well, waddaya know," Nate guffawed. "Marquee o' Queensbury rules!"

Jeremy gulped, wide-eyed, wondering why he wasn't trying to stop this.

"All her cousins are boys," he heard himself saying. "She can look after herself."

O'Dwyer snorted.

"Oh, yeah? Trix fought her way up through the toughest cathouses in the country. I bet a hundred dollars she tears yer gal's eyes out in five minutes flat."

Dubois grinned, surveying the slowly circling combatants with an expert eye.

"I will take that bet, monsieur."

"And I!" snapped Von Seyfritz, cursing as his monocle fogged up.

With a yell, Trixie pounced, her claws swinging. Celia stood her ground. Her left arm snaked out, her fist flickering in a rapid double jab, one-two, splat-splat.

Trixie jumped up in the air, holding her nose. Involuntary tears spurted, blood seeping darkly through her fingers.

"Bitch!" she screeched. "If it's broken I'll—!"

Celia stepped in quickly with a short, clubbing right. Trixie reeled, her arms flailing, off balance. Celia's left swung in an arc, thudding on the side of the blonde head. Trixie flung up her arms and fell flat on her back, her white body sprawling, suddenly slack and uncoordinated.

Celia stood over her, breathing heavily, her shoulders rising and falling. Her bra strap had slipped and was dangling. Beads of sweat were coursing down the furrow of her spine.

"Well?" she panted. "Are you satisfied?"

Dubois whistled lowly. Jeremy beamed at O'Dwyer. The American scowled.

Trixie lay full length, sucking in air, her limbs flung out at crazy angles. She grunted and sat up abruptly. There was a bruise on her cheekbone, a string of blood suspended from her nostril.

Frowning, she kneaded the bridge of her nose, expecting it to crumble. When it didn't she heaved herself to her feet, her movements labored and clumsy. Black dust and bits of grit were glued to her shoulderblades, down the back of her legs, soiling the silk where it stretched tautly across her glorious posterior.

Feet splayed, her head down, platinum strands falling across her face, Trixie rubbed her jaw ruefully. Celia took a deep breath, her shoulders rising, proud breasts thrusting.

"Splendid!" exclaimed Von Seyfritz.

"Well?" demanded Celia.

Trixie scrubbed the sweat out of her eyes.

"Okay," she muttered. "I've had enough."

Celia fixed her with a frosty stare. Then she turned, spinning on her heel.

Trixie sprang. She dropped her shoulder and swung a short, chopping right hook. Her fist jabbed like a dagger into the pneumatic padding above Celia's kidney.

Celia screamed, her back arching. Her legs crumpled and she collapsed on all fours, groaning.

"Oh, I say!" Jeremy protested. "Foul!"

"There ya go," Nate chuckled. "They don't call her 'Trick-sy' fer nothin'."

Snarling, the blonde girl lunged, catlike.

"Ah," said Von Seyfritz. "So it is merely a stage name."

As Celia struggled to her knees, Trixie slammed her down, sitting astride her.

"A nom de guerre," laughed Dubois.

"Oh, yeah," said Nate. "She was just plain Maisie O'Toole when I found her."

Gritting her teeth, Trixie pinned Celia down.

"Say Uncle!" she hissed. "Say it!"

Trixie bounced her rump up and down on Celia's bare middle. Shouting, Celia kicked and wriggled. Trixie rocked her head from side to side, swinging vigorous fore and backhands that resounded like the crack of a whip.

"Say it, damn ya! Say it!"

Jeremy was stepping forward to intervene and the others were reaching out to grab him. Then Trixie went red and let out an ear-splitting screech, and then another, and then suddenly let Celia go and flung herself backwards, rolling around on the ground, clutching at herself, where the scrap of silk girdled her hips.

"Owowowowowo!" she hooted. "Ya dirty pig!"

The men stared in amazement. Puffing out her cheeks, Celia sat hugging her midriff. As she lurched to her feet, the brassiere surrendered. Swaying, she caught up the strap just in time. Nearby, Trixie staggered, bent over double, her hands pressed between her thighs.

"Awwww!" she howled.

"Miss Cavendish learns quickly," Dubois chuckled.

The girls squared up to each other stiffly, gasping, caked in dust and sweat. They jumped as one, meeting with a smack of flesh on flesh, their legs splayed, heaving with all their might.

"Hey!" exclaimed O'Dwyer. "This sure beats Dempsey and Tunney!"

Trixie's fists drummed on Celia's ribs, making her grunt. Then the top of Celia's head cracked against Trixie's chin. Trixie's teeth clicked and she sagged, rubber-legged, her eyes glassy, retreating.

Celia followed, blowing hair out of her eyes. She swung at Trixie's head, but the blonde ducked. Celia lunged and tried to catch her, but Trixie writhed and twisted, slippery, shaking her head to clear the raw buzzing in her brain. Enraged, Celia swung her arms in a frenzy, spitting obscenities, the storm of blows splatting and thudding, punching and slapping and kicking.

Trixie bobbed and weaved, counterpunching. They slugged it out, toe to toe, in a whirling blur of limbs and strained faces.

"Holy.....!"

The big men just stood there, gaping. Then Trixie slipped on a splash of perspiration. She fell face down with Celia on top of her, the impact jolting the breath from the blonde's body.

The red roaring blazed, thunder booming. Celia was only vaguely aware that she was wrapping her arm around Trixie's throat.

"Uh-oh!"

Cursing, Celia squeezed. Trixie struggled, clawing at the stones. A hideous pressure blew up behind her eyes. Her lungs filled with acid. Hot wires twisted in her brain and she thought the top of her head would explode.

Dubois turned to O'Dwyer.

"I believe you owe me a hundred dollars, monsieur."

EPISODE 17:
LUST IN THE DUST

The sun rang like a gong.

The black wasteland shimmered and bubbled, bled white heat to a melting horizon. The heat was crushing. Lava spat and sizzled. Eyes were red-rimmed by the gritty fumes. A bitter tang bit into the back of the throat.

"Aw, c'mon!" Nate rasped hoarsely. "Don't dawdle!"

Trixie stumbled, glaring balefully. She was black and blue and aching all over. Scowling, she fingered the bruises on her throat. The worst was the wound festering deep inside, the worms twisting in her skull.

She tacked across the broken black stones and drew up beside Celia.

"You're dead," she promised. "I'm gonna stiff ya."

Expressionless, Celia accelerated, her body bent beneath the weight of the pack. Her swollen lip was throbbing, and pain jabbed everywhere. Her ribcage pumped like a creaking bellows, the dry air rasping in her lungs.

"Steady, old thing," warned Jeremy.

Head down, she shrugged past him, lengthening her stride. Her heart seemed to jump up drumming. A sudden dizziness wrapped around her. Her legs turned to water, a wavering veil falling across her eyes.

"Steady!"

She felt Jeremy's hand on her arm and leant on him for support.

"Sorry," she gasped.

Jeremy forced a grin, cracking fine lines in a mask of dark dust. He worked his parched lips, trying to concoct saliva. His tongue seemed twice its normal size.

Shading her eyes, Celia squinted at the mocking mountains.

"We're not going to make it, are we?" she asked quietly.

Jeremy gulped. He opened his mouth, then shut it again. He tried to think of Scott and Oates, but the old school tie stoicism and self-sacrifice which had mesmerized a goggle-eyed schoolboy now seemed hugely inappropriate.

Then they gaped at the sight of Mackenzie striding past them.

"Nonsense, Miss Cavendish! Nonsense!"

His head was up and his eyes were shining. He surged past them with a springy, youthful stride.

"Fate has placed us on the verge of discoveries which will shake our conception of the natural order of things!" he exulted. "It will not be snatched from us, not when we are so near!"

Nearby, Von Seyfritz curled his lip.

"The old fool has gone mad," he muttered.

"Outta his mind," agreed O'Dwyer.

Dubois suddenly slipped and fell over. The others all stopped to stare at him.

"Good Lord," noted Jeremy. "The ground is as smooth as glass."

"It is glass," said Mackenzie.

"So what?" barked O'Dwyer.

Where Dubois had fallen the buckled and rubble-strewn desert was abruptly smooth and level, an expanse of black glass gleaming.

Dubois rose gingerly, rubbing his backside.

"Merde!"

Jeremy bent to test the glassy surface. It was faintly rippled, speckled with tiny bubbles.

"I say," he addressed the Professor. "Jolly peculiar, what?"

Mackenzie scuffed the black glass with the toe of his boot.

"Heat," he pronounced. "A great deal of heat."

Trixie shrugged, wringing the sweat out of her handkerchief.

"Yeah, there's a lot of it about Perfesser."

"Yeah," Nate echoed. "C'mon, let's get—"

Mackenzie flapped his hands impatiently.

"No, no!" he cried. "Don't you see?"

"See what?" Celia sighed heavily.

The Professor sawed the air, pointing in all directions.

"There!" he martialled them vigorously. "If you would follow the edge that way.... yes, that's right, and you that way.... that's right, spread out.... that's it....!"

They all stood staring down at their black reflections.

"Alright," said Dubois. "So it is a—"

"A perfect circle!" exclaimed Mackenzie.

They faced each other across a disc of gleaming jet, at least two hundred yards in diameter. The Professor's bright eyes met only a blank stare.

Shrugging, they regrouped.

"Hasn't it occurred to any of you," Mackenzie was practically hopping up and down with exasperation. "That much of what we have encountered on this journey has been somewhat out of place?"

Von Seyfritz tugged off his pith helmet, wiping round the sweatband.

"The only thing that is out of place as far as I am concerned," he stated flatly. "Is us."

He wedged the helmet back onto his cropped skull.

"I suggest that we move on."

Mackenzie opened his mouth to protest, but there was a steely glint in the Prussian's eyes which froze him to the marrow. The Colonel's fingers crept until they were stroking the flap of his holster. Now, he told himself, is as good a time as any.

Then Von Seyfritz relaxed. Where was Dubois? He could not see the Frenchman. That big dumb ox of an American was just standing there glaring at the horizon, and Dubois was somewhere behind him.

Cursing under his breath, Von Seyfritz let his hand drop.

"I repeat," he snapped. "I suggest we move on!"

The night throbbed hotly. A red sky was pulsing, the black plain laced with fire. Fire flowed and bubbled. Tongues of flame licked and crackled, bright blobs squirting.

A glowing red mist was draped all around, suspended in the still, acrid airlessness.

"Ugh!" grunted Trixie. "It stinks!"

She stood quickly. Her shirt lay crumpled on the stones, and her bare shoulders glistened stickily. Looking down at herself, she tugged out the waistband of her trousers, sucking in her middle.

"Yuck!" she lamented. "I'm as high as green cheese!"

Jerking on the belt loops, she made the baggy slacks flap, prompting a tepid ventilation. Then she looked up to see everyone staring at her.

"Aw, heck!"

Trixie rounded on her traveling companions, her pronounced frontage swinging, alarming the little bit of silk that struggled to confine it.

"Put yer eyes back in!"

Grabbing a drab flannel and her last thin sliver of soap, she stomped off across the campsite. Hunkered down by a black blister of stone, Nate heaved his broad bulk upright.

"And where the hell do ya think yer going'?"

Trixie rolled her eyes. She brandished the towel.

"What does it look like?"

A tiny muscle twitched at the side of Nate's jaw. His hands balled into fists, then swung loose again.

"Okay, it's yer ass."

Trixie shrugged, moving on. Mackenzie cleared his throat politely.

"Oh... ah... I would advise caution, Miss Marlowe. Heaven knows what dangers may be lurking out there.

The blonde tossed her head.

"Huh! It ain't likely to be anythin' worse than I got right here!"

She passed by Celia and the worms did their jig inside her skull. She met the dark girl's stare with a mirthless, ugly grin, drew a finger slowly across the fading bruises on her throat.

Naked, Trixie stooped to dip the soap into a pool of steaming water. Glowering sourly, she scraped and scrubbed, the greasy fleck in her hand raising no lather but only a greyish film on her sticky skin.

A slow burning drummed dully in the dark behind her eyes. Celia's white body writhed, wreathed in flame. Celia's screams needled thinly, sucked under by the drums.

Muttering an obscene incantation, Trixie dipped the flannel into the water. She bent and turned and twisted, wiping away the bubbly grey slime. Celia squirmed and bled, her stark, demented features spinning in the blackness.

Small stones skittered, dislodged by a heavy boot. Celia melted. The drums faded as Trixie turned quickly.

"Is that you, Daddy?"

Broad shoulders filled the span of the glowing red horizon.

"D–Daddy....?"

Gruber stared at her. Trixie's eyes widened.

"Oh!"

The Prussian's face was a mask chiseled out of stone. A tiny spark glittered deep within the dull, unblinking opaqueness of his eyes. Beads of sweat glinted amongst the coarse stubble on his jowls.

They stood there looking at each other. The black lands simmered. Gruber swallowed hard. His eyes crawled upwards from the chipped lacquer on her toenails, up the turn of her calves and the long, smooth sweep of her thighs. He lingered over the short curls, truly blonde but not as light as the hair on her head, roamed over the rounded mound of her belly, around and around the heavy breasts that rose and fell in a slow and steady rhythm.

"Well, whaddaya want?"

Trixie slid her palms along the satin span of her hips.

"Dumb question."

She laughed harshly.

"I been waitin' fer one of ya mugs to crack," she drawled. "Though I never figgered on you."

Raising her arms slowly, she struck a pose, a long, slow undulation that shimmered through her from head to toe. Her pale form was vibrant, her gleaming curves tinted with fire.

"Think you're man enough?" she taunted, her eyes rolling saucily.

Gruber exhaled audibly. Sweat trickled down from his temples. His right hand swung up abruptly, a blunt automatic aimed at her belly-button.

Trixie's giggle was fractured, her eyes a little crazy.

"Aw, Jeez, another tough guy what keeps his pecker in his pocket!"

Gruber's eyes narrowed. He gestured with the gun, tilting the muzzle to the ground. Trixie raised her eyes up to the red sky. She turned this way then that, looking for a smooth spot.

"Okay, okay...!"

She sat gingerly, the stone warm and gritty beneath her bare bottom.

"Heck, I only just took a bath!"

Trixie reclined, propped up on her elbows, watching Gruber as he ripped at his belt, hauling down his trousers.

"My oh my," she lay back, her head pillowed on her hands. "What a big fuss over such a little thing."

His pants flapping around his ankles, Gruber stumbled towards her. As he knelt down on the black stone, Trixie stared off into space with a practised air of resignation.

"Just make it snappy, will ya. I ain't got time to—"

Her expression changed dramatically as Gruber clamped his hands around her waist and, with a single quick twist, rolled her over on her stomach.

"OH!"

"OUCH!"

"OW!"

"OH! OW! YA DIRTY—! OW!"

"OWOWOWOWOWOWOW!"

They all came running.

Red-faced and sweating, Gruber struggled to his feet, his trousers tangled round his knees. Trixie's pale form was flopping around on the dark stone.

"Oooh!" she wailed hoarsely. "I ain't gonna be able to sit down for a month!"

Nate swung without breaking stride. Gruber was a big man, but the American's fist fell upon him like a hammer, sat him down hard, blood all over his chin.

Bellowing, O'Dwyer reached down and hauled Gruber to his feet. Spitting teeth, the Prussian batted at him weakly. Nate drew the .45 and split Gruber's face down the middle in a hot wash of scarlet.

"Oh, God!" said Celia, clutching Jeremy's arm.

Rolling around, Trixie grabbed at Nate's ankles. Kicking free, he thumbed back the hammer of the long automatic, jamming the muzzle under Gruber's chin. Von Seyfritz's fingers closed clawlike around his wrist.

"Nein," the Colonel said quietly.

Surprised, Nate let go. Blinking away the blood, Gruber stumbled backwards. He looked around desperately, only to see Mackenzie staring with horror, Dubois smiling coldly, the stiletto balanced on his palm.

"He is my man," Von Seyfritz continued. "I will deal with him."

O'Dwyer lowered the .45. Gruber relaxed. He wiped his palm across his face, smearing the thick crust of blood. Addressing his commander, he began to gabble in a high-pitched, grating whine, gesturing towards Trixie, who was now kneeling with her forehead bowed to the ground, groaning and cursing.

The Luger appeared in the Colonel's hand. Its sharp detonation echoed thinly across the hellish wastelands. A small black dot appeared on Gruber's forehead. He stood there for a moment, looking faintly surprised. Then his eyes rolled up and his knees buckled. With a long sigh, he folded slowly onto his face. The back of his head was pink and pulpy.

"Oh!" said Celia.

Von Seyfritz rotated briskly, the muzzle of the Luger traversing 'til it zeroed in on Dubois.

170

"Drop the knife!"

A pause. Then the slim blade clattered on the stone.

"And now unbuckle your gun belt, slowly."

Cursing himself, the Frenchman tossed the holstered revolver aside. Von Seyfritz sensed a presence at this shoulder.

"The time has come," he stated simply.

O'Dwyer shrugged.

"As good a time as any."

He hefted the big automatic. Wide-eyed, Trixie scrambled to her feet, her hair awry, streaked from head to toe with sweat and grime.

"Hey, Daddy, what the heck are—?"

Nate snarled and she jumped backwards. Cold sweat crawling down her spine, Celia gasped, her throat dry and constricted.

"W–what are you d–doing?" she stammered.

Von Seyfritz gestured apologetically.

"Only what is necessary," he stated matter-of-factly.

Nate nodded. The others just stood and stared.

"I regret to say," Von Seyfritz explained. "That you have become surplus to our requirements."

"Nothin' personal," said Nate.

Trixie stumbled forward, but the unblinking blandness of Nate's stare stopped her in her tracks, her mouth left hanging open, her protest stifled.

"Sorry, Babe," he shrugged. "That's the way the cookie crumbles."

The blonde stood there gaping. Her shoulders drooped. She seemed to sag, to deflate, her startling nakedness suddenly absurd. By contrast, Celia was now dark with fury, her grip bruising Jeremy's bicep.

"You're insane!"

Von Seyfritz smiled indulgently.

"On the contrary," he replied. "I could not possibly be more rational."

The sweat ran down Celia's face. Jeremy felt that he ought to say something.

"I s–say," he offered. "This is not quite the behavior one expects from an officer and a gentleman."

Dubois laughed harshly.

"Ah, non, but it is so typically German."

Von Seyfritz's face darkened.

"You," he hissed. "You I will shoot in the belly. The kneecaps first, and then the belly."

Trixie shook all over. She made a tiny mewling sound deep in her throat. The Frenchman curled his lip.

"There is only ten feet between us," he spat. "You had better be sure and kill me with the first bullet."

Nate cleared his throat impatiently.

"Hey!" he rasped. "Let's quit the jawin' and get this over with, huh?"

Stepping forward, he leveled the .45. Trixie let out a sustained wail and sank to her knees. Celia turned to look at Jeremy, who flung an arm around her shoulders. Dubois hawked and spat, cursing viciously.

Mackenzie sprang forward into the line of fire.

"Surely, gentlemen," he cried. "You cannot honestly propose to commit mass murder!"

Von Seyfritz merely smiled again.

"We simply propose to follow the natural order of things," he said softly. "You of all people, Professor, should appreciate that all creation has but a single common thread, the survival of the fittest."

Nate muttered darkly. The Prussian nodded.

"And now," he declared. "Who shall be first?"

Harness jangled. A cloven hoof scraped the black ash.

"Good God!" cried Celia.

"Eeek!" shrieked Trixie, leaping to her feet and wrapping her arms around herself.

A jagged ridge ringed them, dark against a night sky pulsing redly. The sawtooth rim was occupied, strange figures standing shoulder to shoulder.

They were compact and sinewy. Blue tunics left their strong arms uncovered, their legs bare below the knee. Their rugged, blunt features were framed by a hard leather chinstrap. From a beaten bronze circlet protecting the forehead, red and blue feathers projected, forming a fan that crowned them.

Below a heavy brow, their sunken stare was dark and unblinking. Their skin was coarse and berry brown, weathered by desert winds and baked by the sun. Each carried a long, leaf-shaped blade hanging from his belt, his midriff protected by four bands of bronze. Small, round shields were held at the ready, leather shrunk onto wooden layers and bonded with a simple pattern of square studs. All raised a spear aloft, poised for throwing.

There was a long and screaming silence. The newcomers stared stonily. Below them, the big men shifted their feet, the pistols jabbing in all directions.

"Hey!" snapped O'Dwyer. "Who are these jokers anyway?"

Mackenzie sighed, ecstatic.

"Just as I thought!" he exulted. "Just as I thought!"

Celia rolled her eyes. Trixie stared dumbly.

"I say, Professor," Jeremy entreated. "Let us in on the secret!"

Mackenzie flung out his arms, making the dark men on the rim tense and lift their spears a little higher.

"Ladies and gentlemen!" he trumpeted. "Before you stand the warriors of ancient Mesopotamia!"

No one spoke. The black expanses sizzled.

Then Von Seyfritz cleared his throat.

"Well, whatever," he barked. "They are dead men!"

He aimed the Luger. The spears quivered.

"Uh, that ain't such a good idea," Nate muttered. "They got the drop on us."

"That's right," said Dubois quietly. "One shot and we'll all look like pin cushions."

The spearpoints glittered. A warrior, whose feathered crest stood taller than the rest, thrust his javelin into the ground, unsheathed his sword and took a quick step forward. He pointed at the big men, said something in a strange tongue that was all consonants.

"He recognizes your firearms as weapons," Mackenzie stated. "I advise restraint, gentlemen."

Nate let the tension seep out of his broad shoulders. With a grunt, he let down the hammer of the .45 and tossed it aside. His breath hissing between clenched teeth, Von Seyfritz followed the American's example.

"Bravo!" said Dubois.

The warrior turned away to shout to someone behind him. There were sounds of hooves clip-clopping, harness rattling and wheels crunching.

"Aha!" said Jeremy. "The head wallah, what?"

Shaggy oxen plodded into view, yoked to a high, slab-sided chariot. Behind the driver stood a tall, lean figure, cowled and cloaked in swathes of black and silver.

With an imperious grace, the dazzling apparition descended from the chariot. The silver specter advanced with a long and gliding stride, the warriors parting respectfully. The voyagers stared, awestruck, as it appeared to float towards them, seemingly faceless.

"Well, Professor," Celia said in an oddly brittle tone. "Won't you introduce us?"

Mackenzie just stood there gaping.

"I—! I—!" he stammered.

The shining phantom came down from the ridge, the black and silver resonating. Suddenly, they could not move, their feet clamped to the dark stone, arms locked to their sides.

The silver lit Trixie's pale features with a shimmering incandescence. Her eyes blazed, growing wider and wider. She gasped, trembling. Her bare breasts heaved, sweat trickling on her skin.

"Out of the frying pan," commented Celia. "And into the fire."

The sun skinned their eyeballs.

174

"Aw, goddamn...!" bawled Nate O'Dwyer.

Spearpoints sparked like needles of fire. Fifty armed warriors escorted their prisoners through a desert of broiling ash, amongst the twisted, bleached bones of dead saplings, frowned upon by mountainous whorls and frozen waves of black tar.

The captives stumbled in single file, linked together by loops of rough fiber. The white heat battered them.

"We made a mistake," Von Seyfritz squinted at the molten horizons. "We should not have given in so easily."

Nate lifted his bound hands, rubbing the sweat out of his eyes.

"Yeah, well, I didn't fancy them odds."

He glared at his peculiar escort.

"Don't worry," he rasped. "No feathered monkey is gonna get the drop on me twice."

Close behind, Dubois shook his head, grinning mirthlessly.

The wooden wheels cut deep furrows in the black ash. Clucking his tongue, the driver prompted the plodding oxen. Beside him, the cloaked mystery stood towering over Trixie, who rode the wagon with a stare blank and unseeing, her nakedness concealed by a cape of flowing silver.

"How ingenious," observed Mackenzie. "That cloth appears to be metallic. It deflects the heat of the sun. I'll wager Miss Marlowe is as cool as a cucumber."

Celia's eyes narrowed.

"This isn't the first time that I've wished I was a blonde."

Jeremy frowned.

"I don't know," he said doubtfully. "These blighters have singled her out for something special, and I suspect it won't be pleasant."

Celia snorted.

"Well," she tossed her head. "It won't be a virgin sacrifice!"

Her face was soaking. There were dark, clinging patches under her arms, her shirt glued to the groove of her spine by a broad black band of sweat. When she stumbled, the guards jabbed at her with their spears, shouting angrily. She trudged on, glowering, the cords rubbing her wrists raw.

"I don't think," she gasped. "That any of us is in for anything pleasant."

The night was starless and as black as pitch. Nothing lived in that vast emptiness, and the silence was absolute, ringing tautly.

Dubois lifted his head from the rough carpet of ash. It was the best he could do, spreadeagled as he was, his wrists and ankles tied to stout pegs.

Warily, he twisted his neck, straining to see all around him. He saw pools of an odd, greenish luminescence, cast from crystal globes set on long pikes.

"Strange devices, are they not?" whispered Mackenzie, somewhere close by.

Dubois winced.

"Ssssh!"

Dimly, he saw figures moving, spears resting on their shoulders. He saw a bulky form that was either Von Seyfritz or O'Dwyer, a slender shape that must be Celia, staked out on the ground.

The tall chariot stood out like a beacon, a glowing globe fixed to all four corners.

"Aha.....!"

The silver phantom gleamed starkly, seemingly lifeless. By its side, Trixie stood with that fixed, unblinking stare, her pale face shining eerily.

The Frenchman didn't waste any time. Taking advantage of what little slack he had, he bent and turned his right arm and contrived to press the side of his elbow to the ground. There was a soft click, and a slim blade emerged from his shirt cuff and jumped onto his palm.

It always pays, he grinned to himself, to carry a spare.

Manipulating the thin hilt with his fingers, Dubois addressed the sharp edge to the cords around his wrist.

"Voila," he whispered.

The rough twine parted. In a trice, Dubois was up and moving on tip-toe, grimacing as the ash crunched softly, past the prostrate Professor. He didn't hesitate. I'm sorry, mon ami, but it's every man for himself now.

The blackness swallowed him. He held his hand up before his face and could not see it. He crouched there, breathing evenly. He was on his own, the way he wanted to be.

Someone bumped into him.

Instinctively, the Frenchman attacked. He flipped his bulkier adversary with a dip and twist of his wiry shoulders, then sprang to lock his fingers on a fistful of hair, exposing the throat for the quick cut of the knife.

He froze. His enemy had a belt and buttons and pockets.

"Who are you?" he hissed.

Jeremy's splutterings gradually became coherent.

"Bit of luck, what? One of those bally pegs was rotten, it just fell apart when I tugged it. Couldn't get near C though, dashed goons all around her."

Dubois cursed. He cursed himself and everything he could think of. Meanwhile, Jeremy tingled with excitement.

"Righto, let's go and rescue the others!"

The young man began to crawl back towards the campsite. Dubois stifled a sudden urge to turn and run in the opposite direction.

They peered down through the darkness, at the splashes of ghoulish green light, the spread-eagled figures and the guards moving amongst them.

"Not a chance," Dubois muttered.

He could sense Jeremy's shoulders sagging with disappointment. He grinned suddenly, reaching through the gloom to slap his young companion on the back.

"Don't worry, mon brave. Your Mlle Cavendish is too fine a woman to waste on these savages."

Grinning like schoolboys, they withdrew into the darkness.

The sun rang in a sky of brass.

Mackenzie stood gaping.

"Astounding! Fantastic! Phenomenal!"

Glowering, Nate tugged at his shirt buttons. Beads of sweat glinted in a dark and matted tangle. He scratched himself, shrugging.

"So what?" he growled. "It's just a lotta lines in the dirt, that's all."

Lines. Lines everywhere. Lines spanned and criss-crossed a vast and baking grey plain. Thin lines zig-zagged and intersected seemingly at random, all ways to the melting white horizons. Broad, pale bands were apparently connected in some incomprehensible geometry.

"Hey!" said Nate suddenly. "Don't it look like some kinda airport runway?"

"Don't be ridiculous!" snorted Von Seyfritz.

A tug on his tether jerked Mackenzie onwards, as he stooped to retrieve a jagged shard of pottery. He peered closely at minute incisions etched into the clay.

"This is quite fascinating," he exclaimed. "What do you say, Miss Cavendish?"

Celia hardly heard him. She stumbled as the fibers binding her wrists twanged tautly, gritting her teeth to stifle a cry of pain. She ached all over, the thousand daggers that jabbed into her sinews prompting a sudden rush of scalding sweat. Gasping, she searched the plain, scanning the broiling horizons. Where are you, Jeremy? Come and rescue me, soon!"

The silver figure raised a long arm. The driver hauled on the reins and the chariot creaked to a halt. Trixie stood there staring dumbly, her metallic cloak gleaming.

"Now what?" grated Von Seyfritz.

The war party halted, where lines crossed to form a great triangle.

"Beats me," replied O'Dwyer.

The leader bowed to his silver superior, his long feathers bobbing. Then he turned to the others, pointing and shouting. The prisoners watched as two of their guards were dragged from the ranks and thrown down on their knees, their heads uncovered, the feathered helmets cast aside.

"I assume," observed Mackenzie. "That those fellows are being held responsible for the escape of our companions."

Von Seyfritz summoned up just enough saliva to spit with.

"Trust a damn Frenchman to run away like that!"

Celia's eyes widened.

"I seem to recall, Colonel, that you were about to murder us," she said icily. "It would be somewhat optimistic to expect Mr Dubois to come running to your rescue."

The Prussian curled his lip.

"Well, we are all in the same boat now, my dear," he sneered. "That worthless boyfriend of yours appears to have abandoned you!"

Celia glared. Nate shook his bound fists at Trixie.

"Look at that!" he bellowed. "I'm being dragged around like a dog on a leash and that dumb floozie gets to ride in a carriage!"

Trixie stared blankly into nothingness, long silver talons resting lightly on her shoulder. Observing her, Mackenzie shook his head, his brow clouding.

"The poor girl seems to be in some kind of trance. I fear that…."

A sharp command. The flash of a blade. Heads rolled in a welter of scarlet. Pumping gore, the decapitated corpses crumpled slowly. They fell forward to lie side by side, twitching grotesquely, in a dark pool sucked up eagerly by the dry dust.

"Oh, God....!"

The bodies were still convulsing as the wooden wheels ground onwards and a jerk on the ropes set the prisoners in motion. Jeremy, screamed Celia silently, please hurry!

They staggered on for an eternity. The crazy patterns drawn upon the plain seemed to clash and jangle, the heat pouring down from the metal sky, crushing them.

Mackenzie's legs dissolved beneath him but his guards simply dragged him over the carpet of tiny, sharp stones. Protesting, Celia hauled on the rope until she reached him. Helped back to his feet, the Professor could only gasp gratefully. The blunt end of a spear dug forcefully into Celia's ribs and she threw back her head and screamed with pain and rage and indignation.

They stopped again.

"Good Lord," panted Mackenzie. "If you look carefully, you can just make out a pattern."

They stood within a pale circle. The circle was an eye, the bold eye of a gigantic bird of prey. Its broad wings were spread across the plain, talons clutching at the horizon.

"Who cares!" groaned O'Dwyer.

But he started with surprise as the eye slowly opened, glowing. To their astonishment, they saw stone steps winding downwards, torches flickering in metal brackets.

Mackenzie stared in rapt wonderment. Von Seyfritz's lips were bloodless, working soundlessly. Celia gulped, her shoulders heaving.

No one saw Trixie come alive, her dull eyes suddenly glittering, her blank stare slowly contorting into a cruel and frozen smile.

EPISODE 19:
THAT'S NOT CRICKET!

It was a world within a world. An oasis of green surrounded by the simmering black wasteland.

They had plunged into a jungle, breasting their way through the thick, sun-dappled foliage.

"I say!" exclaimed Jeremy.

"Oui," replied Dubois. "This strange land is full of surprises."

The dripping undergrowth was clinging, grasping, resisting their progress. Cursing, they forced their way through it, ripping it apart with their bare hands.

"Ouch!"

Raked by thorns, Jeremy shouted out loud. Huffing and puffing, he paused for breath, bent over, his hands on his knees.

"W–we…must…go back…for…the…others…" he panted.

Dubois shook his head.

"First we must save ourselves. We must be sure that we are not being followed."

Curling long leaves into a kind of funnel, the Frenchman drank the moisture that ran off them, one by one. Gratefully, Jeremy followed his example.

"Wizard wheeze that!" he smacked his lips.

Dubois grinned, flexing his wiry wrists, where the traces of the binding fibers were still sore.

"The forest will supply us with all that we need," he stated. "Water, fruit…all that we need to keep us alive."

Refreshed, they squared their shoulders and marched on, crashing through the thick undergrowth. High above, the treetops were a tangled canopy, through which the sunlight pierced in narrow shafts and bright needles. Unseen, exotic birdlife chattered, disturbed by their noisy passage. Monkeys gibbered, showing their teeth in a grimace of alarm.

They rested in a clearing, in a pool of thick golden sunlight, bathing them like warm honey.

Jeremy lay on his back, gazing up at the lofty treetops, his hands folded behind his head. Dubois sat cross-legged, staring into the distance.

He patted the many pockets of his stained and torn safari jacket, until he found the pouch with the tobacco and papers.

Deftly, he rolled a cigarette. The brass lighter clicked once, twice, failing to ignite. He shook it and tried again, with success this time.

"I'm low on fuel," he frowned. "Soon I will have to light up your way, my boy scout friend."

He took a deep drag and exhaled, blowing smoke towards the treetops. He glanced at his watch.

"I think we have waited long enough. It is time."

Dubois rose to his feet. Jeremy jumped up eagerly

"Righto!"

They stepped out boldly, shoulder to shoulder.

"Let's go rescue C from those—!"

The ground opened up beneath them. The fall was long and the landing hard.

"Uh!"

Unconscious, they lay in a heap at the bottom of the pit.

"Oh Lord, I'm most terribly sorry…!"

Blinking, Jeremy regained consciousness. The sun jabbed hot needles into his eyeballs.

"Wha…w–what…?"

Beside him, Dubois groaned and sat up abruptly, clutching his forehead.

"Uuuurrgg–ggh…hhh…where am I…?"

The world swam into focus, piece by piece. Bare earth, an expanse of cleared ground, scraped and swept clean, the forest banished. Glowing fire pits, with bubbling cauldrons dangling from squat tripods. Game turning slowly on a spit, fat spitting and crackling. Animal skins and swathes of freshly dyed cloth of purple and green, stretched on large wooden frames. Conical huts made of mud and straw, thin plumes of smoke rising from a hole in the roof.

"I say…?"

A shadow fell across them. Someone was bending over them anxiously.

"Are you alright?"

He was very tall and thin. He would have been taller but for the roundness of his shoulders. A shock of grey hair flopped across his forehead. Piercing blue eyes were mounted above sharp cheekbones, hollow cheeks and a long nose as sharp as a knife blade. His scrawny neck with its prominent Adam's apple projected from the collarless neckline of a baggy white shirt that hung down to his knees, his tan trousers too short for him, exposing bare bony ankles and scuffed sandals.

He had missionary written all over him. The simple wooden crucifix hung on a thong on his narrow chest confirmed it.

Jeremy sat up gingerly. His stomach churned, vision blurring briefly.

"Yes…I think so…"

With a grunt, Dubois heaved himself to his feet. Holding out his hands, the missionary hauled Jeremy upright.

"My dear chap…!"

Hasty footsteps scuffled on the hard dirt.

"I am so sorry!"

He was the missionary's perfect twin. Perfect in every detail. Except that his bright blue eyes were framed by thin steel spectacles.

"We have told them about digging those infernal man traps but they just won't listen."

They stood side by side, like Tweedledum and Tweedledee. The adventurers just stood and stared.

"They're only children really. Such innocents…"

"…in a garden of Eden…"

They even finished each other's sentences.

There was movement all around them. For the first time, they became aware of the crowd watching them.

"Good grief!" said Jeremy.

The inhabitants of the small village were uniformly short and wiry. Their raven hair was trimmed like an upturned basin, the fringe brushing the heavy brow above eyes like black coals. Brown skin was decorated with painted swirls and curls, modesty preserved by a mere twist of cloth.

Some held short javelins, others heavy clubs spiked with shards of flint. Their women, with long lank black hair, peeped out from the dark doorways of the mud huts. A few, bolder, stood just outside, naked to the waist, grass skirts secured to their hips.

"Our flock", said the bespectacled missionary.

"Please allow us to introduce ourselves," smiled his twin. "I am Rupert and this is Thomas Barrington-Carr…"

"…of the White Brethren of Woking…"

"…here to bring the good word to the New World…"

Flashing a grin, Dubois winked at one of the younger and more pneumatic maidens. The men frowned at him, brows knitting, gripping their weapons tighter.

"Um…" said Jeremy nervously.

"Please…" said Rupert, looking anxious. "Don't look at their women that way."

Dubois shrugged.

"Oh, pardon."

He eyed the flint spear points professionally.

"These gentlemen seem to be ready to go to war."

Thomas sighed heavily.

"I'm afraid that they are always ready to go to war."

"Yes indeed," his brother confirmed. It is our greatest burden. They are constantly seeking conflict with the neighbouring tribe."

Dubois nodded.

"Mais oui, it is the same the whole world over. Man is made for war."

Rupert shook his head vigorously.

"No! I cannot believe that. Man is essentially good, he has a noble heart!"

Dubois looked doubtful.

"I admire your faith, monsieur, but history does not agree with you."

Thomas startled them by laughing out loud.

"Ah, faith indeed, my dear chap! And we have faith in the ideal solution!"

He turned on his heel, strode off and vanished into a hut that was larger than the others. Puzzled, Jeremy looked quizzically at Rupert. The missionary smiled mysteriously.

"Here we are!"

Thomas re-emerged, weighed down by two large heavy-duty canvas holdalls, one in each hand. Returning to them, he let the bags drop at his feet. The villagers looked at each other, muttering.

Galvanized by enthusiasm, Rupert slapped Jeremy on the shoulder.

"And you are just in time, my friends, to witness a true miracle!"

There was the harsh braying of a primitive horn. The green curtain of the jungle parted and strange figures stepped into view.

"Ah!" exclaimed Rupert. "Here we go!"

There were perhaps fifty of them, matching the village warriors man for man. They looked taller, an illusion created by their tribal hairstyle, dyed bright orange and standing shock upright on their heads. They too were practically naked, their sinewy bodies adorned with bright white circles and spots. And they also wielded deadly spears and clubs.

The newcomers advanced into the clearing, until the two tribes stood barely ten yards apart, eyeing each other with dark suspicion and dislike, neither wanting to be the first to blink.

The women shrank back into the huts. The two tribes glared at each other, the spear points quivering with tension.

"Oh!"

Raising his hands, Thomas sprang hastily between them. He spoke urgently, in an alien tongue.

"What is he saying?" asked Jeremy.

Rupert looked nervous.

"He is urging peace upon them," he explained. "That is why we invited them here, to make peace."

Stooping, he was undoing the straps and buckles on the large bags.

"And this is how we intend to do it!"

Jeremy could not believe what he was seeing.

"By Jove!"

Amazed, he watched as the missionaries delved from the copious depths of the two bags: half a dozen brand new cricket bats; a heap of shiny red balls; two sets of batting pads and gloves and wicket keeper's gloves with their sausage-like protective fingers; and two lots of wooden stumps, complete with bails.

"You must be joking."

Dubois just stood there scratching his head.

"You're going to teach them to play cricket?"

Snatching up a bat and swashing with it in the air, Rupert was beaming at him.

"Of course!"

Like a wide-eyed schoolboy, Jeremy took one of the balls and tossed it gently from hand to hand.

"But...." He mumbled. "But...."

Still speaking, Thomas was persuading the warriors to lay down their weapons. They did so one by one, reluctantly, eyeing each other suspiciously.

Rupert's eyes were blazing with a messianic fire.

"Yes, cricket! What finer civilizing influence is there?"

"Come, come…gather round!"

Flinging out his arms in an all-embracing gesture, Thomas herded and cajoled the two tribes into a broad circle, surrounding him. A bat in one hand and a ball in the other, he addressed them fluently in their strange tongue.

"He's explaining the rules to them," said Rupert.

"Good luck!" laughed Jeremy. "They're hard enough to understand in the original King's English."

Looking on from the sidelines, Dubois rolled his eyes, bemused.

"Mad dogs and Englishmen," he muttered. "Cricket, bah!"

Taking long strides, Rupert was pacing out the length of the pitch. He pointed at the canvas bags and the equipment heaped beside them.

"If you would, my dear fellow…the stumps…?"

Using the flat of a bat, Jeremy hammered the three short stakes into the ground, side by side. He balanced the little wooden bails across the top, fashioning a serviceable wicket.

"Yes, that's right, monsieur, the other one goes there."

Grudgingly, Dubois joined in, copying Jeremy at the far end of the pitch, assembling the opposite wicket.

"That's it, well done my friends!"

Squatting down, Jeremy examined the ground, running his palm across the gritty surface.

"The pitch is rather hard," he noted. "And there are a lot of cracks."

Juggling a ball from hand to hand, Rupert beamed at him.

"Yes indeed, the bowlers will have something to work with…"

"…and the batsmen will have a jolly exciting time of it", grinned Jeremy.

Dubois snorted, looking skeptically at the foreign object in his hand. Frowning, he tossed the bat away.

"Cricket, bah!" he repeated.

Jeremy stood up straight, holding out his hand. Rupert lobbed the ball to him. He stepped back and took a short run up. His arm came up and over and the ball arced the length of the crude pitch, rotating rapidly as it flew. It bit into the lip of a crack on a line outside of the wicket and looked like it was going to miss by a wide margin, but then it veered dramatically and demolished the stumps, sending the bails flying.

"Oh, bravo," Dubois grumbled, stooping to re-build the fallen wicket.

Rupert clapped his hands.

"Well done! A spin bowler I see."

Jeremy smiled modestly.

"You shall captain one side and I the other", Rupert proclaimed.

"I'd be delighted, sir," Jeremy replied.

"I think we are ready to begin," said Thomas. "Brother, if you would…."

Rupert took charge of the tribe with the orange hair. They were invited to sit on a vaguely defined boundary, in front of the large missionaries' hut, which, according to Thomas, represented the "pavilion."

With Thomas as translator, Jeremy ushered his black-haired team into their various fielding positions. The surplus was sent to the boundary, to be spectators, squatting down uneasily beside their deadly rivals.

It took Thomas a little while to persuade the reluctant "wicket keeper" to don the padded gloves and take up his stance behind the stumps. Meanwhile, Rupert was cajoling his pair of opening batsmen to stand still while he buckled the pads onto their shins. He handed them the bats, which they looked at closely, with interest, hefting them, judging their weight and balance.

"Ah," said Rupert. "I think we have two natural stroke makers here."

Walking with the pads was a whole new experience for the orange-haired tribesmen. One stumbled and almost fell as Rupert led them out. There was a ripple of derision from the black-haired spectators. Glaring, the orange tribe jumped to their feet, their enemies responded and tension crackled in the air.

"Oh dear!" Rupert went swiftly to calm them, stepping in between the two warring factions. They sat down slowly, muttering.

The batsmen were in position, standing by the wickets at either end of the pitch. The fielders stood where Jeremy had placed them, their faces blank, waiting for something to happen.

As captains, Rupert and Jeremy shook hands ceremoniously, for the benefit of the two tribes. Thomas handed the ball to Jeremy.

"I think that you two should do the bowling for your sides", Thomas suggested. "Let them see how you do it."

"Righto!" said Jeremy.

"Will do!" said Rupert, retiring to the boundary and the knot of spectators.

"Play!" called Thomas, taking up his position as umpire, at the bowler's end.

I'll start off with a few soft ones, thought Jeremy, just till they get the hang of it. He trotted in past Thomas and looped the ball gently down the pitch. Holding the bat in one hand, the orange-haired batsman just watched it as it went by. The wicket keeper made no attempt to catch it and simply let the ball go past him.

"Oh dear," said Thomas.

He trotted over to retrieve the ball and tossed it underarm back to Jeremy. On the boundary, Rupert stepped forward.

"Perhaps I had better demonstrate."

Taking the bat politely from the puzzled batsman, he moved him aside and took up the textbook batting stance.

"Give me an easy one, old chap!"

"Coming up!"

Jeremy sent down a slow, straightforward toss and Rupert clipped it neatly away off his toes, sending the ball rapidly along the ground. It disappeared into the dark doorway of a hut. The women's watching faces vanished with a squeal and shrill giggle.

"I don't think we'll get that one back," Thomas chuckled.

He jogged over to the boundary where the warriors sat with stone faces. Selecting another ball from the pile, he threw it from the boundary to Jeremy, who caught it expertly. The throw and its accuracy raised a glimmer of interest and some murmuring.

"Give me another one," said Rupert, swinging the bat. "I'll put one up for them to catch."

Jeremy put something into his next delivery, a bit more pace and some extra spin.

"Oh!"

Rupert misread it slightly. His timing off, he sliced it harder and flatter than he intended.

"Oh Lord!"

The hapless black-haired fielder was standing at silly mid-on, at a shallow angle a few yards to the left and in front of the bat. He made no effort to dodge or catch the ball. It made an ugly sound as it struck him hard on the side of the head. He crumpled and lay motionless.

On the boundary, the red and black-haired spectators jumped to their feet, all exclaiming loudly and exchanging significant glances with their tribal comrades, darting angry looks at their rivals.

The felled warrior groaned, rose to his hands and knees, then fell flat again. Blood was oozing through his black hair.

"Oh my Lord…!"

Standing close to Rupert, the opening batsman showed his teeth in a malicious grin. At the far end of the pitch, his flame-haired colleague laughed out loud, a harsh staccato sound. He brandished the bat high above his head and began to dance, shouting a war cry.

The other fielders were gathering around their fallen comrade. One vented an angry riposte, shaking his fist. Bending, he picked up the bloodied ball. Drawing back his arm, he hurled it with great venom and uncanny accuracy.

"Good grief!"

The round missile struck the dancing batsman between the eyes, splitting his forehead open in a flood of scarlet. He reeled, dropping the bat, putting his hands up to his face, blinded by blood.

Snarling, the opening batsman tried to seize his bat back from a paralyzed Rupert. Alarmed, the missionary backed away from him. Frustrated, the orange-haired warrior ripped one of the stumps from the ground. He stood for a moment, studying it, a short stake with a point at one end.

With a shout, he threw the stump like a dagger. It turned over and over rapidly in the air, flew a short distance and impaled the man who had thrown the ball in the throat. Vomiting blood, he fell and rolled in the dirt, his fingers scrabbling at the short wooden shaft.

"Oh no, no, no…!"

Inside the huts, the women were screaming. On the boundary, the rival spectators were snatching up the heap of balls and were hurling them at each other. The spare bats were being used as clubs, with great effect. The remaining stumps were ripped up and wielded as short stabbing swords.

"No, no, no…!"

The fight spread out across the clearing, intensifying as the warring tribes regained their spears and barbed war clubs.

Thomas was in the thick of it, as the dust of battle rose all around him. Hands flapping anxiously, he pleaded for calm and order.

"My friends, my friends…you must desist…you must—!"

A stocky black-haired warrior stepped up to him and swung a cricket bat. The crack of willow on the missionary's skull echoed across the clearing, cutting through the clamor of the fighting. His eyes rolling up in their sockets, Thomas fell on his back and lay there twitching.

"I say," Jeremy said absurdly. "What a perfect hook shot."

Dubois was at his side.

"I think it's time to leave."

Nearby, Rupert was staggered by a terrible impact between his shoulder blades. Astonished, he stood looking down at the spear point that projected from his chest.

"I think you're right," said Jeremy, turning pale.

They turned their backs and left the battle behind them, running for the green wall of the jungle.

"Merde…!"

They had been seen. They were being pursued.

A squad of orange-haired warriors, spears in hand, were coming after them, deep into the dappled green and gold.

"They're g–g–gaining…on…us…!" Jeremy panted.

Born in the jungle, the warriors weaved smoothly through it, flowing through it, while the Europeans stumbled and staggered, tangled and snared in the thick undergrowth.

Exhausted, they came to a halt.

"It's…no…use…," gasped Dubois. "We cannot outrun them…we will have…to…stand and…fight…"

The tribesmen were upon them, surrounding them in a tight circle, jabbing at them with their spears, taunting them.

We don't stand a chance, thought Jeremy, with startling, stark clarity.

There was a sound, a cry, a call, a signal, coming from somewhere hidden amongst the trees.

"Wha…?"

An arrow transfixed one of the warriors clean through the neck. Gurgling, blood drooling from his twisted lips, he lurched backwards and collapsed. As he lay on the ground, kicking, his comrades froze, staring at him in amazement.

Suddenly, arrows were sprouting from their bodies. Three of them screamed and fell.

The mysterious cry was repeated, a high-pitched, piercing ululation. Fear contorted the warrior's faces. Stiffly, they backed away, and then they turned and ran, disappearing as the green curtain closed behind them.

"What on earth...?"

They stood there looking at each other, baffled. Then they heard someone approaching.

"Hullo, chaps!"

Their jaws dropped.

"Having a spot of bother?"

A vision stepped out through the curtain of the jungle. A spectacular vision, a feast for the eyes, with pale skin and flaming red tresses flowing down from a helm of gold, her breasts cupped by polished steel, her loins girdled by gleaming mail, a jeweled sword hilt flashing at her hip.

The vision strode forward jauntily, extending her hand.

"Pamela Leffingham-Hoare...how do you do...?"

Behind her, tall figures were emerging, fierce warrior women with coppery skin and long black hair. Their swords were sheathed and in their hands they carried short bows, the quivers slung across their shoulders.

Dumbfounded, Jeremy reached out awkwardly and shook Pamela's hand. Her grip was firm and assertive.

"Uh...ah...pleased to meet you..."

Devouring the lithe and supple warrior women with his eyes, Dubois was already turning on the charm, smiling and stroking his thin moustaches. The women stared right back at him, unblinking, appraising him, weighing and measuring him. Suddenly, he felt like a piece of meat hanging in the market.

Grinning broadly, Pamela released Jeremy's limp fingers, as he stood gazing at her raptly, in awe.

She cocked an eye at the fallen tribesmen, lying there riddled with arrows.

"I'm afraid that these poor buggers were trespassing."

Jeremy swallowed hard.

"Oh. Then we must be as well."

Pamela tossed her red mane and laughed.

"Not at all, old thing!" she declared heartily. "You're most welcome!"

She exchanged a knowing glance with her warriors.

"Most welcome indeed!"

Then she laughed again.

"Oh dear, where are my manners? You simply must come back for tea."

A world within a world within a world.

"Be it ever so humble…"

A squat pyramid, blunted by the ages, which rose in crumbling terraces, embossed by lurid friezes of battling warriors, throat-slitting and disembowelling their enemies, bearing plunder and laying tribute at the feet of their long-gone King, dragging prisoners to the sacrificial altar. Here and there were faded traces of color, weeds sprouting from the cracks.

There were long, low buildings that brought to mind a barracks and stone walls creating a grid of large compounds.

"I say…!"

The compounds were busy. Warrior women were exercising their strange mounts, the beasts trotting in a circle or hovering at the end of a long tether, stretching their leathery wings.

"I don't believe it!"

Their short bows twanging, women formed a firing line, aiming at distant straw targets the shape and size of a man, their crude torsos bristling with arrows. There was the flash of ringing steel as they sparred with their swords, their movements swift and supple.

"Oh! <u>Merveilleux</u>! Superbe!"

Naked, save for a tiny scrap of cloth, warrior women wrestled, their lithe bodies gleaming with oil. Jeremy didn't know where to look but Dubois stood and stared in open admiration.

Hands on hips, Pamela made her red tresses swirl and laughed.

"We have no shame here gentlemen."

Laughing again, she slapped her thigh.

"Gosh, where are my manners? I haven't offered you any refreshment."

She was off, her long stride carrying her away swiftly, an armed escort jogging in her wake.

"Follow me…!"

They had to run to catch up, as Pamela veered across a vast open plaza of hard, sun-baked dirt, making for a larger building fashioned from giant stone blocks, with fat columns running along its front, its walls decorated by panels depicting warrior gods and mythical beasts.

"Er…I don't see any men around?" Jeremy asked shyly.

Pamela grinned.

"Oh, we have some of those…"

She gestured towards the distance and in the shimmering haze he saw a patchwork of darker, furrowed ground, and indistinct, melting figures bent in toil, or hauling on the plough.

"They have their uses."

She burst out laughing again and her warrior women, seeing their Queen laugh, laughed also.

"Good…?" Pamela enquired.

Dubois took another sip of the wine.

"Oui, most excellent."

"Not a bad vintage," Pamela commented. "Courtesy of yet another lost expedition."

"Oh dear, really?" said Jeremy, draining his goblet.

Pamela chuckled.

"We get them from time to time. Treasure hunters, missionaries bent on converting the heathen. This lot belonged to some Bible society or another. Died of the fever, poor dears."

She clapped her hands.

"More?"

She sat on a raised platform, on a giant throne of carved stone, padded plushly, leaning back, one spectacular thigh hooked casually over the armrest, a large bejeweled goblet in her hand. The throne room was a great stone chamber, its polished walls gleaming in the light cast by hanging lamps, hung with vivid tapestries that told tales of myth and legend.

"Yes please."

Pamela signaled and young women came forward bearing a jug of wine and golden trays piled high with dainties. As they ministered, smiling, to their charges, Dubois and Jeremy were beaming, reclining like sultans amidst a sea of soft cushions.

This is the life!" declared Dubois.

Pamela sat back in the deep throne and smiled.

"Oh, this is just the beginning," she said.

There was a muffled commotion outside. Sentries posted at the door were shoved aside.

Two women strode across the chamber and stood shoulder to shoulder in front of the throne. They stood tall and proud, fresh from the exercise yard, in their scanty halters and loincloths, their bronzed bodies glistening with sweat.

Her guests looked concerned, but Pamela only smiled again.

"Ah, a challenge..."

Their drawn rapiers quivering in their hands, the warrior women glared fiercely at each other. They brandished their swords, arguing, debating in front of their Queen, who stood suddenly, silencing them.

The women stood side by side, glaring, breathing heavily. Pamela came down slowly, elegantly, from her throne. She nodded at Dubois.

"Yes indeed," she said. "They want to fight for your favors, monsieur."

Full of himself, Dubois stroked his moustaches, sizing up the two warrior women, undressing them with his eyes.

"Ah, of course," he jested. "I have this effect on women."

Despite himself, Jeremy could not conceal his jealousy. Smiling, Pamela held out her hand and an attendant gave her the gold-hilted rapier, sheathed in its decorated scabbard. She drew it with a flourish, tapping him lightly on the shoulder.

"Never fear, my handsome, I want you all to myself."

Jeremy blushed hotly and Dubois roared and slapped him on the back. Pamela turned to the would-be duellists, who promptly sheathed their swords and fell to one knee before her. Suddenly she was tall and stern, the goddess of war. She spoke briefly to the women in their alien tongue. They jumped up, snapping to attention. Pamela spoke again and they turned sharply and marched out of the room.

Pamela slid her blade back into the scabbard.

"Come..."

The sun was a white-hot disk in a sky of brass. Waves of heat rose from the earth trod hard and flat by ancient feet.

The ground had been formed into an arena, a broad square walled by ranks of watching warrior women. Seeking a vantage point, women gathered on the steps of the terraced pyramid. They clustered on the low, flat rooftops, stood on the stone walls.

"Gentlemen…"

Pamela's palace had a long and narrow balcony, supported by the row of columns. She ushered her guests out, blinking, into the harsh sunlight, then followed, flanked by her attendants.

She clapped her hands.

"Begin!"

The duellists stood facing each other at the center of the arena. They were matched in their long and glossy black hair and coppery skin, in the hard muscle tone of their bodies. Their build distinguished them, one long-legged, lithe and tall, the other shorter, more compact.

They were matched in the fierce, proud fire of their eyes, both eager for the battle.

Dubois was rubbing his hands in keen anticipation.

"Merveilleux!" he repeated.

The combatants dipped into a wary crouch, circling each other slowly.

"Does it excite you, *monsieur*," said Pamela. "To have women fighting over you?"

Dubois grinned.

"It's not the first time," he chuckled. "But this is much more exciting than a brawl in a bar in Marseilles."

The tall girl dipped her shoulder in a quick feint but her opponent ignored it. They circled, their blades just touching, tapping, testing each other. Their bodies gleamed with sweat.

Jeremy gulped audibly.

"Not to your taste?" asked Pamela, sizing up the pair with a practised eye.

He shook his head.

"Well…I must say…it's most unlady-like."

Pamela laughed. Her long blade carving the air in a figure-of-eight designed to deceive, the tall girl launched a fast running attack, thrusting repeatedly. Her adversary made a controlled retreat, parrying the thrusts as she stepped backwards.

Their blades flashed in the sunlight, the steel ringing like a bell. Thwarted, the tall girl drew back and they resumed their slow, stalking circle.

"Hmm…," observed Dubois. "Already one can detect a contrast in style, the one more impetuous, the other cautious."

The shorter girl anticipated the next attack and made one of her own, a sidestep, a quick cut and thrust. There was a yelp from the tall girl, who jumped back, a streak of blood on her upper arm.

"I say!"

Dubois was disappointed.

"Ah! It is over already. Blood has been drawn, honor is satisfied."

Pamela looked at him.

"Oh no, monsieur. This is a duel to the death."

Jeremy paled. Dubois was thrilled. Pamela's strong voice rang out and the women watching raised their fists and shouted.

"To the death!"

Breathing heavily, the duellists were now standing and facing each other. The sweat was running down their skin. The shorter girl stamped her foot, once, twice, trying to incite her opponent. The tall girl stood her ground, making little ornate patterns in the air with the tip of her sword.

The tall girl attacked, cutting and thrusting. Her rival was driven back. Then she planted her feet and counterattacked. They came together, their blades a blur of light, in a frenzied clash of steel.

"Ah!"

Suddenly, they stopped. They stood stock still, like gleaming statues, frozen in mid-action.

"Oh!"

A great groan of release rose up from the crowd of watching women. The tall girl stepped back slowly, releasing the hilt of her sword. She was bleeding from several superficial cuts, her hand smearing blood and sweat across her bare midriff.

Her opponent remained where she was, standing at the center of the arena. The tall girl's blade transfixed her body, impaling her and exiting from her back. She staggered, the rapier slipping from her fingers. She opened her mouth but only blood came out. Sinking to her knees, she clutched at the hilt that projected from her flesh. Then she toppled sideways, her legs kicked briefly and she was still.

Swaying, the tall girl raised a clenched fist. Clenched fists rose all around, amidst great shouting.

"Well," blurted Dubois. "I always preferred taller women."

Jeremy stared at him, appalled.

The duellist stepped forward and was bowing towards her Queen. Pamela acknowledged her with a decisive gesture.

The tall girl was devouring Dubois with her eyes. Suddenly he felt nervous. Pamela's laugh had a strange edge to it.

"To the victor goes the spoils...."

Dubois staggered out into the cool blue night.

"Mon Dieu...!"

There was a well. On rubber legs, he lurched towards it, sagging across its stone rim.

"...c'est incroyable...!"

Behind him, from a dark doorway, there issued a voice, low and female, urgent, demanding, summoning him.

"...o–ohh...hhh...!"

Groaning, Dubois hauled on the rope. The bucket rose, water slopping over its sides. He scooped it out with both hands, splashing his face.

Behind him, the voice was commanding.

"...oh...merde...!"

Shoulders drooping, he shuffled back inside.

Shirtless, Jeremy stood on the balcony, gazing up at the brightest Moon he had ever seen. Suffused by its brilliance, his face was a picture of amazement.

"Can't sleep?"

Wrapped in an embroidered cloak, Pamela came out to join him. In the moonlight, his sculpted torso appeared to be fashioned from silver. Her eyes rolled all over him, a shiver of excitement on his skin.

Suddenly, he was blushing.

"I...I've...never done...those...things...before..."

And suddenly, his romps with the fair county debs seemed awfully mundane.

Pamela smiled.

"I'm a good teacher..."

She brushed his bare shoulder with a fingertip and an electric thrill surged through him.

"...and you're an excellent pupil..."

Down below, dark figures were crossing the plaza. A band of warrior women, carrying a heavy burden.

"What's that?"

The smile faded.

"The hunt, returning with its prey."

A shape lay sprawled in the dirt. It had arms and legs, a head, a man.

"One of the slaves tried to escape, it happens every now and then."

The women were lashing the corpse to a wooden frame. Its head hung down, blood pooling on the ground.

"To deter the others," said Pamela. "They will be paraded before it in the morning."

Jeremy looked horrified.

"It is our way, it is how we survive."

He shook his head.

"Am I your slave?"

The Queen laughed.

"No, of course not. You will be my consort."

Jeremy took a step back.

"No," he said staunchly. "I don't want to be your consort!"

He expected her to be angry, but she only looked sad.

"I have to go back and save my friends!" he insisted.

Pamela smiled.

"My brave lad," she chuckled. "Yes, I know, I can't hope to keep you or your dangerous friend, Monsieur Dubois."

She hesitated.

"But…"

"Don't worry," Jeremy assured her. "Your secret is safe with us."

She paused to admire him again.

Oh Celia… she groaned inside…*you lucky cow!*

Jeremy marched between the deep grooves cut by wooden wagon wheels. Head up, his eyes were fixed upon their distant vanishing point, blurred by the hazy horizons.

"Hold on, C," he muttered grimly. "I'm on my way."

The coarse grey ash crunched beneath his boot heels, waves of baking air rising, dry and bitter. The great whorls and mounds of black tar were gleaming, the metal sky resonant. Grimacing, Dubois tested cracked lips with the tip of his tongue.

"Wait, mon ami," wiping his face, the Frenchman ground to a halt. "I admire your sentiments, but let's not push our luck."

Jeremy raised his hand.

"Listen!"

A thin sound, high in the sky.

They looked up and around turning this way then that.

A needling, siren sound, a growing raw-edged whine.

Jeremy pointed.

"Look, there!"

In the vast, glaring dome above them, a spark.

"An aeroplane!" exclaimed Jeremy.

The bright pinpoint was moving, tacking oddly.

"Non," said Dubois.

The spark expanded, became a flashing silver disc. A low pulse underpinned the high buzzing, shivering the taut membrane of the sky.

They stood there stunned, their heads thrown back, hands raised like visors, shielding their eyes.

A momentary silence, the sudden shock of a heart stopping. Then, whistling thunder. The silver circle tilted, dipped and plunged abruptly, falling down and down out of the vaulting sky, hurtling down upon them.

"Run!"

They collided, scrambled frantically, bounced apart. They wallowed desperately, sinking ankle deep into the ash, raising clouds of dust.

"Look out!"

A great shadow fell across the land. The sky was blotted out. A metal roaring battered them. The grey desert seemed to quiver and billow, the grit and rubble bouncing like sand on a drum skin.

Then, all at once, the grinding thunder was sucked in upon itself, gave way to a dull throbbing that pressed relentlessly on their skulls.

"Aaarrgghhhh!!!!"

They reeled, buffeted by a hot whirlwind, baffled by an odd tingling on their skin. Suddenly, the vibrating ground detached itself from the soles of their feet. It fell away beneath them. With a dizzy lurch in their stomachs, they were rising, floating high into the air.

EPISODE 20:
THE DUNGEON

Torches flickered, casting jittery shadows. An oily smoke snaked along dark beams high above. Stone walls were stained and dank with moss. Heavy chains dangled.

A blotched and mottled table top with a windlass-like affair at one end, piled high with knives and tongs and pincers. Nearby, a brazier squatted, slim pokers jutting from its cold black coals. Heavy coils of rope were thrown down everywhere.

"Jeez!" blurted Nate O'Dwyer. "Ain't this a regular chamber of horrors!"

"Crude," sneered Von Seyfritz. "Very crude."

The big men sat side by side, hands tied behind their backs, their ankles locked into a roughly fashioned set of stocks. An egg-sized purple lump just above Nate's eye marked the swift end of a spasm of resistance.

"Oh dear," sighed Mackenzie. "Oh dear, oh dear, oh dear!"

The Professor stood across the gloomy chamber, his arms extended and lashed to a low wooden cross. Despite the tightness of his bonds, his whole being seemed to sag, deflated dismally.

"Keep a tight ass, Perfesser," Nate rasped. "We'll get outta—"

Massive hinges grated and squealed. Distorted timbers protested.

"Swine! Take your filthy hands off of me!"

Their bronzed armor glinting in the murky torchlight, two feathered foot soldiers came in dragging Celia between them. Clad only in her little underthings, she kicked and twisted, spitting with rage.

"Let me go!"

She was sweaty and slippery and hard to keep hold of, but they dragged and half-carried her, backed her up against a broad stone pillar.

"Bastards!"

While one pressed against her, pinning her to the cold stone, the other made busy with a length of cord, binding her wrists to a ringbolt set in the masonry, up above her head. The job done, they withdrew, muttering foully. Celia stood on tiptoe, panting, outraged. Her glistening form contrasted starkly with the dull, dark stone.

She glared at the big men, who squirmed with embarrassment, sat there like naughty schoolboys, in the stocks. Then, seeing the Professor, she mellowed somewhat.

"Oh Professor! Are you alright?"

Mackenzie managed a weak smile.

"Never mind me, my dear," he replied. "What have they done to you?"

Celia's eyes flashed with a dark fire.

"They took me to market!" she snapped.

"Pardon?" said Mackenzie.

"They paraded me up and down and poked and prodded me, while a gaggle of fat black women sat there laughing at me."

Her lip curled.

"I'm obviously not their type," she snorted. "Too thin."

A shimmering electricity seemed to quiver through her gleaming form. The men in the stocks swallowed audibly.

"Oh, nonsense, Miss Cavendish," gulped Mackenzie. "You're a fine-looking…."

"Yes, well, thank you, Professor," Celia cut in dryly. "But that doesn't make me feel any better."

She started, listening intently.

"What's that?"

There was a large metal grating set in the stone floor, its bars furry with moss. From the blackness below came a muffled scrape and shuffle, a low, guttural grunting.

"I've heard that sound before," said Von Seyfritz.

Nate was shrugging, but Mackenzie nodded vigorously.

"Yes indeed," he exclaimed. "Our adversaries from the cliff, Pleisanthropus!"

Suddenly, his eyes were fierce and bright and searching all around.

"And look over there!"

The musty glow of the torches barely filtered into the far, dark corners. Straining their eyes, they saw something move, wiry forms in short skirts of straw, pinioned against the stone, their frightened grins revealing teeth filed to a point.

"Ugh!" Celia shuddered.

"Yes," said Mackenzie. "Our cannibal friends."

There was a grim silence. Then Von Seyfritz cleared his throat and spoke, his harsh tones rebounding thinly off the dank walls.

"Well, it would seem that these fiends have made us the latest addition to their collection."

Nate shifted nervously.

"Yeah, but fer what?"

Celia shivered, a chill slime trickling down her bare back. Twisting her body, she turned to Mackenzie, whose weary features were clouded with foreboding.

"Yes, tell us, Professor. You're the expert."

Mackenzie drooped visibly.

"Oh dear," he said heavily. "I was hoping that you wouldn't ask me that."

Nate showed his teeth in a nervous grimace. The Colonel's eyes narrowed. Celia took a deep breath, and slowly relaxed, letting the tension out of her shoulders. Her steady gaze bore into the hapless Professor relentlessly.

"Well," he gasped at last. "If my worst fears have been realized, we are captives of the cult of Pelath U-Thol, Lord of Chaos."

"Yeah, so?" barked Nate, trying to sound unimpressed.

Mackenzie rolled his eyes dolefully.

"Like so many of the ancient gods," he continued. "Pelath demanded a regular sacrifice from his followers."

His voice faded to a whisper.

"S–sacrifice...?" said Celia.

"I'm afraid so."

Sweat beaded Nate's brow.

"And I guess ya don't mean chickens and goats, huh?"

Mackenzie shook his head slowly.

"No, I am afraid that Pelath demanded the blood and suffering of human victims."

An eerie sound filtered through the stone walls, a thin and distant piping.

"Oh, Lord!" Mackenzie quavered. "I dread to think what they are doing to Miss Marlowe."

Drums.

Drums enveloped and welled up inside her, a dark and slow burning pulse.

Trixie groaned. Raw, inhuman sounds were dragged from the black depths of her soul. Suddenly, there was the weird, high piping treble of the flutes. The dizzy squall of the reeds cut shrilly through the dull, demented pounding of the drums.

Naked, Trixie screamed and writhed insanely. She was floating and turning, around and around, wrapped in a roaring blood red mist. It tossed her this way then that, a raging tide, bending and distending her supple white body. A hideous pain blew up within her and burst from her gaping mouth in a howl of agony and despair.

The drums thundered. The shriek of the pipes was a physical thing, flaying her pale skin. Figures loomed out of the ruby red fog. Horrid gargoyles were capering, feathered demons swooping and soaring up above. Her soft flesh on fire, Trixie clutched and clawed at herself, screaming.

With a hop and a skip, the dancing devils departed. All at once, Trixie was hovering in a ring of broad, brown smiling faces, her scalded flesh soothed by soft hands that stroked and fluttered.

The pipes were cooing like doves, the drums murmuring. Searing pain mellowed slowly to a delicious, exquisite aching. Wide-eyed, Trixie twisted and arched her shining body. The skilled hands caressed and petted her, roamed over her, bold and uninhibited, exploring and invading her.

Agony and ecstacy. Trixie moaned and undulated, her long, lush creaminess quivering. Honey coursed sweetly in her veins. Her whole body tingled warmly, rocked in a cradle of intoxicating perfumes.

Faster and faster. The hands and the flutes and the drums all one, shimmering, then shuddering, an electricity that gripped and galvanized her, her body leaping, out of control.

The cool lip of a bejewelled goblet dipped to let a dark syrup drip down upon her eager tongue. Trixie sighed, as a warm numbness crept along her trembling limbs. The boom of the drums rang hollow, the piping splintered into a brittle clash of echoes. Suddenly, Trixie was falling, plummeting through the red clouds, sucked into a whirling blackness.

Jeremy awoke in a blaze of light.

"Oh, my head.....!"

The young Englishman sat up slowly, blinking, shielding his eyes.

"Good grief!"

A buzzing phosphorescence dazzled him, bright light refracting in a thousand rainbows. The air was crisp and electric, a tinkling singsong floated high above.

Squinting, Jeremy tried to focus. He was dazed by an ever-shifting geometry made entirely of light. Colors were blending, clashing and bursting, starlike.

"Merde!"

Wincing, Dubois clutched his forehead.

"What is this madness?" he exclaimed hoarsely. "What—?"

A dark and solid shape took form in the spark and sizzle of the lights. Something tall and broad lumbered stolidly towards them.

The Frenchman's jaw dropped. Jeremy gasped.

An iron man, seven feet tall. A smooth grey casing, with no head on its massive shoulders, only a great transparent bowl full of winking lights and moving parts, topped by a clutch of curly antennae.

"Aha!" said Jeremy.

"The rock," muttered Dubois. "The thing carved on the rock."

The metal monster towered above them, a low hum droning deep inside its barrel chest. Then, suddenly, a quiver passed through its mighty frame. The light disgorged two whirling columns of dancing silver sparks, glistening clouds that grew milky, solidifying.

Dubois sprang to his feet. Jeremy just sat there, gaping.

Flanking the iron giant, two ethereal beings stood gazing at them calmly. They were cloaked and crowned with light, garlanded with dancing rainbows. Their faces were long and smooth and beautiful, impossibly pale, their wide eyes grey-green and flecked with gold.

Jeremy stumbled upright. Beside him, Dubois clenched his fists.

"No, do not be afraid."

The voice seemed to emanate from the iron man, but it was light and melodic.

"We have come to help you."

This came in a lower tone. Looking closer, they saw that one of the glowing figures was taller and broader than the other, which was slender and unmistakably feminine.

Dubois cleared his throat nervously.

"Who....who are you?"

The slighter of the two strange beings was suffused by a rosy warmth, her eyes now soft amber.

"We are the Watchers," said the lilting voice that came incongruously from the grey giant.

"Ah... er..," stumbled Jeremy. "And... er... what exactly do you watch?"

The colors faded from the taller creature, now as stark and cold as ice.

"There is no time," it struck a note that was dark and stern. "There is no time to lose."

The iron man wheeled ponderously. It clanked away, its great bulk sucked into the giddy cacophony of light. As it disappeared, the two weird figures turned to face each other. A crackling blue mesh enveloped them, bound them together, jeweled by red sparks that popped and sizzled brightly.

Amazed, the humans saw the storm of light take on three dimensions. They watched mighty stems of crystal soar and blossom with energy. Staggering, they felt a vast resonance stir above, below and all around them. All at once, they were rising, as everything surged up into the infinite.

Down in the dungeon, time stood still. The murky dankness was suffocating. Torches glowed fuzzily, exhaled creeping whispers.

A soft click of chain links. The irregular, interminable drip-drip-drip of moisture from slick stone above to mossy stone below. A grunt and shuffle from caged cannibals and shaggy Neanderthals.

Beads of sweat were spiked on the barbs of Nate's dark stubble. Sitting in the stocks, he stared bleakly into the space somewhere beyond his scuffed toecaps. A dull rage smoldering, he saw Gianelli, Gianelli with his feet up on his boss's desk, drinking his best brandy and smoking his cigars.

Close beside the big American, Von Seyfritz sat up ramrod straight, as still as stone, his eyes glittering. His senses were in sharp focus, the spring coiled tight inside, ready for the moment.

"Oh dear!"

Sagging against the ropes that secured him, Mackenzie voiced a sense of impending doom.

"Oh dear oh dear oh dear!"

Celia's chin was down on her chest. Her head lolled, eyes closed, dark hair falling across her face. Glistening all over, her near naked form leant back slackly against the greasy stone pillar.

Bolts clashed and a door groaned open. Celia started and looked up sharply, suddenly upright, her body taut.

"Oh my!" exclaimed Mackenzie.

"Here we go," muttered O'Dwyer.

A squad of feathered warriors entered briskly. Their officer barked at them, jabbing with his leaf-like blade. Pins were knocked out with a sharp tap or two. Hinges squeaked as boards were lifted.

Nate came up swinging, but his legs were like water and his shoulders stiff. A straight right aimed for the chin only scraped a bronzed cheek piece. Then a spear butt poked him hard in the belly. Belching, Nate doubled over, his eyes bugging. Fireworks went off inside his head, fizzing and banging, and then everything went dark.

Curling his lip, Von Seyfritz stood slowly. Spear points poised, warriors ringed him. They watched him massage and flex his limbs, their broad brown features bland, unblinking.

They reached up to free Celia's wrists. She bit her lip as the sudden release sent hot needles jabbing into her cramped shoulders. The armored men stood very close, staring at her. She stood with her back to the pillar, head up, scornful, all too aware of the expanse of flesh exposed to their lusting gaze.

Unbound, Mackenzie slumped to his knees. Poked, he nodded wearily, raising his hands.

"Pigs.....!"

Color springing to her cheeks, Celia moved to help him. The soldiers seized her, twisting her arms up behind her back. She ground her teeth and glared, groaning with pain.

The officer stepped into her field of vision. Their eyes met. Holding her breath, Celia defied him.

His face a flat mask, the officer extended the broad surface of his blade, the cold metal approaching her hot skin. Celia's eyes widened. The short sword halted. With a sharp intake of breath, the officer turned aside. Snapping at his men, he bore down upon the sprawling bulk of Nate O'Dwyer. Celia shuddered in the grip of her guards, her dark eyes glowing.

When Nate stirred and began to struggle, a sharp tap with a wooden shaft sent him back into oblivion. It took four of them to haul his sagging bulk, suspended by his wrists and ankles.

The dripping tunnels wound on for ever, suffused by the rusty glow of torchlight. Gasping, Mackenzie stumbled, but the slab-faced warriors simply caught him and dragged him along. Up ahead, Von Seyfritz maintained a steady marching pace. When the point of a spear pricked him, the Prussian snarled, made the culprit jump, his feathers bobbing.

The rearguard frogmarched Celia briskly, holding her tight between them. Behind her wide and staring eyes, there was a roaring turmoil, while her bare skin crawled with a maddening fire. Forced along at a rapid pace, she moved jerkily, her pale form rigid, like stone in her captors' grasp.

Without warning, the floor fell away, the torchlight muffled, muddy.

At a word from their officer, the soldiers let Nate go. Rolling over and over, he bounced down a broad stone staircase. The jittery spear points gestured, and Von Seyfritz followed with a measured tread, his breath hissing out slowly between clenched teeth. Behind him, Mackenzie was lifted and half-carried. All the energy and substance seemed to have drained from the Professor. Between the stocky figures of his guards, he was grey and boneless.

Her arms gripped tight, Celia descended jerkily. Her eyes adjusted to the gloom. What she saw made her moan out loud.

At the center of a wide, circular chamber, tall cages were glinting dully. They were high, narrow oblongs, the height of a tall man, pointed at the top and suspended just above the floor by chains that vanished into darkness up above.

Ice twisted in Celia's belly, rising to choke her. They wrenched at her arms, making her cry out and lurch forward. She reeled against the bars, felt the chill shock of them on her sweat scalded skin, heard hinges squeal and iron clang shut. For an instant, a black terror washed over her. Her legs melted, the bright blobs of the torches spinning around and around. She swallowed hard, seized the bars and hauled herself upright, gasping, furious.

As her cage swayed on its chain, she watched them fold up a mumbling Nate O'Dwyer and cram him into the barred box on her right. To her left, Von Seyfritz paused to glare balefully at his guards, before stepping inside his allotted prison. Beyond him, Mackenzie peered out dolefully through the bars.

Breathing heavily, Celia fought to clear the roaring in her skull. She blinked, and the warriors were gone. Then a deep tremor rumbled up below her, made the cage vibrate alarmingly. The color draining from her, Celia saw the floor begin to move.

A silver fleck winked once, then twice, spanning the broiling dome of the sky.

Its bewildered passengers wandered deeper and deeper, lost in a dark and humming blue.

"I say," said Jeremy nervously. "Do you think we should be poking about like this?"

Dubois merely shrugged.

"Courage, mon ami."

The brooding blueness had a shape which they were obliged to follow, a maze that turned round and about and in upon itself. They plodded on in silence, nervousness gnawing away inside them. Then the Frenchman seized Jeremy's sleeve, pointing.

"Aha!"

White lights were twinkling in the distance, like a spray of stars floating in the deep blue. Jeremy hesitated, but then jumped to catch up with his companion. As they drew closer, they saw the bright spangles take on a pattern, outlining a forest of tall, transparent tubes.

Dubois ran his hand over the cool crystal. The smooth column was much broader than he was, and he had to tilt his head all the way back, to survey its starry crown.

"Good grief!"

Startled, Jeremy sprang back, as the gleaming curve slid aside.

The white lights ceased their random sparkle and seemed to grow and glow as one, infusing his open, youthful features with bright wonder.

Dubois grinned suddenly.

"Shall we...?"

They looked at each other and then stepped inside. The tubes snapped shut. For a moment, nothing happened. Then they were descending smoothly. They sank into blackness which slowly became blue. The crystal doors opened soundlessly.

They could only stand and stare, dumbfounded.

A glassy forest stretched as far as the eye could see, till the gleaming shafts were the merest glint where the blue melted into black horizons. Each hollow pillar was occupied, by the still, monolithic form of a grey, dome-headed giant.

"Fantastic...!"

Jeremy shuffled nervously. Dubois went to have a closer look. The armored forms were lifeless, save for a single green pin light pulsing slowly somewhere deep inside their glassy domes. Across each mighty iron torso was slung a stubby carbine, all tubes and bulbs and filaments, constructed of an oddly opaque material.

"I say," exclaimed Jeremy. "Very Flash Gordon, what?"

Something had distracted the Frenchman. He was squinting through the semi-darkness, drawn to a bright patch in the distance.

"What's that?"

Glass cabinets bristled with weaponry. A club spiked with shards of flint nestled beside a gaudy matchlock, its ivory stock inlaid with precious gems. Pikes and halbards stood in rows, old muskets interspersed with long, two-handed claymores. A bolt-action rifle lay across a ball-and-chain.

"Look!"

A small table was rising, ascending on stilts that sparked with electricity. They bore down upon it, with exclamations of delight. Amazed, they feasted on the familiar sight of two large, ugly Service revolvers, black from their heavy hexagonal barrels to their bird's head hard rubber grips. They were laid neatly side by side, flanked by fat bullets set up in ranks.

"By Jove," Jeremy exulted. "Just like the one dear old Pater brought home from the War!"

Dubois lifted one of the pistols. The feel of it sent a sharp tingle through him. Thumbing the small side lever, he broke it open and filled the cylinder, plucking up the cartridges and popping them in.

"I think we were expected."

He snapped the gun shut, slid it into his waistband, savoring its potency. Jeremy followed his example and then they scooped up the leftover ammunition and stuffed it into their pockets.

"That's more like it," the young Englishman declared. "Now we can prise C from the clutches of those brown devils!"

Dubois nodded slowly, his eyes narrowing.

"Amongst other things," he muttered grimly. "I have other scores to settle."

Chains rattled, ratchets clattering.

The stone floor parted and the cages sank through a layer of cloud. A choking fog enveloped them, yellow tentacles that stank of decay, winding around the bars.

Mackenzie coughed and spluttered, wiping his eyes. The touch of the sulfurous mist tingled on Celia's skin. Her stomach churned violently. Swallowing hard, she bit back the bitter bile that rose in her throat. She heard a muffled groan that might have been O'Dwyer, heard Von Seyfritz cursing savagely.

The fog thinned slowly and was left behind.

"On my!" gasped Mackenzie.

They were descending into a vast, sunken oval, its high walls punctuated by broad, dark archways. High and low, a thousand torches cast a resounding, brassy glare, and the bare, sandy floor of the great arena was shining starkly.

At the very center of the sand, a shallow ramp led up to a spacious platform, raised on squat pillars, fat columns entwined by a painted orgy of monsters, devouring each other, some even swallowing themselves.

Above the monsters, a long slab of black stone gleamed dully, its flat sides embossed by faces horribly contorted in agony and despair. Tall candelabra stood at the four corners of this gruesome table, and by each an armored guard, short bows slung across their shoulders.

All round the broad sweep of the oval, soldiers flanked the dark archways, the torchlight winking on their helmets and polished bands of bronze. Warriors waited where the cages came to rest, thudding down upon the bright sand.

Jolted, Celia hung on to the bars. O'Dwyer stirred, grumbling. Von Seyfritz glared, while Mackenzie peered out fearfully.

"Oh dear!" he moaned. For once I wish that my theories had been proved wrong!"

Somewhere, drums were muttering. Then a trumpet echoed tinnily. A small army marched out onto the sand. Their armor clanked rhythmically, feathers dancing, spear points glittering viciously. At a word of command, they stretched their ranks out to the cages, stopped in pairs facing each other, marking out a long road to the high altar.

The stone oval swelled with noise. A dark tide came surging out of the archways, filling the arena and turning the bright sand black, jostling and clamoring, held back by the file of armed men protecting the route to the altar.   Battered by the noise, the prisoners gripped the bars till their knuckles bled white.

Then the high sound of a flute cut through the wall of sound.

Silence.

Celia's heart jumped up into her mouth.

Stone thunder. A mighty grinding rumbled, stirring the sand. A great exhalation rose from the dark multitudes.

"Aaaahh.....!"

Behind the cages, the blunt end of the oval was opening. The stone walls parted in a blaze of light.

Strange figures leapt out of the light. Slight, wiry forms came hopping and skipping across the white sand. They were naked, save for a jangle of beads, a belt of shrunken monkey's heads and jumble of whorls and jagged zig-zags painted on their coppery skin. Jumping, twisting and turning, they bounded down the bright road lined with spears, as they raised a crazed shrilling on flutes and crude pan-pipes. While the crowd chattered excitedly, they bounded up the ramp, to dance on and around the black slab.

"Wake up, wake up, wake up!" Celia shook the bars till they rattled.

Tall twins strode out of the light, swathed in leopard skins and jangling with gold, their faces hidden by lurid gargoyle masks. They advanced with a long and stately stride, wielding staffs that tinkled with strange totems and talisman, topped by a grinning skull.

They marched past the cages and on toward the high altar. Von Seyfritz cursed, his face pressed to the bars. Stark against the gold draped across their shoulders, the tall figures wore odd ornaments, a 9 mm Luger and a Colt .45.

The masked apparitions reached the foot of the ramp and stopped there to stand guard. A great shout burst from the crowd. Waves rippled through the vast assembly, as they nudged and jostled, craning to see.

"Wake up! Please wake up!"

In single file, five silver phantoms were gliding out onto the sand. Cloaked and cowled, they floated past the cages. They were liquid metal, like mercury, the light flowing over them.

Mackenzie's chin dropped down to this chest. Celia stared dumbly. Von Seyfritz was watching the masked figures flanking the ramp, fixated by the glint of blue steel.

A solitary drum was booming. Their oiled muscles gleaming, burly guardsmen plodded into view, bearing the weight of a golden throne.

"Oh God!" groaned Celia.

Suddenly, the cold sweat was hot again, sizzling on her skin.

On the throne of gold sat Trixie Marlowe. Her eyes were wide and bright, unblinking, her face a mask of ivory, framed by waves of silver. From her shoulders to her knees, she was wrapped in a cape of tiny white feathers, as soft and dazzling as snow.

She stared, unseeing, out over the heads of the crowd, her gaze arrowing down the white ribbon of sand formed by the guardsmen, to the oval rostrum and the black slab upon it. Looming behind her, swaying in the grip of those laboring to support it, came a stone giant, with the torso of a man and the long features of a jackel.

"Ah," sighed Mackenzie. "Pelath U-Thol."

Celia hung her head. At the sight of the pale, luminescent figure on the throne, a low moan swelled up from those gathered all around. The silver wraiths ringed the raised oval. The throne was set down. Trixie mounted the ramp slowly, turning at the top to face the long road that led to the cages.

There was a steady murmuring, underpinned by the dull throb of the drums. The twin gargoyles raised their staffs, the skulls grinning sightlessly, inciting a single, abrupt exhalation from the crowd.

Two soldiers sprang forward, bearing down upon the iron box that contained a slumped Nate O'Dwyer. Bolts rattled and clashed. They hauled Nate out. He was stumbling, rubber-legged, his slack bulk sagging between them. He shook his head, mumbling. Then his glassy eyes began to focus. He saw Trixie.

"Yeeeeaaahhhh......!"

The soldiers jumped back. The bravest returned, jabbing with his spear. Cursing, Nate swatted the bronze point aside. He reached out and seized the warrior with both hands, shook him till he rattled. The soldier's world turned upside down. Then he was flying through the air, up and over the line of spears and into the crowd.

His hapless companion felt the javelin being wrenched from his grasp. Snarling, O'Dwyer snapped the shaft like a twig. He hurled the point away and wrapped the blunt end around the warrior's head, making his bronze helmet ring like a dull gong. His victim fell flat on his face and lay there spread-eagled, not even twitching.

Bellowing, his heavy features dark with rage, O'Dwyer lumbered up the path. His great arms swinging, he batted the feathered warriors out of his way, bowling them over like so many toy soldiers.

The crowd whooped and hollered. Those in front tried to back up, out of harm's way. Those behind jumped up and down and pushed forward, straining to see what was happening. The silver phantoms were motionless. Trixie stared, inscrutable. The masked twins shook their staffs and made the bony jaw bones clatter.

An odd whistling filled the air. The four guards manning the black altar had unslung their short bows and Nate's mighty frame was suddenly sprouting arrows.

The big man bellowed, like a great bear swatting at flies. A red mist roared before his eyes. Behind his eyes, he saw Trixie. He felt Trixie, felt her flesh yield to his pounding fists, felt her bones breaking, her face mashed into a bloody pulp.

He was on the ramp. She stood just above him, her face a pale, unblinking mask. He reached out to her. A bright spark glittered in her eyes.

His thunder choked abruptly. With a grunt, Nate stumbled, as something struck him between the shoulder blades with tremendous force. Surprised, he looked down, saw something hard and pointed, projecting from the barrel-like swell of his torso.

Everything seemed to swim around. Trixie's sharp, bright form was melting, milky. His breath grating harshly, Nate took a step forward, then another. The spark grew to a slow burning deep in Trixie's eyes. Her eyes grew and grew and were drowning him. She was right in front of him. He reached out but his groping fingers passed right through her.

Bewildered, Nate opened his mouth to curse her, but only a ghastly gurgle emerged, and a great spray of blood. His eyes rolled back till only the whites showed. His broad bulk crumpled, deflating. As his power drained away, he sank down until he was kneeling, his head between Trixie's feet.

His booted foot twitched just once. In a dream, Trixie wrapped her slim fingers around the long shaft of the spear projecting from his back. Her eyes glowed, her lips twisting mirthlessly.

"By Jove!"

"Sacre bleu!"

A great undertow was sucking everything down. The explorers gasped, their faces glimmering in the deep blue-black with a greyish, sickly pallor. They felt their limbs turning into lead, their stomachs rising.

"Look!" croaked Jeremy.

Impossibly, the iron men were floating in their tubes, bathed in a white light that jangled harshly.

"Aha!" said Dubois.

Their vacated pillars of crystal came alive, the rings of tiny lights clamoring insistently.

No hesitation now. Dubois was first, Jeremy close behind him. The transparent surfaces slid and clicked shut. With a schoolboy yell and a shout, they rose and were hovering, suspended in a twist of glowing particles.

"Going down.....!"

The thing that had been Nate O'Dwyer was dragged away, leaving a dark stain on the ramp, his hooked fingers carving furrows in the sand. Murmuring, the crowd swayed and then settled, pressing up on either side of the long road of spears. The low, slow pulse of the drums grew until the entire arena was a drum, booming.

Spear points glittered. The skulls grinned, a twitch of the wrist making their jaw bones clatter. Up above the skulls, the four bowmen slung their bows, stood as still as statues. Her cloaked shoulders rising and falling, Trixie swayed, breathing heavily. Startling in the stark alabaster, her eyes were deep and dark and glowing. Bright beads of blood spotted the snow white feathers of her cape, glinting like rubies. Beyond her, the stone idol stared impassively.

A single trumpet slit the rolling thunder of the drums.

They came for Celia.

When the bolts clanged and hinges squealed, she jumped back and the chill of the bars was an electric shock jangling her spine. She cried out, and in that split second they seized her arms and dragged her out.

The sand was hot beneath her feet. A great gasp burst from the crowd at the sight of her slender paleness, a shout that blew up behind the pounding of the drums, a storm of heat that crawled rawly on her bare skin.

A blind, black madness was roaring in her skull. She struggled furiously. Beads of sweat flew from her dark hair as she tossed her head from side to side. Glaring, gritting her teeth, she twisted and writhed, kicking out viciously. Cursing, she resisted their efforts to march her to the distant altar, her legs splayed, arching her body back against them, digging in with her heels.

Celia's skin was slimed with sweat, and all of a sudden she slipped out of their grasp and for a crazed moment was free with nowhere to go, turning this way and that, while the high walls and the spears and the brown faces whirled around her. Then a spear butt clipped her ankle and she fell heavily. She clawed frantically at the sand, wriggled and rolled, but they grabbed her arms and legs, lifting her.

With a fresh, shrieking surge of panic, Celia felt herself rising. A shout greeted the sight of her thrashing up above the spears. Her long, white body seemed to fly all the way to the altar, shining in the harsh, brassy torchlight. Wild-eyed, she heaved mightily, her body arching, spread-eagled in mid-air. Spitting with rage, she howled lustily, but her voice was sucked away by the demented pounding of the drums.

Staggered by the force of her struggles, the soldiers bore Celia up the ramp. They dropped her on the altar with a vigor that jolted the breath from her body. The black stone was so cold that it burned, and she arched upwards, gasping. Then the soldiers jumped down to the sand and the four bowmen took over. Seizing her wrists and ankles, they spread her out taut, her limbs jarred in their sockets.

The drums stopped. The clamor wilted and stuttered into silence. There was no sound save that of Celia breathing.

The cloak slipped from Trixie's shoulders. The crowd sucked in its breath.

She was naked. She was not flesh but shining ivory, the opulent contours of her body etched with fine whorls and curls of silver, powdered with a winking glister. As she breathed, she gleamed and sparkled, effervescent. Her eyes were half-closed, heavy-lidded, her ruby lips parting slowly.

Trixie turned to face the altar. Her hooded gaze bore down upon the pinioned form of Celia, stark against the black stone. A curved dagger gleamed wickedly. Celia groaned and strained against the iron grip that pinned her down. Her body quivered tautly, the sweat rolling on her skin.

"Wake up, oh wake up!"

Trixie's eyes widened suddenly, reflecting the hard, bright crescent of the blade. Somewhere, the pipes were shrieking.

Her eyes shining with a green, voluptuous and cruel light, Trixie circled the altar with a long and liquid stride. Celia shuddered, shrinking against the stone. Pausing, Trixie bent so close that Celia could feel her hot breath on her face, could see herself reflected in Trixie's eyes, a staring mask of horror.

The drums began to beat again. Trixie stood back from the black slab. Her face distorted by an eager lust, she ran a gloating gaze over her victim's supple body. She made slow passes with the knife, broad, elaborate flourishes that made cold lightning flash from the polished metal. Blinking sweat out of her eyes, Celia panted, her breasts rising and falling.

Long, slow undulations rippled through Trixie's bare body. Her white flesh glistened. She was ablaze, aflame for a victim. The slow rippling quickened until, from head to toe, her silver-tinted lushness was shuddering and shivering, her arms held high, the dagger slashing and stabbing. The pipes wailed and a low moan bubbled up from the crowd.

Trixie froze, poised over the altar. Her eyes were hard and bright, standing out in their sockets, her red lips twisting soundlessly. Celia stared, mesmerized, fixated by the winking point of the knife as it descended slowly.

"Oh, n-noooo.....!"

Summoning up every ounce of her strength, Celia managed to lift herself and twist sideways. With a grunt, the bowmen heaved, jerking her tight. She gave a gasping cry, choked off as she felt the cold metal prick her bare midriff. Raising her head from the black slab, she saw the creamy flesh dimple, a bright bead of blood forming. Screwing her eyes up tight, she bit back the scream that blew up inside her.

She opened her eyes. The knife sprang upwards. Her face alight with unholy passion, Trixie swayed above the gleaming, shuddering form of her victim. Veils of ghoulish green smoke were wreathed around the stone image of Pelath U-Thol, crept across to lick at the corners of the altar. The priests shook their scepters, making the skulls chatter. Tendrils of green mist tickled Trixie's toes, snaking slowly around her shining white thighs. She groaned and rolled her eyes. Her breasts heaved, her hips gyrating.

Tiny whispers of smoke were crawling on Celia's skin. Their touch was cold and clammy, and she gagged on a vile stench of decay. Murmuring a soft, singsong incantation, Trixie touched the place where Celia's pulse was pounding visibly. Galvanized, Celia jerked violently. High above, the blade quivered. Then it struck.

EPISODE 22:
ATTACK OF THE ROBOT MEN

Explosions thudded dully.

The knife froze an inch above Celia's palpitating heart. Trixie staggered, her eyes flickering.

Moaning fearfully, the dark masses swayed. The spears twitched nervously. Yellow dust drifted from the ring of shadowed archways. Lying there pinned to the black stone, Celia saw the sulfurous clouds above begin to writhe and billow.

"Aiiieeeeee!!!"

A single, blood-curdling shriek, a brown hand pointing and then all eyes were directed upwards. The mustard colored gasses were disgorging monsters, iron giants that fell abruptly, slowing to float in wide circles.

No one moved. All stood gaping. Then a single bowman let go of Celia's wrist. He unslung the short bow and with a simple, fluid motion, sent a reed arrow whistling upwards. The slender shaft found a target, only to fall away, shattered, repulsed by the grey armor.

The hovering giant revolved slowly in mid-air, the stubby carbine held at its hip. A fine blue beam was tinted green by the sickly vapors. The bowman shrieked. His hair burst into flame. The flesh bubbled on his skull, his face melting like wax. He stood for a moment, then folded at the middle, toppling across Celia. Winded, she lay beneath him gasping, struggling, red sparks dancing in front of her eyes.

With a yell of alarm, the other bowmen leapt clear of the altar. A web of blue was lancing downwards. The beams raked across the arena, scything down the crowd. The iron men circled slowly and methodically, while below them all was one great shrieking, howling turmoil.

Small crystal globes were falling out of the yellow clouds. Their detonation could be seen but not heard, pressure waves spreading like ripples on a pond. Where they fell, the dark mass seemed to spread outwards in slow motion, like the petals of a flower. Dismembered limbs rose into the air, turning over and over.

The shrieking reached fever pitch. The dead piled up, pinning the dying beneath them. The living scrambled frantically over the heaps of mangled corpses, trampling them and each other into a bloody pulp. The walls of the arena were streaming with blood.

A blue electricity enveloped the silver figures that stood circling the altar. As this crackling lost its color, the silver became transparent, until the strange beings vanished altogether.

Bouncing on the bloody sand, a glass grenade rolled towards the cages.

"Oh—!" exclaimed Mackenzie.

A black flash. Oblivion.

Von Seyfritz blinked the sand from his eyes, shook his head to clear the buzzing. The bars were still vibrating. When his vision cleared, the Prussian was amazed to see the buckled remains of the cage door, lying on the ground some distance away.

"Aha!"

His eyes blazing, Von Seyfritz sprang out into the open. Without hesitating, he set off for the distant altar. The blue bolts whined and spat all around him, the concussion of the small bombs buffeting him. Bodies ran into or fell against him, open mouthed and staring. He shrugged them aside, wading in blood. His advance was relentless and unswerving, his entire being focused on a distant spark of blue steel.

"So!"

All at once, he was standing over a prostrate form still clutching the staff topped by a grinning skull. The priest stirred and groaned, a dark stain sucked into the sand. Von Seyfritz stooped to pluck away the Luger, snapping the thong on which it hung. He straightened slowly, hefting the automatic, his lips twisting into a bloodless smile. Then he turned and was striding through the roar and rush and carnage, head up, looking neither right nor left, making for the dark archways.

"Oooohhh.....!"

The red mists cleared. Gulping, Celia recovered her breath. With a grunt, she heaved the dead bowman off her, gagging on the stench of burnt flesh. Strangely detached from the surrounding turmoil, she sat up stiffly, her bare back parting stickily from the stone. Gritting her teeth, she arched her body, easing the kinks out of her spine.

Pain. Sudden, searing pain, like a white hot iron being drawn swiftly across her skin. A red streak appeared on the creamy curve of her thigh. With a yelp of alarm, Celia rolled backwards across the black slab. She heard Trixie hissing viciously, felt the sickle blade fanning the air close by. Landing on top of the dead bowman, she scrabbled about until her fingers closed upon the hilt of his short sword. She jumped to her feet, pulling the bronze blade free.

"Professor?"

Around the cages, the yellow pall thinned to reveal Jeremy. He cut a bizarre figure, caked from head to toe in dust, wielding the heavy revolver.

"I say, Professor!"

A dull detonation rocked him, but he shouldered aside the pattering rain of shrapnel. With a shout, a bronze-bound figure blocked his path, its eyes demented, the feathers hanging in tatters. A leaf-like blade jabbed at the young Englishman's belly. The sound of the shot was lost in the general din, but Jeremy felt the big gun buck in his hand. The wild eyes rolled up in their sockets, the flat brown face falling away.

Impressed by this neat demonstration of hip-shooting, Jeremy looked about for another opponent. Unrewarded, he shrugged, striding on to the cages.

"Professor, are you alright?"

Mackenzie was crumpled up on the floor of his pen, a shapeless bundle, his chin on his chest, mumbling to himself lowly. Jeremy studied the locks and pins. Then something glinted in the corner of his vision. He turned quickly, to be confronted by another feathered swordsman.

"Ahk–nal Eth–ra!"

Shrieking his ancient war cry, the plumed warrior tensed for the charge. Jeremy fired. The feathers shivered. There was a dull clang. The warrior stepped back a pace, amazed. He looked down at himself, searching for an arrow. He found a small hole in the bands of bronze, fingering it tentatively. A strange glaze came over his eyes, but then he shook his head, raised the sword, and sprang forward again.

Jeremy leveled the pistol and punctured the copper headband where it wrapped around the warrior's forehead. The warrior dropped on the spot, falling as flat as a toy soldier.

"Sorry, old chap," Jeremy apologized, feeling terribly unfair.

A great shadow was a robot man swooping low, the blue death rays spitting venomously. The crystal bombs raised clouds of dust, and a warm wind prompted Jeremy into action.

"Hold on, sir, I'll have you out in a moment!"

Circling the black slab, two pale forms stalked each other. The altar was the calm eye of a hurricane. While the maelstrom roared around them, the women were suspended in a bubble of silence.

Celia put her hand down to her thigh, felt the warm stickiness. Trixie showed her teeth, her eyes gleaming.

"Bitch.....," Celia muttered.

Her thoughts were all scrambled, a raw jangle. The bare expanses of her skin were crawling clammily, a cold fist clenching in the pit of her stomach. The short sword was leaden, dragging at her hand.

Trixie's naked form gleamed like ivory. Her eyes were huge and hard and bright, her ruby lips moving soundlessly. She flourished the curved blade again and made its light dance. Celia's flesh shrank with apprehension, ice twisting deep inside her. A thin bra strap slipped from her shoulder and she tugged at it clumsily. Trixie sneered.

The long knife was neat and sharp and was a thing of light and air. Celia's sword was a brutish, awkward club. A dullness crept into her limbs. Her movements grew sluggish, while Trixie glowed, dancing on her toes.

Then Trixie sprang. She lunged across the black stone, her lips drawn back in a twisted snarl, breath hissing through clenched teeth. The sickle blade swept in an arc of light, fanning back and forth. Celia flapped feebly with the sword and there was a sound like a cracked bell when the blades collided accidentally.

Encouraged by this lucky parry, Celia moved back along her side of the altar. She could feel the sweat trickling on her skin, puffing out her cheeks to blow away dark strands that fell across her eyes. Breathing deep and slow, she tried to still the thunder in her skull.

Trixie was a creature of silver and ivory. She advanced slowly, making strange, low sounds deep in her throat. The reflections from her blade flickered eerily on her pale face, gave her eyes a crazy glitter. Her shoulders heaving, Celia forced herself to stand and wait. She swallowed hard, flexing her fingers on the slippery hilt of the sword. Desperately, she tried to focus, tried to pierce through the odd, dull enchantment which seemed to have fallen upon her.

The blonde was so close that Celia could hear her quick, sharp breath, pick out the glinting beads on her white skin, the intricate patterns of silver glister. A great scream was welling up inside her, growing till she thought she would burst in one vast, black flood of horror.

Up on her toes, Trixie rocked this way then that, flexing her shoulders, making little feinting stabs with the knife. She was smiling. The silent scream was a thousand white hot needles piercing Celia's brain.

The knife flickered, carving towards Celia's eyes. Celia jerked up the sword. She met only air, and the dagger was slashing at her belly. With a shout, Celia wrenched her body sideways, twisting with a jerk that jarred her spine. The sharp edge slit the bit of silk girdling her hip, nicking the skin beneath.

Galvanized, Celia let out a shriek and swung the sword wildly. Blindly, she swung again and again, felt the impact jar her arm to the shoulder, heard the "chock" and "chunk" of the blade in meat like a butcher's cleaver, hot dots of blood spotting her bare skin.

Then Trixie had fallen away and Celia was slashing empty air. The frenzy evaporated and she stumbled dumbly. Panting, she stood over the mangled form which lay twisted up beside the altar. Everything seemed to swim around, and she turned and lurched away, gasping.

A sound made her turn back. Start terror froze the scream that leapt into her throat.

Trixie had risen. Her silver hair was matted with blood, her face split across by a savage sword cut, a ghastly, grinning mask of scarlet. One eye bulged, glaring, the other dangling from its socket. Ragged rents and gashes criss-crossed her body, her white skin laced with crimson. Blood dripped down her thighs, and she left a trail of red footprints, as she advanced, laughing.

The sword slipped from Celia's fingers. Mumbling with terror, she staggered backwards. Her heels slipped on the edge of the raised platform. Her arms flailing, she tipped over backwards and crashed down onto the sand.

The carnage enveloped her. Screams of agony and despair, the thunder of the bombs and sizzle of the death rays, the stench of death and fear.

Up above, the thing that was Trixie Marlowe flung out her arms. Drops of blood flew from her fingertips, as she cackled through broken teeth. The dagger flashed.

Celia got up and ran, stumbling over the dead and wounded, running till she thought her heart would burst, towards the dark archways.

EPISODE 23:
A RECKONING

Beyond the dark archways, lay mile upon mile of dry stone tunnels, bathed in the rusty glow of torches.

The shadows danced as Von Seyfritz rounded a blunt corner. Skidding to a halt, he was casting all around, the Luger jabbing nervously. He thought he heard something. Taking a deep breath, he sprang through a narrow opening in the wall.

"Gott in himmel!"

Gold.

He reeled, dazzled.

A room full of gold.

Gold gleamed. Gold flashed. A fanfare, a symphony, an ecstacy of gold.

Shoving the Luger into his belt, Von Seyfritz stumbled forward like a child. Pyramids of ingots towered above him. Precious pots and plates lay around in heaps. Great chests overflowed with winking coins. Sparkling chains were draped and dangling everywhere.

The Prussian sank to his knees. His wide eyes were glowing, golden. He dug into a deep urn, scooping out a handful of gold dust. Laughing, he let the glittering granules seep through his fingers.

A low hum behind him. Von Seyfritz whirled.

"So!"

An iron giant, lifting its glass carbine. With a shout, Von Seyfritz plucked the Luger from his waistband. He fired once, ducked as a blue bolt spat past his ear, then was rolling and firing again and again.

Slugs whined off the grey armor. Then a lucky shot tore away the curly antennae. Its arms pinwheeling, the monster did a crazy, jerky dance, turned abruptly and walked into the wall. The crystal dome splintered, the pin lights fading. With a sorry drone, the grey figure thudded to its knees. There it stayed, motionless.

Von Seyfritz advanced warily. The fractured dome was dark. Replacing the empty magazine with a spare stowed in his breast pocket, he shoved away the Luger, then stooped to retrieve the odd carbine.

"An interesting toy, mon Colonel."

The Prussian span around. Dubois was strolling towards him, the big pistol held loosely in his hand. Von Seyfritz put the unfamiliar weapon aside.

"It is no toy, my friend."

His hand slipped to his belt, close to the blue-black automatic. The Frenchman's grip tightened on his revolver. Von Seyfritz smiled icily, the gleam of gold in his eyes.

"Our scientists will explain it to us. With such technology at its disposal, the armies of the Third Reich will be invincible."

The air was thick with gold dust, sharp and electric. The gold jabbed like daggers, and Dubois squinted, stepping back a pace.

"We shall return, and this land will yield up all its secrets."

Dubois released his trapped breath, brandishing the big pistol.

"Not if I can help it."

Von Seyfritz stiffened, his eyes narrowing.

"So," he grunted. "The time has come."

Dubois grinned, the gun muzzle tilting idly. He eyed the Luger wedged into the Prussian's belt.

Von Seyfritz's fingers crept closer to the chequered grip.

Dubois cocked the revolver. The click echoed thinly.

"Wait!" cried Von Seyfritz. "Give me a chance!"

The dull mutter of explosions could be heard in the distance. Vibrations tickled the stone walls, bringing down a fine rain of yellow dust.

"Let us settle this like gentlemen!"

His fingertips were brushing the steel.

"A duel! A proper duel!"

The Frenchman's smile vanished.

"I am no gentleman, mein herr."

He fired. Von Seyfritz reeled, spun around. Staggering, he clawed the Luger from his belt. Dubois fired again.

Von Seyfritz swayed and then lurched forward, firing as he came. Dubois back-pedaled, clutching his chest. A pile of gold stopped him, and he sagged against it. As the Prussian lumbered towards him, firing from the hip, he lifted the revolver in both hands, thumbing back the hammer.

Gunfire rolled like thunder. The chamber was clogged with the fog and bitter stench of cordite. Yards apart, the two men emptied their guns into each other.

The hammer clicked on a spent cartridge. The toggle stayed open, with nothing left to feed.

They stared at each other.

"So....."

Von Seyfritz shoved the empty gun back under his belt. Pivoting slowly on his heel, he began to walk away.

He stopped. He coughed. A thin stream of blood ran down from the corner of his mouth. He coughed again, toppled slowly, a faintly puzzled expression on his face, falling forward to lie stretched out on the floor. Gold speckles rose, settled to float on the thick blood seeping from the ragged exit wounds in his back.

A soft thud was the revolver dropping on the sandy floor. Dubois slid down until he was sitting, his back against a mountain of gold. He was grinning.

"I…always w–wanted to…die…rich…"

His light slowly faded, his face lit only by the hard light of the gold. His sharp eyes dulled, his gaze fixed and unblinking.

Celia ran, the sound of her labored breath rebounding off the tunnel walls. Her heart was a frantic hammer, battering her ribs. Her throat was raw and constricted, a great pressure swelling, her whole body bursting.

Dimly, she became aware that the tunnels were getting warmer. The dry, baked walls were now glistening, the torchlight fuzzy and diffused. Her gasps became a high, hoarse wheezing, her lungs grating as though they were full of sand.

The tunnel began to slope downward, a steep incline dipping until Celia was hurtling out of control, wild-eyed, shouting, her legs pumping under their own demented momentum, her thighs juddering, her body jarred to the top of her skull.

"Ah!"

She fell, a diving roll, rolling over and over, till she finished on her hands and knees.

"Oh!"

Ahead of her, the space between the torches widened until their fading glimmer was sucked into a void of hot and humming blackness.

"No!"

Celia lurched to her feet. She stood there swaying, gasping, blinking sand out of her eyes. Then she started, and her stomach was gripped by ice.

It echoed tinnily down the tunnel. A thin, high cackle.

"Oh God!"

The crazed laughter rolled onwards like a peal of cracked bells. Celia's legs turned to water. The spell of black terror fell upon her, the silent scream and cold paralysis. She knelt on the sand, groaning. Far away, down the long, glowing tube, she thought she saw a slim shadow dancing.

She scrambled upright, slipped and stumbled sideways, her arms flung out for support. The stone wall crumbled. She was falling, thrashing in cold blackness, clawing the air vainly for a handhold. Her thin wail of terror echoed into infinity.

Then, nothing. A short sleep full of pain and crazy dreams. She awoke with her mouth full of sand, her belly churning, a band of iron slowly crushing her skull.

"O–ohh–h–h....."

Everything was green and sickly. She lay sprawled on a narrow ledge, one leg dangling in space.

"Aaahhh....."

Celia sat up slowly. For a moment, she thought she was going to be sick, but she puffed out her cheeks, swallowing.

A shadow fell across her. Her heart stopped, her eyes growing wider and wider.

"Oh no!"

Hands on hips, Trixie grinned down at her. She was restored, unblemished, the flawless ivory goddess. Celia struggled to her feet, dumbfounded. She lurched close to the edge, as waves of pain and nausea washed over her. Trixie laughed, her eyes like diamonds.

The laugh was a white light burning away the fog in her brain.

"Cow!"

Glaring, Celia swung with all her might. Her fist cracked on the side of Trixie's jaw. The blonde head jerked back but the bright eyes did not blink, the mad smile never wavered.

Wide-eyed, Celia gulped. Panting, she began to stumble backwards. The curved dagger flickered. Celia yelled and clutched her upper arm, blood seeping through her fingers.

A feint, a dip of the shoulder, and blood beaded on the snowy slope of Celia's breast. She jumped and squealed through clenched teeth, her eyes wild.

A flick of the wrist. A fine red line crossed Celia's bare midriff. It burnt like fire, and she doubled up and fell to her knees, groaning.

Trixie laughed. She lifted the blade to her lips, teasing the bright crescent with the tip of her tongue. With the arch of a pencil-thin eyebrow, she tossed the knife away. Reaching down, she seized hold of Celia and, with a liquid shimmy of her shoulders, hoisted her high above her head.

Howling, Celia kicked and struggled. Trixie only laughed the louder, legs astride, her body a gleaming alabaster column.

Trixie threw Celia down onto the hard ground. Winded, she writhed, her mouth gaping soundlessly. Planting a foot against her ribs, Trixie flexed a white thigh. Then she rolled Celia over the edge.

Falling, Celia screamed, a scream cut short and sharp as she crashed into something, then scraped and slid and hung on by her fingernails, her arms nearly torn from their sockets.

She swung in space, gasping. Sweat was streaming down her, making all the cuts and scrapes sting horribly. She was dangling from an iron spar, suspended above a jumble of twisted spikes, jagged fangs that thrust up greedily, eager to rip into her flesh. Below her, a green glow was pulsing, dark around a bright white core.

Up above, Trixie did a demented jig. Cackling, she began to climb down.

The smoke of battle cleared. In the distance, thin echoes of death and destruction, as the iron men mopped up, probing the tunnels. The bright arena was calm, save for the feeble stirrings of the wounded, the crackle of flame nibbling at twisted black things that once were human.

"I say!" Jeremy strode out of the yellow mist. "Wizard scrap, what?"

Sitting on the sand, Mackenzie stared at him, glassy-eyed. Grinning, Jeremy twirled the revolver on his finger, a steel pinwheel glittering.

"Did you see me, Professor? A regular Tom Mix!"

Something cold settled on Mackenzie. The breed had survived the Great War. The smiling, schoolboy killer.

There was a low, bubbling moan, a brown hand clutching bloodily at Jeremy's leg. White-faced, he jumped. He fired and missed, then made the hammer rattle uselessly on spent shells.

Cursing, he kicked and wrenched himself away. He didn't understand why Mackenzie was laughing.

"Er... ah... well, let's be off, shall we?"

He jumped again when two columns of whirling sparks grew milky as they approached, became shining silver forms with smooth faces and grave, golden eyes.

Iron giants loomed in attendance. The silver beings stared silently. Taking a deep breath, Jeremy pulled himself together.

"What–ho, you chaps! We showed the blighters, didn't we?"

Mackenzie struggled to his feet. Consumed by his thirst for knowledge, he approached the strange creatures with what he hoped was due humility.

"Please tell us what this all means!"

A pause. The bright beings were suspended in a ball of light. Their voices intertwined, high and low, an eerie, shimmering harmony, somehow distant.

"We are the Watchers….."

"…..time travellers….."

"…..many of your centuries ago, there was a rebellion on our planet......"

"..... a conspiracy to divert the flow of time and exploit the corruption of progress for its own ends....."

"…..to seek power and advantage by distorting the course of cultural development in other worlds, in other galaxies….."

"…..the benefits of science were corrupted to serve the need for conquest….."

"…..technical advancement was imposed upon primitive cultures far beyond the natural order of their evolution, so as to give advantage to one society over another….."

"…..thus aiding the cause of the rebellion…."

"..... its effects have been felt throughout the Universe....."

"…..in bloodshed and oppression…"

Mackenzie's jaw dropped.

"Yes, indeed…," he mused. "And so we find the worshippers of a Mesopotamian god here in the New World and weapons of bronze amongst a people still living in the Stone Age."

Eyeing the mists warily, Jeremy reloaded the revolver, scooping the bullets from his deep pockets. Wreathed in a shimmering light, the strange beings continued.

"..... we traced this band of rebels to the cult of an olden god, in a bygone age, in an ancient land....."

"Yes!" interrupted Mackenzie. "Just as I thought! I—!"

"......but sensing that they had been discovered, the rebels fled across time, forward in time....."

".....and were safely hidden here....."

".....until now....."

A thousand questions tumbled over in Mackenzie's brain. His mouth opened and closed, dumbly. The grave golden eyes were cool and steady.

Hefting the loaded pistol, Jeremy shuffled nervously.

"Gosh," he said. "Golly."

Trixie clambered down the iron buttress, light and nimble and grinning like a monkey. The ghoulish green gave her flesh a waxen pallor.

Celia tilted her strained features upwards. Her dangling body shuddered. Pain jabbed into her distended shoulders. The pain grew steadily, making her gasp, her breath rasping harshly.

Trixie perched on the broad slope of the dark rib. She was smiling. Ever so gently, she let her heel rest on the fingers of Celia's left hand. Celia closed her eyes.

Pressure on her knuckles. Celia's eyes popped open. A violent tremor convulsed her. The pain ripped across her shoulders, running down her spine like a red-hot poker. She groaned horribly. It felt as if every sinew was being slowly torn from the bone.

Giggling, Trixie lifted her foot. Celia moaned. Her eyes glaring crazily, Trixie brought her heel down sharply.

"Aaag–ghh!"

Celia hung by her right hand. The pain was numbing. Her mouth opened wide, but only a tiny, strained sound emerged. She hung helplessly. Her head lolled, dark hair falling across her distorted features. Below her, the green sizzled viciously on the spikes.

"Escaped?" spluttered Mackenzie. "What do you mean, escaped?"

The golden beings seemed somehow apologetic, their light dimming just a little.

"We, the Watchers, are immortal....."

"….therefore we cannot destroy them….."

"..... all we can hope to do is to pursue them for eternity across the stars....."

".....to find them before their dark seed is sown....."

".....or nip it in the bud....."

Dismayed, Mackenzie surveyed a scene of smoking carnage.

"All this," he sighed. "All this terrible bloodshed!"

The bright creatures gazed at him somberly.

"There is more to come...."

"..... there are those in your time whose reach would exceed their grasp....."

".....who would gladly take advantage of perverted science to satisfy their thirst for conquest....."

Jeremy brightened visibly.

"Oh, I say! There's going to be another big scrap, what? I missed the last one."

Mackenzie's shoulders drooped.

"It's been barely fifteen years," he muttered. "Will we never learn?"

Cooing softly, Trixie stroked Celia's straining, bloodless fingers. She smiled, her eyes clouding strangely. The green flowed like oil across her bare skin. Celia trembled violently, every muscle protesting.

Trixie's grin grew broader and broader, her white teeth bared to the gums. The clouds parted, her mad glare beaming brightly. She reached down and hoisted Celia by the hair, a fluid ripple of power coursing through her ivory body. She held her out at arm's length, bearing her weight with impossible ease.

Celia's eyes bulged with horror and amazement. Screaming, she kicked and twisted. Her heels thudded on Trixie's ribs. Trixie merely tossed her head and laughed.

"Bitch!"

Celia's body was a living flame. Blind rage consumed her.

"I'll take you with me!"

Jack-knifing, she flung her legs open, then wrapped her thighs around Trixie's waist. Unbalanced, Trixie toppled forward. Locked together, they plunged into the green abyss with its searing white core, hurtling down upon the jagged iron.

"Aaiiieeee!!!"

Celia landed on top. Their faces were inches apart. Gasping for breath, Celia saw Trixie's eyeballs bug out in their sockets, her mouth gape slowly, blood bubbling on her tongue.

The dark girl jumped up, stumbling backwards. Her hand flying to her mouth, she stared in stark horror.

A bright point was protruding from Trixie's body, slowly extending as her weight sank her down. Howling, Trixie squirmed like a pierced insect, her limbs flung out and jerking crazily.

Gagging, Celia turned and lurched away, recoiling as her flesh was exposed to raking metal claws.

A loud sucking sound drew her back abruptly.

Laughing through bubbles of blood, Trixie was lifting herself from the spike. Celia stood paralyzed, her breath wrenched from her in racking gasps.

Smiling, Trixie rose slowly, a long, smooth uncoiling. Pink froth flecked her lips, blood pattering down to puddle between her feet.

Flexing her shoulders, Trixie snapped off the bloody spike. She held it out, shook dark droplets from its tip. She took a short step forward, her eyes fixed and unblinking, looking through Celia and far beyond her. Blood flowed from her smile.

Celia willed her legs to move. Though every muscle was bursting, there was barely a quiver. Trixie took another step towards her, making slow circles with the shard of iron. As she advanced, she drew near to the core of white brightness. Her flowing curves gleamed, highlighted.

Poised to strike, Trixie threw back her arm. Celia's pent-up screams emerged as a hollow moan.

The tip of the spike penetrated the white radiance. The crystal pyramid flared. Blue lightning flashed. Sizzling, a jagged bolt zig-zagged till it bit upon the iron.

Trixie jerked and went rigid. Fanning out from the white core, snakes of electricity were lashing her savagely. She did a ghastly, convulsing dance, shrieking dementedly, her eyes popping.

The cords of power bound her, coiling around her body, criss-crossing her white flesh, which bubbled and smoked where the blue sparks touched it. Writhing and twisting, she was dragged into the heart of sizzling brightness. Her hair burst into flame, her skin blistered and black and melting like tar.

Celia choked on the sickly-sweet stench of burning. She stared at
the twisted black thing that fell at her feet. With a crackle, it was curling,
dark flakes falling from the bone.

"Oo–oh–hh.....!

Her eyes rolled up in their sockets. Her jaw dropped, her body
sagging. The green grew darker and darker, the white core shrinking to
a pinpoint.

"Oooh–hhh.....

"We must go....."

"..... the search must go on....."

Startled, Jeremy pointed to the empty cages.

"I say, steady on! What about our chums?"

Impatience made the spectral aura sparkle. The shimmering voices
seemed ever more distant.

"Your companions are dead....."

Jeremy paled.

".....all except the dark female....."

His color returned. Beaming, he hefted the revolver purposefully.
The glowing figures were floating away. Gasping, Mackenzie stumbled
after them.

"Wait!" he cried. "Take me with you!"

The Watchers paused.

"We cannot...."

".....the journey is arduous, and without end...."

The Professor's eyes were bright with desire.

"You must! I implore you!"

Hovering in their bubble of light, they surveyed him sternly.

"You realize that you will never return....."

Throwing up his hands, Mackenzie shook his head vigorously.

"I don't care! I must know! I have to see what lies beyond the
stars!"

The Watchers turned to Jeremy.

"And you.....?"

Jeremy stepped back hastily, brandishing the big pistol.

"No fear!" he exclaimed. "I'm off to find C!"

Spinning on his heel, he was away and running, leaping over the bodies, his tall figure receding into the mist.

"Cheerio, Professor!"

Mackenzie waved, as the bright bubble expanded to embrace him. Suddenly, he felt himself growing lighter, rising high into the air.

Celia wandered in a dream, a dark dream full of laughing shadows.

Her body was a single, draining pain. It swelled inside her until she thought she would burst. Her groans echoed off the shuddering stone, as she blundered through a fog that glowed with green, stumbling and falling, picking herself up and staggering on.

Dark shapes loomed out of the green mist, deformed outcrops of rock. She shrank from them, her belly churning with fear. The stone monsters flashed by, while the mist wrapped round and dragged her forward, clammy on her skin.

The tunnels were full of glowing green smoke. It receded before her, faster and faster, its oily tentacles sucked in upon themselves, drawn up the long tunnels. Groping, Celia stumbled in pursuit. Her breath was a broken sob, pain wrenching at her joints, red hot needles probing every sinew.

"Ahhh.....!"

Light. Light at the end of the tunnel. The green thinned icily.

With a weak cry, she was running, her feet splayed, a clumsy, rubber-legged shamble. Her battered body howled in protest, but she ground her teeth and willed it to obey. Her strained features shone with sweat, salty droplets tumbling from her hair.

"Oh.....!"

Dismay. A perilous scree of broken rubble was stretching high above her. A pale wash flowed down from a fuzzy scrap of daylight, picking out every jagged edge and dagger point.

Celia began to climb, scrambling upwards on her hands and knees. Each effort brought a new surge of pain.

The brittle stones rattled. Shouting hoarsely, Celia rolled downwards. Raw and bleeding, she lay crumpled at the bottom.

The green tendrils came creeping for her.

Thunder in her skull, Celia's heart pounded, threatening to crack her wide open. Black horror blew up inside her, was vented in a strangled moan. Groaning with terror, she clawed her way upwards, her hands bloody on the stones, her wide eyes stark and staring.

"AH!"

As she lurched out onto the ledge, the day exploded in her face, its brightness shriveling. Gasping, she reeled back against the red cliff face.

Blinking, she scrubbed sweat out of her eyes. Below her, the mottled carpet of the treetops rolled all the way to a shimmering white horizon. The sky above was brass, heat flooding down. Somewhere a bird croaked dryly.

Celia swayed. Breathing heavily, she took stock of her situation. Head to toe, stale sweat streaked a crust of dust and blood. She ached all over, a dull gnawing of nausea deep in her belly. There was no sense of time, and all the events of the ill-fated expedition were mere fragments of a dream.

Frowning, she fingered the dingy remnants of her underwear. Tattered vestiges of civilization, they were suddenly absurd.

A slow burning lit her eyes, smoldered, then sparked into a smile that cracked fine lines in a mask of dark dust. With a hiss of vindictive gratification, she ripped away the scraps of silk. Flinging out her arms, she embraced the shining horizons.

"Me Celia!"

Her fractured tones rang thinly out over the baking treetops. She threw her head back and laughed at the sun.

"Queen of the Jungle!"

Her laughter split the sky.